PENGUIN TWENTIETH-CENTURY CLASSICS

A MAN OF MYSTERY
AND OTHER STORIES

Shiva Naipaul was born in 1945 in Port of Spain, Trinidad. He was educated at Queen's Royal College and St Mary's College in Trinidad and at University College, Oxford. He married in 1967 and had one son. His books include *Fireflies* (1970), which won the Jock Campbell New Statesman Award, the John Llewellyn Rhys Memorial Prize and the Winifred Holtby Prize; *The Chip-Chip Gatherers* (1973), which won a Whitbread Literary Award; *North of South* (1978), the story of his remarkable journey through Africa; *Black and White* (1980); *A Hot Country* (1983); and *Beyond the Dragon's Mouth: Stories and Pieces* (1984). Many of his books are published in Penguin Twentieth-Century Classics.

Shiva Naipaul died in 1985 aged only forty; David Holloway wrote in the *Daily Telegraph*, 'We have lost one of the most talented and wide-ranging writers of his generation.'

SHIVA NAIPAUL

A MAN OF MYSTERY
AND OTHER STORIES

PENGUIN BOOKS

PENGUIN BOOKS

Published by the Penguin Group
Penguin Books Ltd, 27 Wrights Lane, London W8 5TZ, England
Penguin Books USA Inc., 375 Hudson Street, New York, New York 10014, USA
Penguin Books Australia Ltd, Ringwood, Victoria, Australia
Penguin Books Canada Ltd, 10 Alcorn Avenue, Toronto, Ontario, Canada M4V 3B2
Penguin Books (NZ) Ltd, 182–190 Wairau Road, Auckland 10, New Zealand

Penguin Books Ltd, Registered Offices: Harmondsworth, Middlesex, England

The selection of stories in this book appeared first in Shiva Naipaul's *Beyond the Dragon's Mouth*,
published in the United States by Viking Penguin 1984
First published in Great Britain by Hamish Hamilton 1984
This selection published in Penguin Books 1995
1 3 5 7 9 10 8 6 4 2

'The Beauty Contest', 'A Man of Mystery' and 'The Political Education of Clarissa Forbes'
first appeared in *Penguin Modern Stories 4*; 'The Dolly House' (as 'The Process of Living')
in *Winter's Tales 20*; 'Mr Sookhoo and the Carol Singers' in *The New Review*;
'The Father, the Son and the Holy Ghost' in *The Denver Quarterly*;
'The Tenant' in *Winter's Tales 17*; and 'Lack of Sleep' in *Encounter*

Printed in England by Clays Ltd, St Ives plc

For Alexander Chancellor

Contents

The Beauty Contest

There were two hardware shops in Doon Town, and the Oriental Emporium, proprietor R. Prasad, was one of them. There was nothing remotely oriental about the place, but the name had been given by Mr Prasad's father (a man noted for his flights of fancy) and no one cared enough to change it. The other, just a few doors away, was the more aptly named General Store, proprietor A. Aleong. Though selling the same goods, they had succeeded in competing amicably for many years, and Mr Prasad appeared to derive a certain pleasure in telling his customers, 'Me and Mr Aleong is the best of friends. Not a harsh word in ten years.' But of late relations had cooled. The trouble began with Stephen Aleong, who had been sent by his father to study business management in the United States, and had returned not only with pastel-coloured shirts, but new ideas as well. The first blow fell when the General Store put up a neon sign with flickering lights and the picture of a man dressed cowboy style who said: 'Darn me if this ain't the finest store in town.' Mrs Prasad agitated for a sign along similar lines. Her husband was open to new ideas, but having searched the depths of his imagination he surfaced with nothing. This tended to happen to Mr Prasad. He felt that in some inexplicable way, Mr Aleong's sign had gathered up all the possibilities into itself. The nearest he had come to success was to have a picture of the Three Wise Men riding across the desert towards the Oriental Emporium, which was to be lit by an ethereal glow. However, he suspected that this, apart from being derivative, was probably also blasphemous, and therefore he adopted an altogether different line of approach.

'The value of my service lies in the quality of the goods I sell,' he told his wife.

'Don't talk stupid, man, the both of you does sell the same things.'

'I'm a simple man, Tara, selling to simple people. You think they going to care about neon lights?'

But Mr Prasad had misjudged the simple people. They liked Mr Aleong's neon sign, and there was a perceptible drift of custom away from the Oriental Emporium. Then Mr Aleong did another revolutionary thing. It was the custom in Doon Town for shops to bring their goods on to the pavements, where the bulkier items were displayed. Mr Aleong stopped doing this. 'It lowers the tone of the place,' he explained to Mr Prasad. He renovated the front of the General Store and installed plate-glass windows, behind which the goods were now tastefully arranged by his daughter-in-law. From this alteration a new slogan was born: 'Pavements were made to be walked on.' This caught the public imagination and Mr Prasad's simple people deserted him in ever increasing numbers.

'That man making you look like a fool,' Mrs Prasad told her husband.

'You've got to admit it's original, Tara.' And Mr Prasad, who had recently been more than usually prone to denigrate himself, added, 'I don't know how it is, Tara, but no matter how hard I try I just can't think up original things like that.'

'Pavements made to walk on! You call that original?' Nevertheless, she wondered why it was Mr Aleong and not her husband who had thought of that.

'What are you going to do?' The reproach in her voice was unmistakable. Mr Prasad scratched in vain at the thin top-soil of his imagination.

'Why don't you expand?'

Mr Prasad seemed to be thinking of something else.

'You could buy up Mr Ramnath.' Her expression softened. 'Your trouble is you always under-rating yourself. Think big.'

The idea of expansion appealed to Mr Prasad. He thought big for a few moments, then his face clouded.

'It's a pity how Aleong change really. We used to get on so well together until that sonofabitch son of his begin putting ideas in his head. No fuss, no bother. What do you think get into him?'

'That's business. Aleong is a businessman, he not running a charity on your behalf, and it's high time you realise you was one too. Now what about Mr Ramnath?'

'I don't see how I could do anything there, Tara. Ramnath love he money, hard as nails that man.'

'Think big, man. Stop under-rating yourself.' Mrs Prasad was insistent, suddenly alarmed by the empty spaces she discerned in her own imagination.

'You may be right. Maybe I do under-rate myself.' The cloud lifted. 'I don't know what I would do without you, Tara.'

'Chut, man! You mustn't say things like that.'
They gazed happily at each other.

Mr Ramnath, the owner of the shop next door to the Oriental
Emporium, sold chiefly bicycles. He conducted his business with a
misanthropic glee which he lavished on colleague and customer alike.
Mr Prasad, knowing this, was reluctant to approach him, and his
wife had to fan the sinking flames of his ambition for several days
beforehand.

Mr Ramnath was standing on the pavement outside his shop when
Mr Prasad sidled up to him.

'Good afternoon, Mr Ramnath. I see you taking a little fresh air.'

Mr Ramnath spat amicably on the pavement, and taking out a
square of flannel from his pocket, began to polish the handlebars of
one of his bicycles.

Mr Prasad coughed sympathetically. 'Look, do you think we can
go somewhere where we can talk?'

'What, you in trouble or something?' Mr Ramnath seemed happier
suddenly.

'No, no. Nothing like that.' Mr Prasad laughed.

Even Mr Ramnath had his disappointments. He stared gloomily at
Mr Prasad. 'Come on inside and tell me about it.'

Mr Ramnath sat on a stool near the cash register on which had
been painted in neat black letters: 'We have arranged with the Bank
not to give credit. They have agreed not to sell bicycles.'

'It's like this, you see, Mr Ramnath, I want to expand the
Emporium ...'

'Aleong giving you trouble, eh? I was thinking that something like
that was bound to happen one of these days.' He brightened, and
slapping his thighs let his eye roam fondly over the sign on the
register. 'You want my advice?'

Mr Prasad shifted uncomfortably. 'Not your advice so much as
...'

Mr Ramnath grinned. 'It's the shop you after, not so?'

'You could put it like that.'

'Ten thousand dollars, Mr Prasad, not a penny more, not a penny
less.'

'Eh?' Mr Ramnath's alacrity to sell worried him.

'I say ten thousand.'

'You wouldn't consider ...'

'Ten thousand, Mr Prasad. Not a penny more, not a penny less. This place worth its weight in gold.'

'I'll have to think it over and let you know.'

'That's the way, Mr Prasad; and be quick or I might change my mind.'

'He asking twelve thousand,' Mr Prasad said to his wife.

'It only worth eight.'

'I know. Don't worry, I go beat him down.'

'I can't offer you more than eight, Mr Ramnath.'

'Ten, Mr Prasad. Not a penny more, not a penny less.'

'He's a difficult man to budge, Tara, but I manage to get him down to eleven.'

'That place not worth more than nine.'

'You think I don't know that? Don't worry, I go beat him down.'

'I could offer you nine thousand, Mr Ramnath.'

'You know my answer, Mr Prasad. Not a . . .'

'All right, all right.'

'I think I could get him down to ten if I try hard enough, Tara.'

'It's not a bad price when you think about it.'

'I know that. Don't worry, I go beat him down to ten, you wait and see.'

'All right, Mr Ramnath, have it your way. Ten thousand.'

'In cash?'

'Yes, yes, in cash.'

'Consider this place yours, Mr Prasad.'

'Well, he come down to ten.'

'Good man. You see what a little firmness will do? Twelve thousand! Who did he take you for, eh?'

'I told you I could beat him down. All it needed was time.'

But the General Store was not resting on its laurels. The shop assistants appeared in uniform and Mr Aleong retired from the public gaze to the fastnesses of an office at the back of the shop. It was the next move, however, which really shattered the long-standing friendship. Mr Aleong began to cut his prices. Mr Prasad watched helplessly as the General Store, succumbing to a kind of controlled frenzy, announced new give-away offers and bargains each week. His own plans were proceeding feebly. When he had bought out Mr Ramnath his wife's joy had at first known no bounds. The prospect which opened before her promised a shop of palatial grandeur and spiralling profits. She was disappointed. Mr Prasad did not know what to do with the additional space. He demolished the dividing wall and spread his stock more thinly over the enlarged area. The emptiness was embarrassing, and later on he added a few secondhand items. After he had done that his imagination spluttered and died, and his wife's dreams of glory faded. Mr Prasad, sinking deeper into despondency, found fulfilment in prophecies of doom for Mr Aleong, the General Store, and more recently himself.

'Man, I know what you could do,' his wife said one day, visibly excited. 'It's a great idea.'

'What?' The joy of life, never strong in Mr Prasad, seemed to have deserted him entirely.

'You could enter someone for the Miss Doon Town contest. Imagine you get a really nice girl, Miss Oriental Emporium – you know they have to say who sponsoring them in a sash across they chest – and if she win Aleong go come crawling back to you. He'll keep his tail quiet after that.'

'But that need money, Tara, and anyway who go want to be Miss Oriental Emporium?'

'Man, remember what I was telling you. Think big.'

And Mr Prasad did think big, and as he did so a vision of success and revenge rose before him and the fires of hope kindled once again.

If one were to judge by the rancour it aroused, the Carnival Queen contest was without doubt the most important event in Doon Town. The winner was in due course offered up to the National Queen contest, where she had been consigned by tradition to that group of contestants universally acknowledged to have no chance of winning; though their presence there did have one advantage: it gave the other more plausible contestants an occasion to be magnanimous. One year, the national winner, Miss Allied Electrical Traders Ltd, had said afterwards, 'I thought Miss Doon Town looked stunning as Aphrodite,' and Mr Prasad had commented, 'It's she conscience bothering she.' Such lack of grace was understandable. The competition had degenerated into a self-lacerating exercise to which the people of

Doon Town felt obliged to submit themselves annually. Mr Prasad, as a member of the town's Chamber of Commerce, took a keen interest in the affair. 'You just wait,' he would say, after Miss Doon Town had made yet another poor showing, 'one day we are going to shock them out of their boots. Let us see who will be laughing then.'

And now, the more he thought about it, the more the conviction took hold of him that it had fallen to him to deliver the people of Doon Town from their bondage. His flights of enthusiasm scaled such heights that even his wife was worried.

'You forget Aleong. He entering this too, you know,' she reminded him.

'Aleong? Who is Aleong?'

The confidence that comes from a sense of divine protection and mission had descended upon Mr Prasad, and despite herself, his wife was impressed and eventually infected by his fervour.

Mr Prasad discovered in Rita, one of his former shop assistants, the candidate he was looking for. She worked in one of the big department stores in Port of Spain. Rita was good-looking in the generally accepted way, and her stay in the city had given her 'poise' and 'confidence'. Mr Prasad had no doubts about her suitability while she on her part was eager 'to show Doon Town a thing or two.'

'But what do you know about this beauty queen business, Mr Prasad?'

He had to confess he knew nothing.

'Well, it got to be done professionally for a start. Professionally.'

'Sure.'

'It's not simply walking across a stage, you know. It takes money and . . . and know-how.'

The transformation in Rita's grammar and vocabulary since she left the Oriental Emporium surprised and unnerved Mr Prasad.

'Don't worry. I ain't going to spare no expense.'

'I know a hairdresser who is experienced in these matters. We better go and see her.'

'Sure, sure. Anything you say.'

Whenever Mr Prasad tried to speak 'properly' he ended up with a mock American accent. He was aware of this and it made him uncomfortable. He left Rita, his sense of mission and divine protection shaken.

The hairdresser was attractive and supercilious. She had been trained in New York.

'So much depends on what you parade as,' she told them. 'From my experience I would say it's either got to be Greek or Roman.' She stared at her long, impeccably polished fingernails. 'Or Egyptian, perhaps. That's quaint.'

Mr Prasad nodded, striving hard to control the threatening American intonations. 'What do you like, Rita? Greek or Roman or Egyptian?'

Rita pondered. 'How about Egyptian? Everybody will be doing something Greek or Roman.'

'You could be Isis for instance,' the hairdresser said.

'What's that? Some kind of god or something?' Mr Prasad asked.

Rita looked embarrassedly out of the window.

'A goddess, Mr Prasad. An ancient Egyptian fertility goddess.'

'You like Isis, Rita?'

'Isis sounds fine to me. It's original.'

'Now there's only one more thing,' the hairdresser held her fingernails up to the light and squinted at them. 'Do you have any hobbies?'

'I does . . . I read a little.'

'We'll use that. What else?'

'To be frank . . .'

'Modelling?'

'Well . . .'

'We'll use that all the same. Now we must have something quaint or as you would say, original.'

'What's wrong with two hobbies?'

Rita looked out of the window.

'It's *de rigueur* to have three hobbies, Mr Prasad.'

'Try gardening,' the hairdresser suggested.

'But . . .'

'No. We'll use gardening. It sounds bohemian. That always helps.'

'What's bohemian?'

'Mr Prasad . . .' Rita looked out of the window.

'Well, she going to be Isis,' Mr Prasad informed his wife.

'Who's Isis?'

Mr Prasad was incredulous.

'It's an Egyptian fert . . . fertiliser goddess. And she also have three hobbies, reading, modelling and gardening.'

'Gardening?'

'You've got to have something bohemian, you know.'
'Oh.'

Mr Aleong's plans remained wrapped in secrecy. Whereas Mr Prasad splashed the walls of the Oriental Emporium with pictures of Rita and the pyramids and talked incessantly of the competition, the General Store continued to prosper amid a reticence so blatantly discreet that Mr Prasad's conversations gradually assumed a tone at once hysterically boastful and anxious.

'Maybe you shouldn't have advertise it so much,' his wife said to him. 'That kinda thing does bring bad luck.'

'Bad luck! We go see about that when the time come. But all the same I know that man and he bound to be making mischief somewhere.' He peered at her. 'Do you think he bribing the judges?'

'No, man. We would be sure to hear about it if that was the case.'

'All the same.' And the shadows of suspicion chased each other across his face.

However, Mr Aleong appeared to have only the civic virtues on his mind. He issued a pamphlet appealing for 'common-sense and good order' on carnival days, reiterating what he called his 'unshakeable belief in the native tolerance and forbearance' of his fellow citizens. But about his entrant for the contest, not a word. 'He want to be Mayor,' Mr Prasad said.

The contest was held in a cinema. When the Prasads arrived they were conducted to their seats by a girl in mock tropical costume. The Aleongs were late. Mr Aleong smiled pleasantly at Mr Prasad and elbowed his way across to him. 'Well, Mr Prasad, the night we've all been waiting for.'

'Yes. I expect you have a little surprise for us, eh?'

Mr Aleong laughed. 'Oh no, Mr Prasad, nothing like that. For me it's just a bit of fun. I don't suppose you look at it any different yourself?' Mr Aleong patted him on the shoulder. Mrs Prasad frowned.

'The best of luck, old man. Oh, by the way, Mrs Prasad, you look . . .' Mr Aleong, waving his arms delightedly, backed away in a cloud of good will.

'The son of a bitch,' Mr Prasad whispered.

There were ten contestants and they were to parade three times: in bathing costume, in evening dress and in a 'costume of the contestant's choice'. The last was crucial. The urbanity of the master of ceremonies, whose presence there was a concession to Doon Town, was paper-thin. His jokes, so successful in Port of Spain night clubs, tended to fall flat, and he had even been booed by the audience. The people of Doon Town were not kind.

'And now we come to the first important business of the evening – the parade in bathing costume attire.' The master of ceremonies rocked delicately on his heels as he made the announcement.

The first six girls sauntered across the stage. They looked identical and were evenly applauded.

'Contestant number seven, Miss Ma Fong Restaurant.'

Nothing happened.

He glanced hastily at his programme. His professionalism was at stake. 'Miss Ma Fong Restaurant.' Good humour and contempt struggled for dominion over him. He addressed the audience. 'I suppose she take Chinese leave.' They stared at him stony-faced. He grimaced and prodded the back-drop curtain. 'Where is Miss Ma Fong Restaurant?'

At last she appeared, wearing a bikini emblazoned with dragons. The audience gasped, and even the master of ceremonies was unable to control his astonishment. Rita, who came next, seemed pallid by contrast, and Miss General Store, though attractive, was conventional.

The parade in evening dress followed the same pattern, with Miss Ma Fong Restaurant again providing the focus of interest. While the other girls were content to wear eighteenth-century ballgowns, she slithered across the stage in a close-fitting red sheath with a daring slit up the sides. 'The world of Suzie Wong,' the master of ceremonies explained, 'and man, what a world.'

Mr Prasad's impatience melted into irritation. Rita so far had made no impact at all.

'It's that damn Chinaman. They too cunning, I tell you.'

The 'pageantry' (so the programme described it) of the final round unfolded slowly, the goddesses of the Graeco-Roman world following each other in ponderous progression.

Mr Prasad relaxed.

'These people have no imagination at all. With them it either have to be Greek or Roman. Like they never hear of Egypt at all, but . . .' he turned to his wife, 'they go hear tonight, eh?'

'You getting too excited. Control yourself, man.'

Miss Ma Fong Restaurant was disappointing. Being a Chinese pagoda did not suit her. Anyway, the pagoda was tilting dangerously.

'A Chinese pagoda,' the master of ceremonies intoned. 'From Pisa.'

Again the audience failed to respond. Miss Ma Fong glared at him, and the master of ceremonies, sheltering behind his professionalism, rocked delicately on his heels.

'Miss Oriental Emporium as Isis, the Egyptian fertility goddess.'

There was a rustle of interest. Rita walked circumspectly across the stage, her movements restricted by the shaped tightness of her costume, and the precarious balance of a squat head-dress surmounted by what looked like a pair of bull's horns. In one hand she carried a staff and in the other a scroll of what was presumably 'papyrus'.

'Isis?'

'But I never hear of that one before.' Whispers like these reached Mr Prasad, and he prodded his wife in the ribs and smiled.

'Miss General Store as Fruits and Flowers.'

Mr Prasad stiffened. The audience digested the significance of this before bursting into rapturous applause. Miss General Stores wore what was basically a grass skirt, hidden behind bunches of hibiscus, oleander and carnations. Her bosom and back were encased in banana leaves overspread with wreaths of fern and more flowers, and on her head she balanced a fruit-filled basket from which hung chains of roses reaching to the floor. People rose from their seats and applauded. Someone threw a straw hat on the stage.

'Original!'

'Fruits and flowers, a local thing.'

'Look, she have a real mango and orange.'

The voice of the master of ceremonies rose above the uproar. 'Ladies and gentlemen, you should be here to see this.' He had forgotten he was not on the radio. This time the audience did laugh. Miss General Store tossed a rose into the audience. A man shouted, 'Strip!' She blushed. Everyone knew then that Miss Doon Town would have to be reckoned with in Port of Spain that year.

The Prasads left the cinema before the results were announced. They drove home in silence and went to bed. The next morning they read in the paper that Rita had come third. She had hinted in an interview that she would have done better but for her sponsor. She was quoted as saying, 'You must have a professional, not an amateur to look after you in this business.'

When Miss Doon Town came second in the national contest Mr Aleong's fellow citizens expressed their gratitude by electing him their Mayor. His rise in fame was paralleled by a rise in his fortunes. The General Store became one of a chain, Proprietor A. Aleong, and above each of his establishments there blazed forth the slogan, 'The finest store in town'. Mr Prasad, who now owned Doon Town's only secondhand shop, would say, pointing to the General Store, 'Our one claim to fame. You wouldn't believe this, but there was a time when me and Aleong – sorry, I mean the Mayor – used to be good friends. I know it hard to believe what with all them stores and things he own now, but we used to be rivals in the same business. I and that man used to compete. Imagine that!'

He would laugh for a long time after he said this, but there was no unhappiness or regret in that laugh. Mr Prasad was content. After all, the Oriental Emporium *was* the only secondhand shop in Doon Town.

A Man of Mystery

Grant Street could boast several business establishments: a grocery, a bookshop that sold chiefly Classic comics, a café and, if you were sufficiently enthusiastic, the rum-shop around the corner (known as the Pax Bar) could also be included. On week-ends a coconut seller arrived with his donkey cart which he parked on the corner. The street's commercial character had developed swiftly but with the full approval of its residents. Commerce attracted strangers and the unbroken stream of traffic lent an air of excitement and was a source of pride. In time a group of steelbandsmen had established themselves in one of the yards, adding thereby a certain finality and roundness to the physiognomy of the street. However, long before any of these things had happened, Grant Street could point to Mr Edwin Green, 'shoemaker and shoe-repairer', whose workshop had been, until the recent immigrations, the chief landmark and point of reference.

From the first Mr Green had been considered by his neighbours to be different from themselves. There were good reasons for this. Grant Street lived an outdoor, communal life. Privacy was unknown and if anyone had demanded it he would have been laughed at. There were good reasons for this as well. The constant lack of privacy had led ultimately to a kind of fuzziness with regard to private property. No one was sure, or could be sure, what belonged to whom or who belonged to whom. When this involved material objects, like bicycles, there would be a fight. When it involved children, more numerous on Grant Street than bicycles, there was a feckless tolerance of the inevitable doubts about paternity. Young men in pursuit of virility made false claims, while at other times the true father absconded. No one worried, since in any case the child would eventually be absorbed into the life of the street. Romantic relationships, frankly promiscuous, were fleeting rather than fragile, and the influx of strangers accelerated this tendency. Unfortunately, the results then were less happy. Grant Street was communal, but only up to a point, and any attachment one of its women might develop for a man from another street was looked upon with distaste. The inevitable child became the centre of a feud. Paternity in the stricter sense was of course not the issue. To which street did the child belong? It was over this problem that argument and acrimony raged.

Mr Green had been deposited in their midst like an alien body. Not only was he married, but his wife, a woman of half-Portuguese, half-Negro extraction, was pale-complexioned, good-looking and 'cultured'. In the late afternoon when Mr Green had closed his shop for the day, she would bring an easel out into the yard and paint for an hour. She had a fondness for sailing ships sinking in stormy seas and vases of flowers. The street, to begin with, had gathered solemnly around her and watched. She enjoyed their bewilderment.

'Lady, why you does paint when it so dark for?'

Mrs Green would stare seriously at her questioner.

'It's the light. There's a certain quality to this tropical twilight which I find so . . . exhilarating.'

Her accent was 'foreign' and when she spoke her bosom heaved cinematically, suggesting a suppressed passion. This impressed her audience. Mrs Green also frequented the public library. On Saturday mornings the street saw her struggling under the weight of half a dozen books, the titles of which were conspicuously displayed. The women sitting on their front steps would laugh in awed disbelief and shout after her, 'Soon you go read up all the books they have in the library. You go have to begin writing them yourself then.' Mrs Green, looking martyred, would disappear into her yard.

All of this was curious enough, but what really intrigued the street was her attitude to Mr Green. They could not understand it. They were never seen together. During the day while he hammered in his shop, she was nowhere in evidence, while during her afternoon painting sessions, he in his turn seemed to have been swallowed up by the silence in their house. That silence was another cause for speculation. It was an unnatural, abnormal silence which many believed to be in some strange way a counterpart to the suppressed passion they thought they detected in Mrs Green's voice.

Nevertheless it was on her husband that the street's perplexity and wonder finally came to rest. The incongruities were not hard to find. Mr Green was spectacularly black, he was ugly, and he betrayed none of the outward signs of culture which his wife exhibited. Stated so baldly the problem was insoluble. That could not be tolerated. Therefore, the belief took shape that Mr Green was something other than he appeared to be. He was not a shoemaker at all; on the contrary, he was a man of the highest education who had chosen that lowly profession out of a profound and philosophic love for the 'simple life'. Mr Green, it was claimed, was in revolt against the hypocrisy and useless trappings of modern civilisation. Also for a time it was fashionable to uphold the theory that Mr Green spent much of his time in a trance, but that was soon abandoned as being too improbable. Nevertheless it did not hinder his transformation into a man of mystery.

His shop became the centre of romance for children on the street. It was a small wooden hut situated at the front of the house (itself an enlarged hut on stilts) under the shade of a tall tamarind tree. Above the door there was a sign which claimed he had the ability 'to fit all sizes and conform to all tastes'. This was a piece of rhetoric. As far as anyone could tell, Mr Green had not once been commissioned to make a pair of shoes; he simply repaired them. Inside there was a clutter of old, unreclaimed shoes overspread with dust. On a sagging work-table he arranged those recently brought in for repair and, always in the same place, an American trade magazine for the year 1950. Mr Green worked facing away from the light. He sat on a bench, holding several tiny nails between his teeth, occasionally extracting one which he would tack with exaggerated care into the shoe he was holding. After each such operation he examined the shoe from all angles and shook his head mournfully. The children crowding near him savoured the smells of leather in various stages of decomposition and the bottles of glue which lay open beside him.

Gradually from his conversations with the children a picture of his past was pieced together. He had lived in Brazil for many years where he had worked as a tapper on a rubber plantation. There he had met his wife, the daughter of the overseer, a hard and unfeeling man who kept his daughter a virtual prisoner and beat her regularly and viciously. She had begged him to take her away – he was the only foreigner working on the plantation – and together they had fled to British Guiana where she had borne him a child, a daughter. They had named her Rosa. The overseer having by that time repented, and they being extremely poor, the child was sent back to Brazil to live with her grandfather. In the meantime, they had saved sufficient money to buy a house and it was thus they had come to Trinidad and to Grant Street. His one sadness in life was never to have seen his daughter – 'a full and grown woman now' – and it was only the hope of seeing her again that kept him 'alive'.

This was a far cry from the picture that had been built up, and while no one really believed the story, it did have its attractions. Therefore the street pretended to believe that it believed Mr Green. He made their task easy. He was everything they expected him to be: kind, gentle, and a little sad. His eccentricities pleased them, especially his dress for occasions, which was invariable and immaculate. He wore a starched and ironed white tropical suit and a cork hat, and when he began taking the children for walks the men lounging on the corner murmured as he passed them, 'Make way for the Governor, everybody make way for the Governor.'

On his Sunday walks Mr Green took the children to the zoo and botanical gardens. They went early in the afternoon, marching in military formation behind Mr Green, who walked stiffly ahead of them. When they had come to the highest point in the Queen's Park Savannah, he would gather the children more informally about him and show them the sea and the ships in the harbour. 'The Brazils,' he would say, 'lie in that direction, and Venezuela, which from certain points you can see on a clear day, in that.' His arms extended in a sweep that embraced the harbour and the glittering sea beyond. When this ritual had been performed, they crossed the road to the zoo. He appeared to have a taste only for those animals he had seen in the wild. 'They call those jaguars? Who they trying to fool? I'll tell you about a jaguar I saw in Brazil one time.' And he would relate a long and tortuous tale. The birds, though, were his favourites and he was at his most lyrical when talking about them. 'They call those parrots? I've seen them in the wild. The colours of the rainbow and more besides. Wonderful creatures. They belong in the jungle,' and adjusting his hat he led them to the alligator pond, as if what he had just seen had been calculated to offend him personally.

Afterwards, they went to the botanical gardens, which, at six o'clock, would be nearly empty. There he allowed them to rest, and while they sprawled on the grass he wandered along the gravelled paths, staring up at the trees, occasionally bending close to read the labels attached to the trunks. Sometimes, perhaps struck by the sudden recall of an incident or a landscape long forgotten, he left off his examination of the trees and gazed abstractedly at the flag flapping limply above the roof of the Governor's house, itself hidden by a bandstand and the clumps of trees growing thickly nearby. At such times it was not difficult for the children to make believe that he was indeed the Governor, and that these were his private grounds. There was something truly proprietorial about Mr Green as he stood there, oblivious of their presence, hostage to some troubling recollection. However, a gust of wind through the trees or a fight among the children and the melancholy would be set aside, to be resurrected and resumed the following Sunday.

His shadow stretched out before him on the path, the harshness of his dress muted in the softer light, he led them through an avenue of trees to the greenhouses where the more exotic exhibits were on display and there showed them insect-devouring plants, fruit one bite of which sufficed to kill a man, and a tree that 'bled'. Mr Green lingered over these things longer than the children cared for. The botanical gardens, so alien, so distinct, seemed hardly to connect with the street they had left three hours before. It was a swept, ordered profusion, a region of shadow on cut grass and strange fruit made stranger still by Mr Green's heady fascination for malignancies they did not understand and which appalled and frightened them. Some of the children cried, but Mr Green, ignoring, or perhaps ignorant of their distress, touched and smelled everything, delighting in the heat and spray of water from the pipes, his suit and helmet tinted green by the light filtering through the vines that crept up the sides of the glass and spread out over the roof. He would leave only when one of the caretakers looked in and told them it was time to go.

If these visits were not the undiluted pleasures they ought to have been, there were some advantages to be had in associating with Mr Green. He was a skilled carpenter and built stools and chairs and desks which he gave to the children. However, the most prized of all his accomplishments were the telephones he was able to make out of bits of wire and old tins. This sustained his popularity and at the same time it allowed him to continue his excursions to the zoo and botanical gardens.

Time having smoothed the rougher edges, the street learned to accept the Greens, bestowing on them the respect that springs from incomprehension. Crowds no longer gathered to watch Mrs Green paint, and although the men lounging on the corner still shouted 'Here comes the Governor', when Mr Green appeared dressed in his white suit, it was done less from malice than a desire to acknowledge his presence. Yet the Greens did come to have one thing in common with their neighbours: they shared their unchanging way of life. In that life, no one ever got richer or poorer; there were no dramatic successes or, for that matter, dramatic failures; no one was ever in serious trouble. Basically, they were cowards. Now and again Grant Street spawned a prodigy, a policeman for instance, but that was considered an aberration and did not happen often. Nevertheless, unheroic as it undoubtedly was, the street did have its heroes: the man in the Western who, flying in the face of the odds, conquers all, and his corollary, the loser, riding off, but with dignity, into the sunset.

The Greens succumbed to this pattern. The shoe-shop maintained a steady trickle of customers; Mrs Green continued to paint ships in distress and vases of flowers; the same silence swallowed now the husband, now the wife; and the tamarind tree, a prisoner of its own maturity, grew no taller. The changes Grant Street knew centred on the succession of carnivals, of births, and of deaths. Marriage, like the policeman, was an aberration that occurred infrequently. Ephemeral groups of children called Charlie and Yvonne and Sheila gathered round Mr Green and were introduced to the wonders of the zoo and botanical gardens and they cried as their predecessors had done. Mr Green, in his turn, saw them grow up, become mothers and putative fathers, fading away from him to the street corners and front steps of hovels.

Therefore when Mrs Green started work as a receptionist to a doctor it was considered almost an infringement of the established order, and when he was seen to come for her in the mornings and bring her back in the afternoons, it amounted to a disturbance of the peace. It soon became apparent that her suppressed passion had found an outlet. All the symptoms were there. When the doctor brought her back in the afternoon they talked long and earnestly in the car before he left, and Mrs Green, who, though distant had always been friendly, now abandoned her friendliness altogether. One change led to another. The painting sessions stopped and so did the visits to the library on Saturday mornings. From these occurrences was dated the commercialisation that was to sweep Grant Street, as if there were some species of sympathetic magic at work connecting the two sets of events. And it certainly was the case that hard on the heels of Mrs Green's liaison the Pax Bar and grocery first made their appearance. Mr Green alone seemed unaware of what was happening. He worked in his shop as usual, smiled benignly at the children and took them out for walks. Unfortunately it was noted that he had recently begun to make more telephones than he had ever done. Mr Green's sadness ceased to be speculative. The street had its standards. There were limits to what anyone could do, and one of the unspoken rules in their

relationship with Mr Green was that their standards did not apply to
him: he had a role to fulfil. They felt not merely that his wife was
'wronging' him, but more peculiarly, that her manner of doing it was
sordid. For them, morality was a matter of form, of 'style', and they
did not approve of Mrs Green's style.

Grant Street's commercialisation proceeded apace, and in the rush of
cars and business and the sounds of the steelband, the Greens
receded. The steelband was the street's pride and had rapidly
become the focus of its loyalties. They practised every night and were
good enough to merit being recorded. The radio spread their fame and
eventually even the American tourists came to marvel at the men who
could produce such sweet and coherent sounds from oil drums. Mr
Green, his accomplishments thrown into shadow by the influx of
visitors, was deserted by his youthful congregation The telephones
which he made in increasing quantities lost their market and lay in
untidy heaps on top the trade magazine for 1950. He had to entice the
children into the shop and as before tried to talk to those who did come
about his life in Brazil and the daughter he longed to see, but they
were impatient and not interested in these stories. Formerly, they had
begged him for his telephones and compliance had had to be dragged
out of him. Now to hold them in his shop he had to promise
instruments of greater sophistication. The next day he would be sure
to see his efforts abandoned in the gutter outside his house or being
kicked along the street. He stopped making telephones and on
Sundays he took his walks alone. One or two people remembered to
say, 'Here comes the Governor', but it was done without any enthusiasm, and Mr Green to avoid them went another way.

  One morning some workmen arrived and they produced the first
noises to come from the Greens. A crowd gathered on the pavement to
watch. The house was being pulled down. Mr Green was detached.
He worked in his shop all day amid the crashing of timber and
galvanised iron sheets. The doctor arrived to supervise the demolition, leaving later with Mrs Green and two trunks, an action sufficiently daring to mollify the neighbours. There was no silence for Mr
Green to return to that night. The house was already roofless and
instead he went to the Pax Bar.

  Everyone there recognised him and looked up with unconcealed
surprise when he went in. He bought half a bottle of rum and sat alone
in a corner. He wore his white suit and did not remove his cork hat.

Towards morning Mr Green shook himself and got up a little unsteadily from his chair. He fixed his hat more firmly on his head and felt his way across the room, holding on to the sides of tables and backs of chairs in his path. The few remaining drunks eyed him disconsolately. 'Good night, Governor.' Mr Green went out into the dark, empty street. A chain of red beacon lights punctured the blackness of the hills. Grant Street was unreal in the stillness. Gazing up at the street lamps and the shuttered houses he walked slowly back to the workshop. He fumbled for a long time before he found his keys. There was no light in the shop and he lit a candle. Half-made telephones littered the bench and table. He picked up one, held the receiver to his ear and laughed. The trade magazine caught his eye. He leafed through it, glancing at the advertisements. The Baltimore Shoe Corporation claimed to be able to 'fit all sizes and conform to all tastes'. Mr Green laughed again and put the magazine back on the table. He closed the door, snuffed the candle and went to sleep on the floor.

When he awoke the demolition men were already at work. The doctor was giving them instructions. Mr Green examined his suit in the semi-darkness. It had changed colour, and circular brown patches showed where rum had fallen on it the night before. He started brushing it, then, frowning, he gave up the attempt. He opened late and worked until lunch-time, when he closed the shop and went to the Pax Bar. It was the last time Edwin Green, 'shoemaker and shoe-repairer', ever opened for business.

It was a small house and in three days the demolition was complete. The street salvaged what it could from the piles of timber laid out on the pavement. There was no one to stop them except the doctor, and even he, after an argument in which he called them 'carrion crows', allowed them to take what they wished. The new house took shape slowly. Grant Street had never seen anything like it. It was large and rambling in the Californian fashion, surrounded by a lawn and fenced in from the street. The outside walls were painted a bright pink, and wooden louvres were used instead of windows. There were wrought iron gates surmounted by wrought iron lanterns. But by far the most impressive innovation was the chimney on the roof.

Mrs Green returned when it was finished. She behaved as if she had come to the street for the first time. In the afternoons she watered the lawn while the doctor fussed with the potted plants and orchids which hung from the eaves. Mr Green was banished to his reservation. His shop had not been touched and stood in ramshackle and bizarre opposition to the modernity that seemed poised to devour it.

The street had long ago surrendered its illusions about him. The evidence to the contrary was too overwhelming, and anyway they did not need these illusions. Mr Green's fall had been public and obvious, and any private sorrow which he might still have had could not compensate for or hide his humiliation. Now all they could see was the physical shell whose disintegration they studied with a passive morbidity. Grant Street had a clear conscience. It had expressed its sympathy for Mr Green and its horror of what his wife was doing. There were many other things demanding their attention.

Mr Green lived in the shop. His revelries in the Pax Bar ended late in the evening, and as he crept down the street on his way home he sang noisily, pausing to swear when his steps stuttered uncontrollably. Occasionally he stumbled and fell on the roadway and then he would lie there for some minutes without moving. Sometimes he urinated as he lay there, taking fresh swigs from the bottle he always carried with him. He delivered his final orations outside the shop, laughing and cursing in turn as he kicked at the door until it gave way. Then, suddenly, he would fall silent and leaning against the fence, stare at the freshly watered lawn and the curtains in the new house drawn tight and secure. At noon the next day he emerged, his suit tattered and frayed beyond recognition, the cork hat dented and twisted at an odd angle on his head, to make the journey once again to the Pax Bar. Mr Green's metamorphosis had been quickly absorbed into the landscape. The world had come to Grant Street and it would take more than the ragings of a drunken man to disturb them.

Sunday afternoon was hot. The men on the corner had sought the shade of the bookshop and in the yards the children played and the women sat on their front steps fanning themselves and gossiping. The steelband maundered sleepily to itself; the Pax Bar would not open until evening. Grant Street was in limbo.

Tamarinds were in season and several children were collecting the fruit that had fallen off the tree and littered the yard in front of the shoe shop. Mr Green watched them from the doorway. His eyes were red and he blinked painfully in the harsh light. He reached for the bottle of rum on his work table, uncorked it and drank some. With a faint smile and still holding the bottle he approached the children gathering the tamarinds. He picked up a handful and offered it to one of the smaller girls. She shook her head and backing away began to cry. The other children retreated, dropping the fruit they had collected. Mr Green laughed, and stepped out on to the street. He looked at the house. The louvres were opened and even in the gloom he could see that the walls were covered with pictures. One stood out. It was a painting of a ship with only its rigging visible, on the verge of being totally annihilated by a mountainous sea. He threw the tamarinds in the gutter and started up the street. His walk was studied and tenative. The urine stains on his trousers showed clearly. He took another sip from the bottle and shielding his eyes from the sun he gazed up at the sky. There were only a few clouds about, and they were small and white. He quickened his pace when he saw the coconut seller turn the corner with his donkey cart.

The donkey, a shaggy, morose, under-fed creature, had been tethered in a patch of weeds. Mr Green stopped to examine it. He passed his hands over its shanks and patted it. The men in the shelter of the bookshop laughed. Mr Green turned to address them. 'Do you call this a donkey? Poor creature. I've seen them in the wild . . .' The rest of what he said was lost in their laughter. The coconut seller advanced on him. 'Mister, you better leave my donkey alone, or you go know what.' He traced patterns in the air with his cutlass. 'Friend, I was only pointing out . . .' The coconut seller spluttered into obscenity and Mr Green, shaking his head sadly, drank some more rum and walked away.

On the Queen's Park Savannah people were playing cricket and football and horses were cantering on the exercise track near the racecourse. Families out for their Sunday walk paraded amiably on the perimeter. Mr Green sat on a bench under a tree and stared at them, eyes half-closed. A clock struck four. He was tired and sleepy and beads of sweat watered his face and arms. An attack of nausea frittered itself away, but the tiredness, reinforcing itself, would not go. He opened his eyes. There was a breeze and the dust was rising in clouds, hiding the horses and people. The colours of the sky and grass melted and footballers and cricketers wandered through a golden, jellied haze. A voice unattached to a body spoke near him, then receded. Someone tapped him on the shoulder. A dog played round his heels and barked from many miles away. Beyond the Savannah the sea was a sheet of light. The sun fled behind a cloud and the sea was grey and rose up to devour him. He shuddered. For a moment the disoriented world re-grouped, but it needed all his energy and all his will to keep it that way. He let it dissolve and shatter. The rum was everywhere, flowing from chimneys and lanterns and tumescent seas, soaking his clothes. He kicked feebly and the bottle rolled into the dust. He got up. The ground shivered. He swam to the iron railings protecting the Savannah from the road. Another dog barked, a herald of the loneliness descending on all sides. Someone said, '. . . back in time for dinner,' and someone laughed. Weariness called on him to surrender, but he was already on the road, creeping between the cars, and not far away was a refuge of shaded green. A flag danced in the sky. The brown, lifeless hills wavered. A gust of wind blew through the trees; blossoms floated in the air; trees and trunks and labels whirled towards him. The tree-lined avenue was cooler and he was startled by his reflection looming up to meet him out of the foliage. In a moment he was inside. There was a sound of spray, and water dripped on to his hat and trickled down his face. The desolation deepened. Stalks and flowers stumbled in the effort to make themselves seen. He noticed the green light flowing through the glass, becoming one with his nausea, and he tried to remember why the children had cried. The tree that bled. He moved towards it, but darkness closed in, confounding his desire, bringing with it the smell of fruit even stranger than those he had described, of flower-laden jungles and muddy rivers, landscapes of the mind more real than any he had roamed. Then, mercifully, there was only the darkness.

When the caretaker found him he had been dead for an hour.

Two days later Mr Green was buried in the Mucurapo cemetery. His body, contrary to custom, had been kept in the funeral home, returning to Grant Street for the brief religious service which was held in the drawing room of the new house. Some hitherto unsuspected relations of Mr Green turned up and wept, but no one from the street was allowed in. They gathered on the pavement and stared through the louvres at the coffin.

The procession did not have far to travel and a sombre crowd of neighbours walked behind the hearse to the cemetery. Mrs Green drove in a car. The sky clouded and it began to rain, delaying the burial. It was already dark by the time it was completed and the few limp wreaths had been scattered on the grave.

Within a month the workshop was pulled down – it took one morning to do the job – and for days afterwards the children played with the unreclaimed shoes that had been thrown in the gutter. The tide of grass invaded the spot where the shop had been, and the fence was extended.

Grant Street prospered. The borough council gave it concrete pavements and running water, and the Central Government, a sewage system. Commercialisation had stimulated its ambitions and several of the residents built new houses, none of course as grand as the Enriques' (Mrs Green had remarried), but all with pretensions to modernity. The grocery had become a supermarket, the café a restaurant; and the steelband went on tours to the Bahamas and United States. Romantic relations were regularised, and there were even a few marriages. Children were still numerous, but the index had changed: they were more numerous than motor cars.

The street had undergone a series of changes that went beyond carnival and birth and death, and this had brought nostalgia. Grant Street had acquired a past whose sharpness had been softened by the passage of time and now glowed with a gentle light. Those who were no longer there or had died shared that softness and were transfigured by it. Mr Green had left no physical reminder of his presence to trouble them and as a result his legend revived. His style of death, a memorial to his dreams, was beyond reproach, and in the end it redeemed him. Put in another way, in terms of the Westerns Grant Street loved, he had ridden into the sunset.

The Political Education of Clarissa Forbes

Clarissa Forbes had a mind of her own, a peculiarity sufficiently strange for her family to have recognised and sanctified it. The source of this independence of spirit was a mystery to her family, her friends, and, in due course, her employers. But first to bear the burden was her family.

The Forbes were poor and relatively humble. There had been a time when they were poorer and straightforwardly humble, but a new government had been voted into favour with help from people like the Forbes and in an initial flush of gratitude decided, among other things, to build new roads. The Forbes benefited from this.

Mr Forbes was a semi-skilled manual labourer, chronically out of work and compelled as a result to do jobs like sweeping the streets and cleaning windows, which he considered to be beneath his dignity. However, with the advent of the new government, the situation improved.

The extensive road-building programme left Mr Forbes with little spare time, but that spare time he spent not in a hovel wracked by the coming and going of cars and lorries, but in a new house, another of the government's gifts to its supporters, laid out side by side with other houses minutely similar to itself and inhabited by people indistinguishable from the Forbes.

Mr Forbes was understanding. 'If we was not all the same, there is bound to be some unreasonable people who go be sure to get up and ask why Tom different from Dick and Dick different from Harry. This way, nobody have reason to complain and we all happy.'

Mr Forbes was only partly right. True, his wife was happy. She applauded these sentiments. 'If everybody was like you, Ethélbert, there wouldn't be no trouble in this world today.' Clarissa, however, was less easily swept off her feet.

'Huh. I just don't understand people like you two. Is as if you have no sense of pride, no dignity, wanting to live and be just like all these foolish people you see around you.' She was sprawled on the sofa reading a copy of a cheap English magazine given her by a school friend whose aunt had emigrated to England.

'But what you mean, Clary?' her father objected gently. 'Don't tell me you prefer that other place we used to live in.'

'I do in a way, if you must know. At least there we was different, not living exactly like everybody else.'

'I just don't understand you, Clary.' Mr Forbes scratched his thinning hair, always a sign of perplexity. His tone, nevertheless, was mild and questioning. The disharmony his daughter had injected into the idyll he had been painting was not an entirely unfamiliar experience.

'Well take this, for instance.' Clarissa flourished the cheap English magazine. There was a picture on the cover of a woman in a bikini, sitting on a rock and gazing into the far distance. 'You should read this and get an idea of how other people does live abroad, the different kinds of thing they does do.' Clarissa sat up. 'You know, over there they does go to places like Spain and Portugal for they holidays. Have a look at that.' She thrust the magazine near her father's face and showed him another photograph, this one in colour. It was a picture of dozens of pale-skinned people gathered round the edges of a swimming pool. The sea, in the distance, was hidden by a jungle of umbrellas. 'Tell me, where we does go for we holidays? I never even set foot in Tobago once in my life. We never hear of that kind of thing. But over there they does take it for granted.'

Mr Forbes studied the photograph carefully. 'It look very nice,' he said. 'Let me see it, Ethélbert.' Mr Forbes gave his wife the magazine. 'Yes. Ethélbert right. It look very nice.'

Clarissa snatched the magazine from her mother. 'You don't have to tell me that. I know it nice.' She flicked through the pages of the magazine in search of further evidence. 'Ah yes. All you ever hear of Torremolinos?' Her parents shook their heads. 'I thought so. That's exactly the kind of ignorance I mean. And another thing. Here we only have horse racing, not so?' Her parents nodded. 'Well over there in England they have something else. Greyhounds. You ever hear of that?'

Mr Forbes scratched his head. 'Greyhound is a kind of dog, not so?'

'That's right, Pa. You smarter than I thought. Everybody does go to the dog races over there.'

'Dog races?' Mrs Forbes was incredulous. 'You mean they does race dogs against each other?'

'I remember now,' Mr Forbes said. 'They does call it greyhound racing.' Mr Forbes was pleased with himself, hoping this display of knowledge would further impress his daughter.

'That's right, Pa. I glad to see you know a few things.'

'And they have jockey riding these dog?' Mrs Forbes inquired.

Mr Forbes laughed loudly, slapping his thigh.

'No, Ma. They does have an electric hare out in front which the dogs does chase around a track.'

Mrs Forbes did not fully understand, but she was happy to let the matter drop. Mr Forbes, however, was determined to press home his advantage. 'Hear she. Jockey riding dog. Have to be a very small jockey or a very big dog.' He spluttered into fresh laughter.

Clarissa warmed to her theme. 'Someone like you, Ma, if you was living in England, could go in the evening to one of them bingo halls.'

'You mean they have places where they does only play bingo?'

'Every night without fail,' Clarissa assured her.

Mr Forbes whistled. 'I could go to the dog races and Maisie could go to them bingo halls.'

'Exactly,' Clarissa replied.

'I think I would really like them bingo halls.' Mrs Forbes, closing her eyes, surrendered to the seductive pictures of her imagination.

After this the Forbes were more circumspect in singing the praises of their new home in front of their daughter. Each new issue of the cheap English magazine brought its fresh dose of invective and a further unsettling of the Forbes household. To avoid this, Mr and Mrs Forbes did as much as was within their power to placate Clarissa. They responded with the same look of simple-minded amazement to everything she said, the same expressions of astonished incredulity and the same anxiety lest their ignorance should annoy her. Unhappily, try as they might, they could never quite escape the taint imposed on them by the limitations, the 'inferiority' as Clarissa never tired of describing it, of their situation.

Nevertheless, Mr Forbes's political consciousness continued to grow, doubtless stimulated in part by his daughter's incessant attacks. Despite Clarissa's scorn or, most probably, because of it, he developed in response to the pleadings of the politicians a sense of the injustices done to him in years, centuries, gone by. And this by the very people Clarissa would have him imitate. For the moment, however, he was reticent. Mr Forbes was still unsure of his ground.

This process the Prime Minister called 'political education', and to put his loyalty beyond all reasonable doubt and also as an expression of his gratitude for all the government had done for him, Mr Forbes joined the Party. He adopted its tie, whose motif was a yellow sun (presumably rising) over a blue sea. For some time Mr Forbes kept this a secret from Clarissa and listened in silent submission to her ravings about Torremolinos, the greyhound races and the bingo halls. But as the months passed his confidence grew and he began wearing his tie on Sundays when he went to the local Anglican church with his wife. Clarissa did not accompany them. 'It too low class,' she told her parents. 'If I go to any church at all it got to be Catholic.'

Mr Forbes was an admirable pupil. 'Nowadays,' he said to his wife, 'it ain't have a soul who going to push we around like they used to before. Let them just try it and the P.M. go take care of them.' Then he explained the facts about slavery and colonialism as described by the Prime Minister. Mrs Forbes applauded and was unable to decide whom she loved more, her husband or the Prime Minister. In time, Mr Forbes joined the ranks of the active Party workers and scoured the countryside showering leaflets on the peasants. His enthusiasm stimulated gossip about the Party nominating him to run for the local council. Unfortunately, though, to Clarissa's unbounded relief, he was not chosen. She was aware that people in the best circles rather despised the proletarian character of the present government and her father's activities had consequently become a great drain on her pride. Clarissa reproached him.

'You mean after all I teach you, you still think that running for the local council is the greatest thing in the world?'

Mr Forbes was apologetic. 'I didn't have anything to do with it, Clary. It was other people who was talking, not me.'

'People like you will never learn,' Clarissa said despairingly.

Mr Forbes hid his disappointment well and vowed to his wife that he would continue to serve the Party faithfully. Mrs Forbes, however, was greatly distressed by the turn of events and her fervour for the Prime Minister abated perceptibly.

'You been working for these people so long, Ethélbert, breaking your back to please them. You would think they could at least give you a seat on the council as a kind of reward.'

'These decisions have to go through a lot of channels we don't know about, Maisie, and I feel sure that if they didn't give me a seat it was for a very good reason.'

'But you would think the Prime Minister . . .'

Mr Forbes waved his hands angrily. 'He don't have nothing to do with this. You think he ever even hear my name? He is a busy man. And another thing, if I was a councillor I couldn't take you with me to functions and things like that. Is not that I insulting you, but you don't have . . .' Mr Forbes, scratching his head, searched for the right words.

'I know what you mean, Ethélbert. But you could have take Clary with you.' Mrs Forbes was not used to compliments and by the same token she was only able to recognise the crudest insults. Political education had hardly made any impact on her.

'Me!' Clarissa cried, looking up with a start from her magazine, 'Me! What you take me for, Ma?'

'Your mother was only using you as an example, Clary.' Mr Forbes was embarrassed.

'I hope so! I really hope so! Anyway, what's the point in working yourself up over a stupid thing like that for? Who would want to be a councillor in a stupid place like this? If you was in Port of Spain I could understand. But in a place like Paradise. It beats me!' She gave the rocker on which she was sitting a gentle push with her feet and creaking demurely back and forth continued reading her magazine.

Mr Forbes, catching his wife's eye, shook his head sadly. In a world where the cheap English magazine was not to be denied, the Forbes, husband and wife, had come to feel themselves and their activities insignificant and Lilliputian. They began to wish Clarissa would leave home.

The object of their concern was not particularly prepossessing. Clarissa's face was moon-shaped and faintly scarred by chicken-pox. Her round, black eyes were heavy-lidded and hemmed in by the bulging flesh that pressed in upon them from her cheeks. She had a boxer's build, squat and thick-set, her diaphragm giving the impression of having been added to the rest of her as an afterthought. As a result, one thought of it as being misplaced, another person's property which Clarissa had appropriated and turned to her own uses. Yet it was the attentions allegedly paid to this unlovely exterior which ultimately were to lead to the gratification of her parents' unspoken wish.

Clarissa, despite her irredeemable unattractiveness, took great care with her appearance. She was extremely vain. This, however, had not always been the case. As a child, she had shown little inclination to improve upon her looks and indeed, up to about the age of sixteen she had tended to emphasise her ugliness by the clothes she wore and the way in which she carried herself. Clarissa had, in other words, made a fetish of her ugliness. Then she met the girl whose aunt had emigrated to England and who, unaware of the revolution it would stimulate, introduced her to the cheap English magazine. Overnight Clarissa's world was transformed.

The first symptom of this transformation was her obsession with personal hygiene. Her cleanliness became mythical. She bathed twice each day, once in the morning before she went to school, and again in the evening before she went to bed, when, to the never-ending wonderment of her parents, she followed the exhortations of the toothpaste manufacturers and brushed her teeth as well.

Her clothes, which she now chose with the greatest care, were always neat and well-ironed and her hair, which formerly she kept plaited close to her scalp, she let down and attempted to comb straight with the assistance of the village hairdresser. Clarissa took copies of the English magazine to her and explained she would like it done just as in the particular photograph that had caught her fancy.

'That style not make for hair like ours, Clarissa.' The hairdresser herself had adopted an 'African' hairstyle. Her political education was well advanced.

'I don't see why. Why only they must have it for?'

'Because they have softer hair than we, Clarissa. That's why. Look, I'll draw a picture so that you could see the difference.' The hairdresser illustrated the difference with two rough diagrams. 'You see how theirs does fall without any trouble? Now you try doing that to ours and see what go happen.'

Clarissa twisted her face sourly and glanced quickly away from the sheet of paper. 'You only making that up,' she said. 'You just like my father. I don't see why you can't use a really hot comb. That bound to get it straight.'

'But it might burn you.'

'I don't care. Is my head that go be burning. Not yours.' Clarissa stared wistfully at the photograph in the magazine.

The hairdresser was resigned. She did as she was told and applied a very hot comb. Clarissa grimaced but did not complain. 'You see what I tell you,' she said, gritting her teeth, 'our hair not really all that different.' The hairdresser was silent. When it was all over, she brought a mirror and Clarissa examined the result. Her cheerfulness disintegrated instantly. 'You call yourself a hairdresser? Like you out to spite me or something?' She began to cry.

'You looking just like one of them Amerindians you does see in British Guiana,' the hairdresser giggled. And then, being a woman of some sensitivity, she realized her mistake and added, 'I was only joking, Clarissa. Don't mind me. It not looking all that bad.' She compared it with the picture in the magazine. The resemblance was tenuous. 'I could fix it up for you in no time at all.'

'You do it on purpose,' Clarissa sobbed. 'You was jealous of me. Everybody in this place jealous of me. You 'fraid that I was going to look too pretty, so you take the chance of spiting me.'

The hairdresser endeavoured to soothe her. 'Come, Clarissa. Don't cry. I'll fix it up for you so it wouldn't look too bad. I'll give it a few curls and it will look real nice. You wait and see.'

Thus Clarissa had no alternative but to submit to a more discreet hairstyle, more in keeping, as the hairdresser put it, 'with our stiff kind of hair'. In the end, all was forgiven. Paradise had no other hairdresser.

However, Clarissa's programme was not confined to improving her appearance. She stopped going to any and every film that happened to be on at the village cinema. Now she went only to light American melodramas and musicals; every other kind of film she considered beneath her. Westerns, especially, she condemned as 'unrefined'.

In addition, many of her friends fell under the withering contempt of Clarissa's new austerity. One of the few survivors was the girl whose aunt had emigrated to England. Without her, Clarissa's supply of the cheap English magazine would have been strangled at its source. Her reputation in the village grew. Young men took to roaming near the house in the hope of catching a glimpse of the renovated Clarissa and their girlfriends, when they saw her on the street, usually on her way to school or, if to the hairdresser's, with a copy of the magazine rolled under her arm, shrieked insults at her: the kind of insults which Mrs Forbes would have had no trouble in understanding.

Clarissa thrived. Her favourite place of repose was the little veranda at the front of the house where, in the afternoons after she had returned from school, she rocked gently in the sunlight, filing her nails and reading. The boys would arrive on bicycles and leaning against the gate try to hold her in conversation.

'Hey, Miss Forbes, give we a smile, eh!'

'You looking real sweet today. How about a little kiss?'

Clarissa would frown into her magazine, brushing imaginary flies away from her face. Then, with a shiver of annoyance, when the chorus seemed on the verge of melting away, she would rise and say, 'I don't see why you hooligans can't leave decent people alone. I can't even read in peace in my own house now.' And she would flounce inside, slamming the front door.

Clarissa's academic pretensions were never very great, but she took a stubborn pride in her poor performances, refusing to believe that they indicated any more than her own preoccupation with matters of greater importance and the spiritless mediocrity of those around her.

One day she returned home from school earlier than usual, and throwing her books on the floor, collapsed on the sofa with apparent disgust. Mrs Forbes was concerned. 'Clary! You sick or something?'

'Sick! I wish I was.' She stared at the books scattered on the floor. 'It's not me who sick, Ma. Is the people who live in this town sick, if you ask me.' She searched in her pocket for her nail file.

'Somebody trying to take advantage of you?'

'He would have if I had given him half a chance. Vulgar beast!' She filed minutely at her nails.

'Who you talking 'bout?' Mrs Forbes knelt down and began collecting the books.

'One of them masters at school. He was trying to be fast with me this afternoon.'

'You mean . . .' Mrs Forbes gazed in scandalised disbelief at her daughter.

'That's right, Ma. If I had give him half a chance he would have rape me right there and then.' Clarissa studied the neat edges of her nails. She did not appear to be particularly shocked or distressed. She relished using the word 'rape' and Mrs Forbes, consequently, was inclined to treat what had happened as merely an echo from that larger, melodramatic world which Clarissa inhabited. It paralysed her normal response.

'I going to leave that school,' Clarissa added. 'I can't stay there after today. Anyway, that place don't have anything for me.' She replaced the file in her pocket and hugged herself. 'God! I can't tell you how much I wish I was abroad some place. Torremolinos. That's where I should have been born.'

'But that kind of thing might still happen there, Clary,' Mrs Forbes ventured timidly.

Clarissa was appalled. 'People like you does never learn,' she said. 'How many times I have to tell you things different over there?'

Mrs Forbes acknowledged her mistake and said no more.

Mr Forbes's reaction when he heard the news (he had been to a

Party meeting) was similar to his wife's, but nevertheless he felt it his duty to go and see the schoolmaster. Clarissa was not pleased.

'What's the point of doing that, Pa? I leaving the place after all and I didn't even give the man a chance to touch me. I suppose he was just overcome by desire. That does happen to men sometimes, you know. I sure even you does feel like that sometimes.'

Mr Forbes was enveloped in a thickening mental fog. 'Overcome by desire.' Attempting to gain a securer foothold, he pushed it away from his mind. 'All the same,' he continued tentatively, 'it not right to have a man teaching there who is liable at any time to grab you in the corridor and . . .'

'I didn't say anything about a corridor, Pa. Maybe he's frustrated.'

'Look here,' Mr Forbes replied with abrupt resolution, 'I going to have it out with that man whether he frus . . . whether he is like what you say he is or not.'

The schoolmaster was jovial about the affair. 'I don't know how Clarissa get an idea like that into she head, Mr Forbes. I treat she the same as I does treat all my pupils. And anyway, she tell me the other day that she was leaving school, so I thought I could ask she to go and see a film with me. Mind you, if she was still going to be my pupil I would never have dream of doing a thing like that. It wouldn't have been ethical, if you see what I mean.' He gestured attractively with his cream-coloured palms. 'Not ethical at all, Mr Forbes. But I don't see where she get this idea about my wanting to rape she from. Is not a nice thing to say about a man, you know, Mr Forbes. Is not a nice thing to say at all. That kind of gossip could ruin people, especially a man in my position.' He rubbed his palms together, wagging his head mournfully from side to side.

Mr Forbes was convinced by the sincerity of this defence and he returned home to Clarissa worried and confused.

'He say he only ask you to go to a film, Clary. And besides, you had make up your mind to leave school. You didn't tell we anything about that.'

Clarissa shrugged her shoulders. 'That's not the point,' she replied, but did not bother to elaborate.

'Anyway,' Mr Forbes persisted, 'it would have been unethical for him to try to do a thing like that.'

'I don't like all them big words,' Clarissa said, 'and anyway, I don't like talking about such things. It's better to leave that sort of thing to the other girls. Let them keep their "men".' She twisted her mouth in distaste. 'If I ever go with anybody it will have to be for love and love alone. I'll only become pregnant in wedlock.'

Clarissa's alternating use of the vernacular and that other vocabulary which stifled the judgement baffled Mr Forbes. Torn between the crudity of the former and the elegance of the latter, he listened uneasily to his daughter. Again he strove for the concrete.

'But did he really try to . . . to . . .' Mr Forbes scratched his head and avoided looking at his daughter.

'Really, Pa! Next you go be accusing me of lying.'

'Well I just wanted to . . .'

'If you must doubt me. Yes. He did want to have sexual intercourse with me. But I'm a virgin and will remain one until the day I get married.'

Mr Forbes's perplexity deepened. Sexual intercourse. Virgin. The gap between him and his daughter widened. It was not Clarissa's knowledge of the world that worried him: it was the way she communicated this knowledge. Somehow she managed to make the world seem a much more threatening and mysterious place than he had ever imagined it to be. He dropped the matter and awaited with mounting impatience Clarissa's decision to leave home and begin that inevitable pilgrimage to the land of her dreams.

For some weeks, however, Clarissa did nothing. She remained at home, clean and fragrant, rocking with determined obstinacy on the veranda, occasionally taking time off to rail at the smallness and pettiness of Paradise.

'Look at this place,' she exclaimed, 'a main road with a lot of houses on either side. What do they expect people to live here and do, eh?'

'Me and your father live here all we life. We never complain about it,' her mother answered.

'That's because you and he have no ambition.'

For the first time, Mr Forbes lost his temper.

'It's because we know we place. For people like we it all right, but for people like you . . . well, you could only make trouble for yourself and everybody else. You is the sort of person who have to wait for people to spit in your face before you come to your senses.' Mr Forbes watched his daughter narrowly. 'Why don't you go to Port of Spain, then and live with your aunt?'

'With Auntie Selma! You must be crazy or something, Pa. She does live in John-John with all kinds of louts and riff-raff. What you take me for, Pa?'

'You might find a nice job there and get married,' Mr Forbes went on. His tone was simultaneously conciliatory and goading.

'I could see you out to insult me, Pa. If all you want to do is get rid of me why don't you say so right out instead of beating round the bush?'

'Who say we want to get rid of you?' Mr Forbes replied soothingly.

'Get married!' Clarissa snorted. 'What do you take me for, eh? You think I like all these girls you see running round Paradise?'

'Nobody say that. We know you different.'

'I'll make up my mind in my own good time, you hear. Nobody going to push me around.'

Nevertheless, Clarissa announced her decision the following week.

'I think I'll go and find work in Port of Spain after all. I sure to meet a different class of people there.'

'That's a good idea, Clary,' Mr Forbes said.

'You don't have to tell me that, Pa. I know.' Clarissa was filing her nails. 'I'll go and be a nurse to some rich people children. They does do that kind of thing down there, treating you like one of the family.'

'You need qualifications to be a nurse.' Mr Forbes fingered his Party tie. Political education had gradually enlarged his idea of the complexity of things (due in large part to his failure to gain a seat on the local council) and he derived some comfort from being able to hint at the snags in any undertaking.

'I will learn, Pa. I not stupid you know.'

In Port of Spain, Clarissa discovered that while the wealthy did indeed want 'nurses', they were, none of them, prepared to treat her as one of the family. She would be subject to all sorts of regulations and restrictions which, needless to say, she found offensive. The charms of the Opposition faded and she detected in her heart small, but undeniably sympathetic sentiments towards the government. Clarissa, however, was not yet prepared to surrender to these baser instincts. She would compromise.

Day after day she ran her finger down the classified column of the newspaper. Too many of them asked for 'servant'. That was taking compromise too far, since for Clarissa it was metaphor alone that made the present world habitable. She persevered until at last she noticed that the Gokhools wanted a 'maid'. Clarissa arranged to be interviewed.

The Gokhools lived in a large, rambling house in Woodlands. It was surrounded by a well-watered lawn and two cars were parked in the garage. She hesitated on the pavement, studying the other houses on the street, nearly all as prosperous as the Gokhools'. Unconsciously she had allowed an expression of mild astonishment to form on her face, then, suspecting this, her eyes narrowed into a harder stare.

She rattled the gate. A small white dog came bounding out of the house, barking furiously, a frail woman in pursuit. 'Stop that, Nelson. Get back to your kennel.'

Nelson, ignoring her, barked frenziedly at Clarissa.

The woman looked at Clarissa. 'You are the girl who come for the servant job we advertise?'

Clarissa, shrinking into her obstinacy, nodded briefly.

'Come inside, then. Nelson bark is a lot worse than his bite. Pedigree dogs tend to be rather highly strung, you know.' The woman tittered, and Clarissa opened the gate, her hostility focused on the yapping dog. Nelson subsided instantly, cowering behind the woman who had bent down to stroke him.

'So you are the girl, eh?' She examined Clarissa's clothes with the barest slinking displeasure. 'You ever do servant work before?'

Clarissa shook her head, gazing, her eyes dull and lifeless, at the woman crouched at her feet.

'I'm Mrs Gokhool.' The woman stood up, smoothing her skirt. 'Come this way into the kitchen where we can talk.' Mrs Gokhool, adopting a more business-like manner, led the way briskly, leaving a faint trail of perfume in her wake. Clarissa shambled negligently behind her. They entered the kitchen, a spacious tiled room, obviously newly built. All the equipment was electric and extremely modern. Clarissa had to struggle to control the look of astonishment that was about to descend on her again. The expression she assumed implied that nothing could surprise her. Mrs Gokhool threw herself into a chair.

'We had to send the last girl away because she got pregnant.' Mrs Gokhool twirled a strand of her hair around her fingers. 'She was having a baby, that is,' she explained, smiling more genially at Clarissa. 'My husband didn't want to have yet another mouth to feed and anyway she started having all kinds of riff-raff hanging round the house. It's amazing how quickly that kind of thing can happen. Overnight.' Mrs Gokhool wrinkled her brows and smiled up at Clarissa. 'But I don't expect you are the sort of girl to go and do a thing like that.' As she had done earlier, she glanced at Clarissa's clothes with the same hint of muted displeasure. 'Still,' she waved her hands, running her eyes over the shining kitchen equipment, 'all that's over and done with now, thank God.' She sighed. 'Well, I suppose what you really want to know is what your duties would be if we decide to give you the job.'

Clarissa stood withdrawn and unmoved before Mrs Gokhool.

'You wouldn't have to do any cooking. I have someone else for that.' Mrs Gokhool paused, waiting for a reaction, but none forthcoming, she went on. 'But you would have to help with the washing up. Adeleine suffers from rheumatism and it's not good for her to be in water too much.'

Clarissa's gaze travelled over the varnished wooden ceiling, returning to rest for an instant on the tip of Mrs Gokhool's nose, before settling on the floor. She gave the impression of not having heard a word.

'Your main job, though, would be the cleaning of the house, the making of the beds in the morning and looking after the children generally. Saturday afternoons will be yours and you can do anything you want then, within reason of course. There's a cinema just across the road.'

Clarissa had drawn herself tightly together as if striving to efface the image of the woman speaking to her. Nelson came running into the kitchen and crawled under the table. Mrs Gokhool picked him up and put him on her lap. She stroked his long, furry ears. 'Naughty boy. I thought I told you to go to your kennel.' She turned to Clarissa. 'You just leave school?'

'Uh huh.'

'Your parents still alive? This last girl we send away was from the Belmont Orphanage.'

'Uh huh.'

'What does your father do?'

'He's a councillor.' Clarissa hardly parted her lips as she spoke and the sounds emerged as if wrapped in cotton-wool.

Mrs Gokhool, herself a supporter of the Opposition, was condescending.

'A councillor! That's nice. So you come from an important family?' She grinned at Clarissa.

Clarissa twisted her face sourly. She did not answer the question. Instead she asked whether she would have a room of her own if she, and Clarissa laid special emphasis on this, if she 'decided to take the job'.

Mrs Gokhool looked at her queerly. 'Yes, yes. I was forgetting. Come and I'll show you.' She got up hurriedly, Nelson sliding from her lap, and went out through another door into the backyard and pointed at a small, low shed with a corrugated iron roof kept in position by strategically placed stones. Next to it was Nelson's kennel with 'Home Sweet Home' painted in neat red letters on the front. Clarissa stared at it, trying to disguise her interest. She had never seen a kennel before, not even in the cheap English magazine.

'It's not as bad as it looks,' Mrs Gokhool grinned cheerfully at Clarissa. She was referring to the shed, not the kennel. 'It's much better inside than out and it has everything you will need. The other girl was very happy until she began getting ideas above her station.'

They went inside, having to stoop slightly so as not to brush against the roof. The shed was furnished with a bed and a battered wardrobe. Along one wall there was a sagging bookshelf, filled with old text-books. The floor was of bare concrete and there was no electric light. 'You will have to use candles, but I don't suppose you do much reading anyway, so that doesn't matter.'

'I read a lot,' Clarissa said.

'Do you? Oh, I forgot to ask. What's your name?'

'Clarissa.'

'What do you read, Clarissa?'

'All kinds of things.'

Mrs Gokhool giggled. 'Well, you won't have much time for that here, Clarissa. But what little reading you like doing you can do in the daytime. It's a nice little room, don't you think? The electric light is the only drawback.'

What Clarissa thought was written plainly on her face. She did not attempt to hide her disappointment. She puffed out her cheeks and with that look of sourness that had become habitual to her, stared morosely round her future surroundings, refusing to be drawn by Mrs Gokhool's forced enthusiasm.

Mrs Gokhool giggled uncomfortably. 'It used to be a chicken-run at one time.' They went out into the yard.

'When do you think you can start work? If you want the job, that is. I have lots of other girls like you breathing down my neck.'

'Tomorrow. I can start tomorrow.' Nelson sniffed at her heels.

Mrs Gokhool promised to have the room cleaned. 'I'm sure you will like the rest of the family. My husband is the easiest man in the world to get on with, once you do your work properly.' Mrs Gokhool escorted her to the gate. 'Till tomorrow then, Clarissa.'

'So you going to be a nurse after all,' Mr Forbes mused. 'Well, I must say that really surprise me.'

'I keep telling you I not stupid like you think.' Clarissa was arranging her clothes with great care in a suitcase. 'People know they can't push me around.'

'They giving you a uniform to wear?' her mother asked.

'Nothing like that, Ma. The woman say they going to regard me as one of the family. Mind you, I don't think I going to stay with them all that long. What I really want to do is a commercial course.'

'But you haven't even start the job as yet and you already talking about leaving. You is a funny girl, Clary.' Mr Forbes scratched his head.

'A long time ago I set my heart on a commercial course. I don't want to be a . . . a nurse for the rest of my life.'

'What you want to do a commercial course for?'

'What do you mean, Pa? I going to be a top class secretary one of these days. I don't mean any ordinary secretary like you does see running about all over the place. I mean really top class. I intend to work in a bank or something like that.'

'You ever see a black person working in a bank?'

'You wait and see,' Clarissa said. 'Mrs Gokhool say she going to use she influence to find me a really first-class job some place. They is important people, you know.'

'They sound really nice. You is a lucky girl, Clary.' Mrs Forbes looked at her daughter admiringly.

'People know they can't push me around,' Clarissa insisted.

Clarissa and the Gokhools were destined not to like each other. At almost every point her duty came into conflict with her dignity. They quarrelled on the first day when Mrs Gokhool insisted that she wear a special blue and white uniform when taking the children for walks. Clarissa refused.

'I don't want everybody taking me for a common servant, Mrs Gokhool.'

'But what do you think you are, Clarissa? You mustn't forget that I am employing you. Just because your father is on some borough council or other and you want to take a commercial course – I don't know who put that idea into your little head – that doesn't make any difference you know.'

'I not a common servant, Mrs Gokhool, and you wait and see, I going to take a commercial course, no matter what you say.'

'Why you working for me then? I didn't ask you to take the job. If you feel like that you shouldn't have come here in the first place.'

'I doing a job for money, Mrs Gokhool. But I not nobody's servant. I won't let anybody kick me around.'

'You must be mad.'

In the end it was Mrs Gokhool who capitulated and Clarissa took the children for walks dressed as she pleased. She avoided those places where the other 'maids' on the street congregated with their charges; but, in the succeeding weeks inevitably having to meet and talk with them, let fall that she was a friend of the family and doing them a favour. Thus having established her position relative to them, they no longer sought to chat and gossip with her about their employers. However, the full flight of Clarissa's fancy was reserved for the rheumatic Adeleine with whom she was in daily contact.

'I'm really a kind of au pair girl,' Clarissa told her.

'A what?' Adeleine had not heard of such things before.

'An au pair girl. They have them in places like England and that.'

'Oh. But I never hear of them in Trinidad before, Clarissa.' Adeleine was as guileless as Mrs Forbes, slow to suspect or take offence and willing to believe anything she was told.

'Is not a common thing as yet. But it just starting to happen here. I'm not really a servant at all, you see.'

'I understand now. But . . .' a doubt formulated itself hesitantly in Adeleine's mind, an unusual thing with her, 'but I don't see you eating with them and things like that. You does eat in the kitchen just like me and the other girl who used to be here. How is that?'

'That's because,' Clarissa replied readily, 'I like keeping myself to myself. I don't like mixing with all different kinds of people. I is a fussy person. I like to pick and choose.'

Adeleine nodded slowly. At last she understood. From then on she kept a suitable distance between Clarissa and herself.

These rumours drifted back to Mrs Gokhool. She liked them even less than Clarissa's refusal to wear a uniform. Nevertheless, she bided her time and said nothing. These stories were an unfailing source of amusement to her friends and they urged her to keep her on for a while longer. 'You can't get rid of such a gem,' they said.

But the causes for mutual complaint grew apace. Mrs Gokhool also read magazines, though of a different kind, and, like Clarissa, they were the source of many of her ideas on elegant living.

'I want you to call Jerry Master Jerry from now on,' she informed Clarissa one day. 'I don't think you should be so familiar with him.'

Clarissa laughed, unfeignedly astonished and amused by this latest directive. 'But I so much older than him,' she protested.

'That's not the point. At this rate you will be calling me Mavis soon.'

'You older than me. But Jerry?' She burst out laughing again.

'Master Jerry.'

'But Jerry . . .'

'Master Jerry.'

'. . . he is not even ten years old and I is seventeen.' Clarissa puffed out her cheeks, shaking her head, and Mrs Gokhool knew she had lost again. She did not retail this 'story' to her friends. It was embarrassing and she was not even sure whether they would approve. They might laugh at her, not at Clarissa. Therefore this refusal rankled more than the rest.

Reluctant as she was to fall back on her father's political teachings, nevertheless Clarissa's injured pride fled there to nurture its grievances. She had divided her world into two quite separate spheres: a present full of injustice, a future laden with promise. The one fed the other. The nature of this future was unclear, except for her conviction that, in it, all wounds would be healed. In the meantime, hoping to further extend her horizons and prepare herself for that great day, she read, furtively, all Mrs Gokhool's American magazines and experimented with her expensive perfumes. Mrs Gokhool caught her. 'So, like you want to take my place as mistress of this house, Clarissa?'

'I was only trying the perfume out, Mrs Gokhool.'

'What make you think this kind of perfume is for you, child? That is proper French perfume you know. I just don't know who is putting all these grand ideas in your head.' She took the bottle away from Clarissa. 'This sort of thing wasn't meant for people like you.'

'I don't see why.' Clarissa puffed out her cheeks.

Mrs Gokhool stared at Clarissa for some moments without speaking. Her status had never been seriously called into question before. 'Get this into your head, girl. You are not like me. We are not the same kind of people.' She paused, scrutinising Clarissa's face, before turning away discomfited by what she saw there. She lowered

her voice. 'Look, here, Clarissa. I don't want you to feel I'm doing
you down, but what I'm telling you is going to be for your own good.
My husband is, as you must know, an important man. We belong
to . . .' Mrs Gokhool groped for words, her eyes wandering painfully
over the room.

'I know,' Clarissa replied. 'You believe that you is really high-class
people and I is some kind of dirt which you can sweep anywhere you
want. That was what you wanted to say, not so?'

'That is not what I want to say, Clarissa.' Mrs Gokhool's composure was cracking fast. 'I've been very reasonable with you before
now. Believe me when I say that none of the people I know would
stand from a servant . . .'

'I is not a servant, Mrs Gokhool. I doing a job for money.'

'. . . none of them would stand from a servant what I have stood
from you. You would've been out on your ears after two minutes.'

'I is not a servant,' Clarissa intoned, but she seemed to be trying to
convince herself rather than Mrs Gokhool.

'. . . there was that business about Jerry, for instance, then your
telling everybody that you were a friend of the family. A friend of the
family! And not wanting to wear a uniform . . .'

'I is not a servant . . .'

'. . . and what was that phrase you used? An au pair girl? For a
servant you have a lot of false pride. Not wanting to call my son
Master, well I never . . .'

Clarissa roused herself. 'I wouldn't call that boy Master if you was
to pay me a million dollars. Not even for a million dollars, you hear.'

'Look here, girl!' Mrs Gokhool shouted suddenly. 'Watch how you
talking to me. I'm not your equal, get that straight. My husband is a
rich, important man. He has more money in his pocket alone than
you will ever see in your entire life and I'm employing you and that
means you are my servant. My servant. Get that straight in your
head.'

'Having money don't make you God, you know. And he only get
that money by robbing poor people. But the government going to fix
all of you soon.'

'Who going to do that? Your councillor father? Is he going to come
and dispossess us?'

'I warning you not to insult my father, Mrs Gokhool . . .'

Mrs Gokhool took a step nearer Clarissa. She spoke slowly, measuring each word. 'You are a servant, Clarissa, not a friend of the

family as you keep lying to everybody on the street. A servant! A servant! A servant!'

'I'm not yours or anybody's servant, Mrs Gokhool. My father is a respectable man. He didn't want me to take this job in the first place and if he ever get to hear of the way you treating me . . .' Clarissa glowered at her. Mrs Gokhool laughed shrilly.

'He's going to come and beat me up. Don't tell me.'

'That's the sort of thing only you would do.'

'Oh! So you are more respectable than us now. Good. I'm grateful to you for telling me. You have any work for me to do? Maybe I could wash your feet for you and spread a red carpet everywhere you walk.'

'I didn't come here for you to insult me, Mrs Gokhool.'

'Sorry, Miss Clarissa. Sorry.' Mrs Gokhool bowed her head low, bringing her palms together in mock obeisance. 'Well, I don't suppose we can continue to be honoured with your presence.'

'Don't think you can tell me to go, Mrs Gokhool. I make up my mind to leave here a long time ago.'

'Don't let us keep you, Miss Clarissa.'

'Stupid, stupid people,' Clarissa muttered and stumped heavily out of the room.

'Clarissa!' Mrs Forbes, astonished, watched her daughter come stumbling up the path. 'What happen?'

'I give up the job.' Her tone was matter-of-fact. She threw her suitcase on to the steps.

'But why? I thought they was such nice people wanting you to be like one of the family and that.'

'Nice people!' Clarissa spat, and pressing her lips tightly together, kicked the suitcase. 'They wanted me to be too much like one of the family, if you ask me. The woman husband try to rape me.'

'You mean to say . . .'

'Exactly, Ma. You hit the nail on the head. He wanted to sleep with me.'

Mrs Forbes gazed more with puzzlement than with alarm at her daughter. 'Sleep with me.' The phrase echoed in her ears. She had never heard it put like that before. Her judgement clouded.

'Imagine that,' she murmured, unable to suppress the note of admiration creeping into her voice. 'Imagine that. A big, respectable man like that wanting to . . . to sleep with you.'

Mr Forbes when told was tempted to intervene. Clarissa dissuaded him. 'It's not that important, Pa. After all, for a man, especially a frustrated man, to want to sleep with a woman is only natural.' And he too, falling victim to the magic phrase, decided the matter was outside his competence.

During the time she had been at the Gokhools', Clarissa had saved sufficient money to enable her to enrol for the commercial course she had long set her heart on. She relented on the matter of accommodation and in the end agreed to live rent-free with her Auntie Selma in Port of Spain.

'When I finish this course,' Clarissa declared, 'I could get a job anywhere in the world. And not any old job either. You mark my words.'

Clarissa bought all the necessary books and a fountain pen. The books she covered carefully with waterproof paper and her name she wrote on specially chosen pink and white labels. It looked extremely pretty. Each day Clarissa wore a different coloured cotton blouse and a neatly pressed skirt. She was the best dressed girl at the college, and for a month all went well. The reports she sent home were enthusiastic. She even dropped hints about being 'dated' by the man who ran the college. Her parents, poring over the cryptic language, marvelled at their daughter's success.

Unhappily Clarissa was dogged by the same kind of mediocrity that had crippled her performance at school, and, to make matters worse, thrifty though she had been at the Gokhools', she had been buying too many clothes and cosmetics and thus was unable to finance more than her first month's attendance. She was summoned by the head of the college.

'Now, Miss Forbes,' he said, 'you owe us fees for four weeks. We are not running a charity here, you know.'

'I expecting some money soon, Mr Roberts, in another month or so. I'll pay you then.'

Mr Roberts shook his head mournfully. 'A bird in the hand is worth two in the bush, Miss Forbes, and your birds are too much in the bush for my liking.' The phrase pleased him. He smiled dreamily, playing with his thin beard. 'I will tell you something, Miss Forbes. I was a very trusting man when I first began running this business and everybody was taking advantage of me right, left and centre. Hundreds of dollars are still owing to me all over the place. I'm sorry, but I must have it now.'

Clarissa fixed her eyes on the floor. 'I not the sort of person to run away without paying, Mr Roberts. Give me a chance. I'll be getting money soon.'

'I have heard that story too many times, Miss Forbes. Anyway, your work here doesn't justify my giving you a chance.'

Clarissa closed her eyes, her lips pinched together. She seemed to be trying to ward off some unpleasant image or memory.

'You mustn't think me hard-hearted, Miss Forbes, but I must draw the line somewhere.' He spoke as if from a prepared speech.

'I'll do anything you want me to do, Mr Roberts. Just give me one more chance.' Clarissa's eyes strayed over his face.

'What are you suggesting, Miss Forbes?'

Clarissa did not answer. Her eyes, leaving him, swept across the walls and ceiling.

'You're a nice girl, Miss Forbes, and you take a lot of care of yourself. I can see that. But don't go and spoil it . . .'

'I'll do anything you ask, Mr Roberts. Anything.' Clarissa no longer struggled to hold back her tears.

'No, Miss Forbes. That won't do. It's a bad policy to get . . . how shall I put it? . . . to get involved with one's students in this kind of business. I speak from bitter experience.' Mr Roberts, unruffled by her tears, stared steadily at Clarissa, displaying the professional concern of the undertaker.

'You is a stupid, stupid man. I could tell you how much people try to make it with me, getting down on they knees and begging me. Is not everybody I does offer myself to and don't think I haven't seen how you been watching me out of the corner of your eye these past few weeks.'

'I'm surprised to hear you talk like that, Miss Forbes. Truly surprised.' And he could not resist adding, 'If I was watching you it was only because you hadn't paid your fees.'

'You're a stupid, stupid man. Don't believe you will ever have another chance with me. I warning you. Your face not all that pretty.'

'I never said it was, Miss Forbes.' He got up. 'I think you better take your things and go. You can pay me when you get the money you were talking about.'

'You is a real nigger!' Clarissa screamed. 'Is people like you who is the cause of our people downfall, making everybody treat we like servant. They should throw you in jail. In jail, you hear!'

'Yes, Miss Forbes, I hear. But you better go now before you say anything you will really regret.' Mr Roberts pushed her gently towards the door.

'In jail, in jail,' Clarissa whimpered.

'Here, Miss Forbes. You are forgetting all your nice books.'

'You could eat the damn books, for all I care.' Clarissa brushed her tears away in quick violent movements. Then, pushing him aside, she ran abruptly out of the room, slamming the door hard behind her.

Once more Mrs Forbes was confronted by the sight of her daughter struggling up the path with her suitcase.

'You finish the course already?' she asked.

'I give it up.'

'You give it up? But think of all that money you waste, Clary.'

'Is not my fault. Is the blasted man who own the school to blame.'

'You mean . . .'

'Yes. That's right. He try to rape me like the rest of them.'

Mrs Forbes nodded. This time Mr Forbes did not even suggest intervention.

Clarissa sought and found comfort in the pages of the cheap English magazine. However, she was altogether quieter and more withdrawn. Her parents, especially Mr Forbes, were distressed by the change in their daughter.

Mr Forbes was not an entirely stupid man. It struck him as distinctly odd that three quite different men at one time or another should have tried to rape his daughter. He studied her. She was not beautiful. He mentioned this to his wife and she agreed. 'I never think of it like that before,' she said. Mr Forbes brooded over Clarissa's history and, as he brooded, his distress gave way to ill-temper. His political education was by now very far advanced.

'Clary,' he said one day when she had been more than usually reticent, 'what would you say about my paying your passage to England?'

Clarissa brightened. 'You really mean that, Pa?'

'Yes.'

'That's the place I feel where I really belong. Living in a flat and that sort of thing.' Mr Forbes scowled. 'Mind you,' she went on, 'what with all that rain and fog and thing is not an easy life. But I really feel that's the kind of life I was made for. Still, it's expensive getting there.' She glanced doubtfully at her father.

'Not if you take one of them immigrant ships and travel third class.'

'Immigrant ships! Third class!' Clarissa flung the copy of the magazine she was reading on to the floor. 'What do you take me for, Pa?'

'Shut up, child. You'll do as I say or not at all. I'm damn tired of all your stupid prancing around the place. Is high time you learn some respect for me.'

'Ethélbert!' Mrs Forbes groaned, alarmed at the prospect of their daughter's scorn falling on their heads. She worried needlessly. Clarissa did not rise to the bait. Her reply was defensive, self-pitying.

'You just like everybody else, Pa. Trying to take advantage of me.'

'Nobody taking advantage of you. Is your . . . is your . . .' He flung his arms about excitedly.

'Ethélbert,' Mrs Forbes groaned, 'don't excite yourself so.'

'Keep quiet, Maisie, and mind your own business.' He turned again to face Clarissa. 'Is your damn colonialist mentality that taking advantage of you. Yes, that's what it is. Your colonialist mentality.' It was a phrase the Prime Minister had employed recently against a renegade Minister who had embezzled large sums of money and fled to Switzerland. Mr Forbes waved a threatening finger in front of Clarissa's face.

'You always blaming your failure on people wanting to rape you. Well, let me tell you something. You got to have sex appeal for people to want to rape you and you have about as much of that as I have. But you go to England and we go hear how much of that kind of nonsense you go still be talking when you come back.' The magazine caught his eye. He picked it up from the floor and flipped rapidly through the pages. 'Is this what you consider so great? Is this where you does get all your stupid ideas from? You should be shamed of yourself. Let me see.' He read aloud from the magazine. 'They met on holiday in the Riviera, he, unmarried and bronzed as a Greek god, a happy-go-lucky man of the world, she, good-looking and with a husband suffering from leukaemia . . .'

'Give me back my magazine, Pa. What I read is my own business.' Clarissa lunged at him.

'Tell me first what all this Riviera business got to do with a little nigger girl like you, eh?'

'Give me back my magazine please. Please.' Clarissa wrung her hands. Mr Forbes let the magazine slip through his fingers and fall on to the floor. Clarissa picked it up and hugged it close to her bosom.

A few weeks later Clarissa took passage to England on an immigrant ship, third class.

London was not all Clarissa expected it to be. True, there were fogs and days when it drizzled without cessation. But the fogs were not as thick or as yellow as she had been led to imagine and there were many days when it did not rain. Neither did Clarissa share a flat with a friend. She lived in a bed-sitter in a dilapidated immigrant section of the city. Her landlord, a West Indian, charged her six pounds a week for it. It had peeling wallpaper, a leaking ceiling and a stove that filled the room with smoke. She had no friends. The cheap English magazine, and others like it, existed in abundance, but she had lost her taste for it. Where were the Greek gods? The leukaemia-stricken husbands? The world pictured there hardly corresponded with what she saw around her every day, and on the rare occasion when the veil did lift, Clarissa took fright and ran away.

She was two months finding a job, as a ticket collector on the Underground. Week after week she stood outside her cubicle, her hands stretched forth to trap the stream of tickets thrust at her. At nights she crept slowly back home, cooked supper and went to bed to the accompaniment of the trains that rattled past beneath her windows. Her landlord was sympathetic.

'I know how lonely it does get when you away from home so long and all by yourself. But you does get accustom in the end, like me.'

'I leave a good home to come to this,' Clarissa replied. 'My father is a councillor. He would dead if he was to see me living like this.'

'I been here ten years. Take me a long time to save up to buy this place.' He surveyed the decaying room with pride. 'Ten years,' he repeated. 'Is warming to meet a really nice local girl like you after such a long time. From the moment I set eyes on you I know you had class. Real class. What you say your father is?'

'A councillor.'

'A councillor. Yes. You is a girl with real class.' He put his hand on her shoulder. Clarissa did not protest. 'I tired of these English girl.' He felt her hair. Still Clarissa did not protest. The landlord grew bolder. He swayed slightly as he bent low over her.

'You want to sleep with me?' Clarissa asked suddenly.

The landlord, taken aback, laughed. 'Real class,' he said.

'You want to sleep with me?'

'What a funny girl you is.'

'You want . . .'

'Yes, yes.'

And so Clarissa Forbes lost her virginity. But it was not for love and certainly it was out of wedlock.

Clarissa worked hard and this time she did not spend her money on clothes and expensive perfumes.

'But what you killing yourself so for?' the landlord asked.

'I going back home. I saving up for a tourist-class passage.'

'But, Clarissa . . .'

'No, Frankie. You was enough.'

A few weeks later she was back home.

'You see them dogs race?' her mother asked.

'No, Ma.'

'No bingo halls either?'

'No, Ma.'

'And I don't suppose you ever get to that place you was telling we about. Torr . . . something or the other.'

'No, Ma, I didn't manage to get to Torremolinos.'

'And nobody try to . . .'

'No, Ma. Nobody try to rape me.'

'But like you didn't do anything at all while you was there?'

'It was too cold out there, Ma,' Clarissa replied. 'It was much too cold.'

Mr Forbes's political fortunes had improved during Clarissa's absence. Recognition of his unswerving devotion to the Party came eventually and he was, after all, elected to the county council. Clarissa was proud of her father, and Mrs Forbes, whose ignorance was still an embarrassment to her husband, gratefully gave way to Clarissa who accompanied him on all important official occasions. And thus she too was brought to the attention of the branch Party. Her international experience stood her in good stead.

'We need more people like you,' the local party manager confided to her. 'People with experience of conditions abroad will be an asset to the Party.'

Clarissa was flattered. She joined the Party and was unanimously elected secretary of the Paradise Women's Federation. The head of the local branch visited the Forbes often. The rumours circulated. He proposed. Clarissa accepted.

'Your daughter is a terror,' he said to Mr Forbes some time after they had been married. 'A real fanatic about everything local. She does say that she wouldn't even let our children read any of them foreign magazines. Yes, man. Clary is a real terror.'

'It take she a long time to learn,' Mr Forbes confessed. 'There was a time . . .'

'I owe it all to my father,' Clarissa interrupted hastily. 'He it is who teach me all I know. He was my first political mentor, right through from my childhood . . .' Clarissa elaborated. Her voice drifted sonorously through the sitting room.

Mr Forbes laughed and patted his daughter. He settled back more comfortably into his armchair and as he listened to her conversation, his judgement clouded, but in a manner he was quite content to leave well alone.

The Dolly House

The neighbours had seen Roderick first: a dark, slender young man with the beginnings of a manly air and a moustache. A gold watch was slung loosely on his wrist and he was neatly and nattily dressed. He had come to look at the single room with jalousied windows and doors, which, because it was divided by partitions into a warren of tiny cells, its owner called a house. It had been unoccupied for some months.

They examined Roderick with interest; while he, pretending to be oblivious of their scrutiny, inspected the property with an air of knowing, businesslike efficiency. Using a measure – the kind that shoots out several feet of limber steel at the press of a finger – he strolled purposefully about the muddy, poultry-soiled yard, recording lengths and breadths and heights in a red notebook. He pounded the woodwork with his fists, crawled among the supporting pillars and examined the floorboards for signs of decay. He frowned, drummed thoughtfully on his head with the pencil and scrawled more jottings in the notebook.

'What are you taking all them measurements for, Mister?'

Roderick surveyed the faces staring at him from the surrounding windows. 'I like doing things properly,' he answered. 'Sci-en-tif-ically. I don't believe in hocus-pocus.'

The neighbours were impressed.

'Like you thinking of renting the place, Mister?'

'Not renting.' Roderick pounded the woodwork and listened. 'Buying.'

The neighbours were even more impressed.

'Buying!' They assessed him. 'What somebody like you thinking of buying house for?'

Roderick did not answer immediately. He scrawled another observation into his notebook, muttering to himself and frowning. 'I getting married,' he announced casually when he had done. And then added offhandedly: 'A married man must have somewhere for his wife and family.'

The neighbours stared at him. '*You* getting married? But you hardly out of short pants!' They laughed. 'You bound to be making joke with us, man.'

Roderick was peeved. 'I don't see what's so funny about it.'

The neighbours were conciliatory. 'Don't take offence. Is just that you look too young to be thinking already of wife and family and what not.'

'I'm twenty years old,' Roderick said sourly, putting the notebook into his shirt-pocket.

'And your wife-to-be? How old *she* is?'

Roderick grimaced and departed without another word.

They had their first glimpse of Clara the following week when Roderick brought her to see the house. An arm circling her waist, he led her somewhat defiantly – he was aware of the neighbourly scrutiny – into the yard and up to the front steps of the house.

'This is it,' he said. 'What you think?'

'It's nice,' Clara replied. 'It's very nice.'

'A bit on the small side,' he conceded. 'But that's not the main thing. The construction' (he kicked one of the supporting pillars) 'is basically sound. What I like best about it is the possibilities. This place has a lot of poss-i-bil-ities.'

Roderick waved his free arm optimistically.

'I like it,' Clara murmured. 'It's very nice.' She pressed closer against him.

The neighbours gaped.

'So this is the wife to be, eh!'

Clara blushed, raising and lowering her head quickly. She clung to Roderick, endeavouring to conceal herself as much as possible from their naked curiosity. There was much laughter.

'Don't be bashful, doux-doux. What you hiding yourself behind him for? Come where we could see you.'

Roderick had done his best to outface them. However, they could not be outfaced indefinitely. 'You don't have to be frightened,' he whispered. 'Let them look at you.' He removed his arm from her waist and stepped back, giving them an unobstructed view. Having done so, he looked round challengingly. 'Yes,' he said aloud. 'This is my wife to be.'

Clara bowed her head. Roderick, who was of average height, seemed to tower over her. A rich, unschooled mass of curling black hair spilled in natural ringlets across a smooth forehead. It emphasised her childish aspect; as did the prim, oval face and upturned nose. Her eyelashes were thick and curving, veiling her brown eyes. Prominent veins buttressed her narrow neck: it seemed that the weight of her abundant hair might almost prove too much for that neck to support. Her legs tapered down to tiny feet. The wind stirred the folds of her light cotton frock and she smoothed it absently with the hand which bore the engagement ring. The ring flashed when it caught the sun.

This slip of a girl was soon to be a wife! This slip of a girl was soon to possess a husband!

'She must still have a few milk-teeth!'

Kindly laughter floated from the windows.

'What's your name, doux-doux?'

'Clara.' Her voice was an undertone.

'And how many years you have, Mistress Clara?'

'Sixteen.' The ring flashed.

'Your mother and father – what they have to say?'

'That's enough questions,' Roderick said.

But Clara answered. 'They don't approve.' She exchanged an uneasy glance with Roderick. 'We having a love marriage.'

The neighbours clucked their tongues. 'Ah, doux-doux. A love marriage. I hope the both of you know what you doing.'

A month later a truck backed into the yard. A sheet of tarpaulin protected the furniture stacked on its open tray. Clara was huddled affectionately against her husband in the high driver's-seat. Roderick jumped out and eased his wife gingerly to the ground. Then he hauled off the tarpaulin. There was revealed a wardrobe, a rolled mattress, a double bed, a chest of drawers, a two-burner kerosene stove, assorted pots and pans; and, crowning it all, a cane-bottomed rocking-chair. The latter was resplendently new but the rest had obviously been acquired on the cheap: they were ancient, battered things.

'How you going to carry all that inside your dolly house?' the neighbours enquired.

'We'll manage,' Roderick said. He stripped off his shirt.

'You'll manage, eh! Don't be stupid, man. Just take one good look at the doux-doux.'

Roderick, despite himself, obeyed. He looked at Clara. His assurance wavered.

'And you is no superman either, come to that.' They eyed his naked torso.

'We'll manage all the same.' Nevertheless, he stared disconsolately at the massed furniture.

'Tcha!' They sucked their teeth. 'Stubbornness will be the death of you. Wait there.'

Their faces disappeared from the windows. The women trooped into the yard. 'We'll help you carry it to your dolly house.'

'This is a nice-looking rocking-chair you have here,' one of the women said to Clara.

Clara beamed. 'You like it? It's he who buy it for me as a wedding present.' She pointed proudly at her husband who was struggling up the front steps under the weight of the mattress.

The woman grinned.

Every morning at eight o'clock, Roderick, dressed in the khaki uniform of a sanitary inspector, wheeled his bicycle out of the yard. Clara, her arm linked in his, walked with him out to the road. There, unashamed and undaunted by the passers-by, they kissed each other goodbye. Clara spent the time until his return in the evening – the day for her was, essentially, nothing but a waiting and longing for his return – performing the necessary wifely duties and chatting to the neighbours over the rotting wooden fence, giggling girlishly at all their jibes. They had had to teach her those necessary wifely duties. For Clara, they had not been overly amazed to discover, did not know much about anything.

'Like your mother didn't learn you nothing at all?' they asked.

To which Clara replied that her mother had tried; but that she could not be bothered to pay a great deal of attention.

'Telling us!' the neighbours retorted. 'But now you give yourself a husband you have to pay attention – even though you had a love marriage with him.' Their lectures were grave. 'He is the only thing you have to have on your mind from now on. Because no matter how much a man in love with you, he will still expect you to be able to cook his food and wash his clothes.'

These were unpalatable truths but Clara accepted them without complaint. The neighbours set in train her domestic education; and Clara, urged on by the threat of forfeiting her husband's love, learned with remarkable rapidity.

The daily routine accomplished, Clara readied herself for Roderick's homecoming. Sheathed in a petticoat, she splashed herself with buckets of water in the corrugated-iron cubicle near the back fence which served as a bathroom. After her bath, she dressed and sat on the front steps combing out her hair, letting it dry in the sun. Finally, she powdered and 'made up' herself. The morning kiss of farewell was matched by the evening kiss of welcome; and, as Roderick wheeled his bicycle into the yard, Clara provided him with a running account of the day's adventures.

From the neighbours' point of view, the house next door remained a dolly house. Clara and Roderick were playing at life: playing 'wife'; playing 'husband'. Life, as the neighbours knew it, was something hard and intractable; a maze of thwarted desire. Thus they could not treat the young couple seriously. It was impossible to put the two on an equal footing with themselves. Equality would have required of Roderick and Clara a knowledge – or if not a knowledge, at least an awareness – of the quicksands that might be lying in wait for them. But neither knowledge nor awareness seemed to be present in the smallest degree: they had no notion of tragedy. This ignorance did not diminish the neighbours' fondness. They did not wish the slightest harm to befall the young couple. Indeed, had it been within their power, they would gladly have conferred upon them an eternity of blissful play in their dolly house.

Not even Clara's pregnancy could make them alter their attitude. Improbability was merely being piled on improbability: from playing wife Clara was only about to make the natural progression to playing mother. She thrived on her pregnancy and discussed with them suitable names for the child.

'I hope it's a boy because then I could call him after Roddy. What's another nice name for a boy? I can't think of any.'

The neighbours tried to discourage these speculations: they were superstitious; they felt fate was being needlessly tempted.

'Leave all that until the child born, Mistress Clara. Is never good to count your chickens before they hatch.'

'It's not a chicken I going to have,' Clara said, contemplating her swelling stomach delightedly.

The neighbours clucked their tongues.

Their fears were unfounded. When the time came, Roderick called a taxi and took Clara to the General Hospital. A week later she was back home – with a baby girl. Her initial disappointment at the child not being a boy was soon quelled by the praise which the neighbours lavished on mother and infant. There was no formal christening – Roderick dismissed the suggestion as a piece of hocus-pocus; but, at the insistence of Clara, he did agree to have a small party to mark the event.

All the neighbours were invited. In addition, Clara asked some of her old schoolmates; while Roderick, less prodigal, contented himself with the friend whom he had chosen to be best man at his wedding. Archie appeared to be – so far as it was possible to tell – the only person in the world outside (that mysterious world to which Clara consigned her husband every morning and from which he was returned to her every evening) with whom Roderick was on anything like intimate terms. In fact, apart from a shared interest in things mechanical, they were a strangely contrasting pair: Roderick, slender to the point of being gaunt and reticient to the point of being surly; Archie, plump to the point of being fat and flamboyant to the point of being vulgar in dress and manner.

Clara presided from the rocking-chair, cooing to the baby and smiling amiably at everyone. Archie, behaving like a host, distributed the cigars he had brought and poured the drinks.

'Come on, ladies,' he would shout from time to time. 'Drink up! Drink up!'

The room filled with smoke and laughter and the smell of rum. Roderick, a little drunk, flourished his cigar and began to enlarge on his plans for the future now that he was a father. The neighbours listened attentively: they had never seen him in so expansive a mood. He said he intended to build an extension; to install a 'real' bathroom and a 'real' kitchen. Clara beamed at her husband in the thickening haze. Her face was barred by the sunlight falling through the jalousied window under which she was sitting.

'That is what I liked about this place from the first – the poss-i-bilities. All it need is some imagination to make this into what people would call a desirable residence.' The cigar stabbed the soupy haze. He repeated the phrase, rolling his *r*s. 'A desir-r-rable r-r-residence.'

'Imagination – and money,' a neighbour ventured. 'You might have the imagination. But where you going to get the money from?'

'I will. Don't you worry.'

They studied him sceptically.

'America is the place for money,' Archie said. He rubbed his reddened eyes and swayed a little as he spoke. 'If is money you after, America is the place.'

'But I hear it not so nice for black people,' another neighbour observed mournfully.

'Am-er-ica.' The glow of Roderick's cigar had been extinguished. He tapped it and watched it shed its load of dead ash on the floor. The guests were oddly subdued.

'You shouldn't throw ash on the floor, Roddy,' Clara scolded mildly.

Roderick grimaced. 'I'm still a young man,' he went on, as if speaking only to himself and with a sudden access of belligerence. 'I don't intend to remain a sanitary inspector all my life. I don't want to spend the rest of my life spraying drains, throwing lime down cess-pools and poisoning rats. That is no kind of life for a man.'

'That remind me of something I wanted to tell you,' Clara said. 'Now we have a baby I don't think you should keep all that rat poison hanging about the place.'

He paid her no attention. 'I have a brain. A good brain. Why should I let it rot? The world . . . the world is such a big place. It have so many things a man could do. So many things for a man to be.'

Clara looked up at him, surprised. 'I never hear you talk like that before, Roddy. What get into you so sudden?'

His mouth contracted. 'Do you want me to remain a sanitary inspector forever? Is that what you would like the father of your child to be?'

'You know I want whatever you want, Roddy. Whatever will make you happy.' Clara smiled timidly at him. 'But up until now I thought . . . well, it's just that I never hear you talk like that before. That's all.'

'You like living in this shack? You like bathing yourself with a bucket instead of a real shower?'

'We been happy,' Clara said. 'And that is what count most. So long as we happy I don't mind living in a shack or bathing with a bucket.' She appealed to the room for confirmation and support.

The neighbours nodded approvingly. But they were solemn. The party spirit had fled from the room.

'That is the kind of talk I would expect to hear from stupid country people,' Roderick said.

An uneasy silence ensued during which the neighbours pondered the speeches they had heard and Roderick twirled his dead cigar. It was the baby who came to the rescue: she began to cry vociferously – as if the silence disturbed her.

They were recalled to the purpose of the gathering.

'Ssh . . . ssh . . . I not going to starve you.' Clara unbuttoned her blouse and proffered a full breast.

'What name you choose for the baby?' one of the old schoolfriends asked.

'Paulette,' Clara replied.

Everyone agreed it was a pretty name.

'Come on, ladies. Drink up! Drink up!'

The neighbours channelled their attentions to the feeding operation. They cautioned and recommended and praised. Clara giggled. Archie filled the empty glasses. Roderick relit his cigar. Soon the talk became cheerfully general.

The next year Clara was pregnant again. It astonished the neighbours that so fragile a frame could produce babies with such apparent ease.

'I praying for it to be a boy,' she confided to them. 'Roddy would like a son. Somebody to follow in his footsteps.'

'Tcha!' they rebuked her. 'Leave that to God. He know best whether to give you a boy child or a girl child.'

'Roddy say it's nothing to do with God,' Clara replied. 'He say it's to do with something he call the genes.'

The neighbours crossed themselves and rolled their eyes heavenward.

Clara wept copiously when she was delivered of a second girl. The neighbours sought to console. 'Is not your fault, doux-doux. Nobody could blame you because is a girl child. Roderick is a intelligent man. He will understand.'

This time, however, Clara was not to be so easily comforted. 'It's all my fault,' she wailed. 'I let him down.'

The neighbours were right. Despite his unscientific desire for a son, Roderick was sensible about it. With all the patience and resourcefulness at his command, he explained to Clara that it was not within her power to determine the sex of her child; her 'foetus' as he called it. Consequently ('though I admit a boy would have been nice') she could not be held responsible. But, he added as a footnote, the wonders of modern science were such that in the not too distant future . . . etc. . . . etc.

Clara was inconsolable. 'I know it's all my fault,' she wailed. 'I let you down.'

Roderick gave up; and Clara's distress remained acute until he was driven to relent and permit a final assault on the recalcitrant genes. 'But remember I mean final,' he warned. A third child was going against his principles: Roderick was fond of denouncing the practice of indiscriminate child-bearing. 'It's because they have no self-control that all these stupid country people will go on starving and being stupid.'

And Clara's luck held! The third child was a boy. Even Roderick – stern in the preceding interval – could scarcely disguise his pleasure. The child was named after his father. Clara's happiness was now complete. In the eyes of the neighbours, they were still the enchanted couple playing at life in their dolly house.

Yet it was the very completeness of Clara's happiness which worried the neighbours. Her happiness was too perfect; too simple. In that perfect simplicity lay its great strength – and, alas, its fatal weakness: for it depended on everything remaining more or less the same. Her happiness was not adaptable. It could never accommodate itself to a change of circumstances. The neighbours knew that things never remained the same. All was flux. Once let that happiness fracture and it would vanish all of a piece. It would be as if it had never existed. Clara, they saw quite clearly, could be easily – and dreadfully – hurt; though they could not predict from what quarter that hurt might descend; what awful shape it might assume.

Roderick's outburst at the 'christening' had not been forgotten by the neighbours. It could not be lightly dismissed. From time to time it surfaced to haunt them. Unconsciously – against their wills – they searched for fresh signs of restlessness in him. The evidence did not reassure them. Roderick, they observed, had slipped gradually into the habit of treating his wife much as he treated his children. This was not a deliberate policy of his. On the contrary: in conformity with his progressive views Roderick had accepted the theory that a wife was not a mere 'chattel' – as he expressed it – but a 'companion'. Confronted with Clara, the theory collapsed. She agreed with automatic (and unfeigned) enthusiasm to everything he said or did. Clara had willingly sunk herself in his authority and, with the passage of time, she was increasingly hypnotised by it. His theories having been sabotaged, the decline from the heights was inevitable. He could be magisterially stern with her in moments of displeasure; and, occasionally, he exceeded magisterial sternness.

One morning – it was a Saturday and Roderick was not at work – a wandering preacher came into the yard. There was nothing extraordinary about this visitation. Such characters were a familiar and accepted part of the social scene; a kind of travelling circus providing an innocuous diversion. Robed and bearded, they were an exotic sight. Clara was a trifle disappointed by this one: he was neither robed nor bearded but conventionally dressed and carrying a briefcase. He looked more like a door-to-door salesman than a preacher. It was only the big silver cross hung round his neck which belied the resemblance. He was tall and thin and stoop-shouldered.

Clara greeted him banteringly. 'I never see a preacher dress like you before. You look more like a salesman.'

He bowed gravely. 'I'm a salesman for the Lord. How a man dresses is not important. Our souls go unclothed before God.' He opened the briefcase he was carrying and drew out a magazine from it. 'I would like you to read this.' He held it out to her. Clara hesitated. 'Take it – it is given free of charge.' He smiled.

Clara accepted the magazine from his outstretched hand. She saw Roderick approaching and fumbled guiltily with it.

'What is all this?'

'I take it you are this lady's husband?' the preacher enquired politely.

Roderick was not welcoming. 'That's right. But I want to know who *you* are and what *you* are doing in my yard.'

'My name is Horatio Reuben and I am a servant of the Lord.'

Roderick turned to Clara. 'What's that he give you?' He took the magazine from her and leafed through it, his expression darkening as he did so. 'So this is the kind of nonsense you like to fill your head with. You not interested in what I try to teach you. You prefer to addle your brain with this rubbish. Eh? Answer me.' He shook her.

'It's only a magazine, Roddy. What's the harm?'

His indignation waxed. 'Only a magazine, you say. What's the harm, you say. How do you know there's no harm in it? Who tell you that? Tell me!'

'How can God's Word possibly do any harm?' Reuben asked with undiminished politeness.

'If you know what's good for you, you had better keep out of this, Mr·Preacher.' Roderick ripped the magazine in two and flung it at Reuben's feet.

'Blasphemer!'

Roderick advanced on him. 'Haul your tail from my yard, Mr Preacher.'

Reuben retreated with as much dignity as the circumstances permitted.

'You shall regret having done this,' Reuben shouted when he had gained the safety of the road. He waved a clenched fist. 'God will not suffer his servant to be humiliated by the likes of you.'

'Make sure,' Roderick said to Clara, 'that that is the last time you ever let him – or anybody like him – enter my yard. I won't have it.' He shook his head at her. 'I can't help feeling that all my efforts are completely wasted on you.'

Clara clutched at his arm. 'Please, Roddy. Don't say things like that. I don't mean to be always letting you down. But . . .' She started to cry.

He gazed at her with a sorrowful, surrendering anger, still shaking his head.

Acting on the assumption that there was nothing a man could do or understand which was beyond the capacities of an 'intelligent' woman, Roderick had tried to instruct Clara in the elementary principles of mechanics. She was not an amenable pupil, accusing him of 'confusing' her. Her concentration would quickly wilt and, rather than listen, she preferred to run her hands through his hair. 'Please pay attention,' Roderick would plead, fending off her flirtations. 'Pulleys are no joke business, you know.' Ultimately, he was forced to give up his attempts to educate her. Hence Clara was deprived of place and function in this important area of his life. She was simply an obstacle to his efforts to 'improve his mind'.

Even though she boasted about her husband reading books laden with numbers and mysterious diagrams, it was apparent to the neighbours that Clara was not overly keen on Roderick's determined struggle to educate himself. His reading seemed to stir a latent unease in her and, either through wilful neglect or an apprehension dimly formulated, she refused to credit it with any real significance; refused to admit the danger. For instance, she had never referred to the incident with the preacher: it appeared to have slid completely from her memory by the next day. She confined herself to saying things like: 'I wish Roddy wouldn't read so much. I'm sure it's not good for his eyes.'

For a while it was Archie who filled the gap of 'companion' left vacant by Clara's desertion. He would come on Sunday mornings and crouch on the front steps with Roderick. Together they would work through various complicated calculations and have long and earnest discussions. Clara was not jealous. Glad at her release, she was content to circle hennishly around them, bring cups of tea and shoo the children away. Then, without warning, Roderick suffered his second desertion: Archie suddenly announced he was going to America.

'Sorry, old man.' Archie looked guiltily at him.

'You have nothing to be sorry for,' Roderick said quietly.

'I know I should have tell you before but . . .' Archie laughed nervously. 'Well, to be frank, I wasn't sure how you would take the news.'

Roderick laughed heavily.

'I thought you mightn't take it too well,' Archie said.

'I don't know why you should think that,' Roderick replied.

Archie rested a hand on his friend's shoulder. 'Thanks, old man. I was so worried that you would . . .'

Roderick gathered up the books on the step. 'No use for these today.' He removed Archie's hand from his shoulder and carried them back inside.

Roderick did indeed appear to take Archie's desertion in his stride. But it unnerved the neighbours when, throwing his books aside disgustedly, he paced aimlessly about the yard in his short, fraying khaki trousers and vest, his sabots clicking; plucking at the leaves on the bushes with unnecessary violence, his mouth contracted. The click of those sabots sounded like a warning in their ears. They could interpret its message; Clara, it seemed could not.

And what could they tell her? After all, they could be wrong. In any case, Clara would not have believed them. Even worse, she would not have understood. She would have scorned their fears. Therefore, they said nothing. Impotent observers, they could only hope for the best. Above all, they did not wish to hasten by foolhardy meddling that which they feared. They suspected that, if and when the eruption did come, it would do so suddenly; as suddenly as it had come at the christening: like the crash of thunder in a clear sky.

But nothing untoward occurred and the fear, though it did not vanish, lessened. On the surface at any rate, life in the dolly house proceeded smoothly. Motherhood had filled out Clara's figure. Her breasts had expanded to ample and womanly dimensions and her arms and legs were well fleshed. She had become altogether sturdier. The changes wrought were not negligible – but they could not be described as dramatic. Now she could, without arousing incredulity, pass muster as a young wife. However, as mother of three, Clara was still not convincing.

She looked after her children reasonably well – as reasonably, that is, as the salary of a sanitary inspector would allow. She was not afraid to beat them when the occasion demanded. The spectacle of an angry Clara pursuing her children around the yard with a broom caused the neighbours much amusement. Clara herself, realising how comic and absurd she must appear to them, would sometimes pause in the midst of one of these sessions and share in the merriment before resuming the chase. These beatings were done largely at the instigation of Roderick: he was a kind but not a lax father. 'If you spare the rod you spoil the child,' he said to her. 'That is a sci-en-tif-ic fact.'

Despite the additional cares imposed by the children, Clara managed to maintain most of the rituals of the early days of their marriage intact. She walked out to the road with Roderick in the mornings and delivered on his lips the kiss of farewell; and the evening found her waiting to give him the kiss of welcome. Once or twice a month, having left the children with the neighbours, they went to the pictures. At four o'clock on Sunday afternoons, after dressing carefully, the entire family would set out on a leisurely parade around the Queen's Park Savannah. As a special treat, Roderick would buy them all coconuts from one of the many carts which lined the perimeter of the park.

The extension had not been built; the kitchen stayed a lean-to shed tacked on to the house; Clara had not ceased to splash herself with buckets of water in the corrugated-iron cubicle near the back fence; and Roderick never stopped talking about the possibilities of the property. Still, they were not years totally devoid of achievement: there had been a few tangible improvements. Celebrating a marginal increase in his salary, Roderick painted the partitions of the house white and repaired the broken slats in the jalousies; and, after an orgy of measuring and jotting in his notebook, he had slowly and painstakingly raised the wooden fence to the front. The wood was not new – he could not afford that – but it looked as good as new. Clara and the neighbours brimmed with admiration.

'It's because I do it sci-en-tif-ically it turn out so well,' Roderick commented, surveying his handiwork with ill-concealed pride.

The neighbours had almost persuaded themselves to forget their fears; had almost come to believe that Clara and Roderick led truly charmed lives in their dolly house, when the crash of thunder came out of a clear sky.

*

After three years in America, Archie returned to the island. During the first year he had written regularly to Roderick; the second year saw a gradual tailing-off in their correspondence; and, latterly, there had been nothing at all. 'He become a real sweet man' was the verdict of the neighbours when they heralded his unexpected entry into the yard with cries of warm greeting.

Archie was dressed in a suit of black-and-white houndstooth check. A thin, cultured line of moustache adorned his upper lip. His loss of weight gave him an air of springy, dandified alertness. He radiated confidence, knowledge and success. Next to him Roderick felt as though he were made of a heavier, earth-bound material. He greeted his friend awkwardly.

'And how's the Dawson family?' Archie grinned affably at Clara and the children. He was sitting in the rocking-chair, the seat of honour.

'All of us fine and well,' Clara said. She too smiled affably and turned to Roderick for confirmation as she spoke.

'You back for good or . . .' Roderick's tone was heavy and a little sullen. He stared at the shimmering houndstooth.

Archie laughed loudly and slapped his thighs. 'Not on your life, old man. Not for all the tea in Boston harbour. This is just a little holiday to see how the old folks are getting on.' He winked at Roderick. 'Gotta fine woman in Noo York City keeping my bed warm.' He tucked a finger into the fob of his trousers, leaning farther back into the chair. 'I'm through with this dump.' He shivered with prefabricated distaste.

'You think it's a dump?'

Again Archie laughed loudly. 'I don't *think*, old man. I *know* it's a goddam dump.' He half-closed his eyes and smiled as if at some lascivious memory. 'Whaddadump! Whaddadump!' He drummed on the arms of the rocking-chair.

'A dump. . . .' Roderick echoed, savouring the word.

'Tell me something.' Archie opened his eyes and stilled the motion of the rocking-chair. 'How much are you earning these days in that so-called job of yours?'

Roderick told him.

'Peanuts!' Archie snapped his fingers in his confident, knowledgeable and successful way and set the rocking-chair in motion again. 'In Noo York City you would be earning nearly four or five times as much for the same work.'

'It's enough for our needs,' Clara intervened. 'We don't need more.' She glanced appealingly at Roderick. He was silent, staring intently at Archie.

'Any man could do wonders over there if he had a bit of initiative,'Archie flowed on. 'Of course, it's a little hard at first. I'm not denying that. But if you could stick that out . . . why, old man, it's a land of limitless opportunities. The sky's the limit over there.'

'They don't like black people,' Clara put in, dredging up the flotsam of another conversation.

Archie laughed. He was a little contemptuous; a little pitying. 'I can tell you a story or two about some of those white chicks. Some of them are really hot for it. . . .' His eyes closed lasciviously.

'Lim-it-less opp-or-tun-ities,' Roderick echoed.

'We have enough for our needs,' Clara said. 'We don't need more.'

Archie shrugged.

'Let me get you something to eat,' Clara said.

Archie dismissed the offer with a small flutter of the hand. 'In Noo York City. . . .'

'Something to drink then,' Clara urged with a hint of desperation. 'Something to drink if not something to eat.'

They ignored her.

'It's easy for you to come here and say these things, Archie.' Roderick's voice was leaden with reproach; and something more than reproach. 'You don't have a family.'

'Quite right, old man. I was forgetting. Let's drop the touchy subject.' He smiled amiably. 'How are the mechanics coming along?'

Roderick did not answer the question. He stared at the shimmering houndstooth.

It was a difficult evening. Neither for husband nor for wife was the reunion a great success.

The following evening Roderick was late home from work. This was virtually unheard of and Clara was frantic.

'Maybe he had an accident. Maybe he dead!'

'Tcha! The man must have a good reason.'

'But he was never so late before.'

'There have to be a first time for everything, doux-doux. Keep calm.'

It was past ten when Roderick wheeled his bicycle into the yard. Clara, notified by the neighbours, rushed out of the house and overwhelmed him with her tears. Roderick brushed aside her lamentations and cries for explanation. He did not let her kiss him. 'Let's go inside,' he said brusquely. 'I want to talk to you.'

The neighbours strained their ears but they could hear nothing.

In the morning Clara was unusually subdued. She and Roderick did not kiss goodbye.

'Did he say why he was late?' a neighbour called anxiously over the fence.

Clara was silent. There were tear stains on her cheeks and her eyes were puffed and red.

'What's wrong, doux-doux? What you been crying for?' They could not control the catch of fear in their voices. 'He didn't tell you why he was late? It can't be some woman friend....'

Clara shook her head. 'It wasn't a woman friend.' She spoke so softly they could barely hear what she was saying. 'He was drinking with Archie.'

'Archie!'

Relieved laughter rolled across the yard.

But Clara was weeping.

'Doux-doux ... doux-doux. It was only Archie. A man friend. What could be so bad about that?'

'I wish he had never come back. I wish Roddy had never know him.' Clara thumped her breast. 'Archie only bring trouble for me. So help me God, I could take all that rat poison Roddy does keep in the kitchen and poison him. Kill him dead with it!'

'What a thing to say, doux-doux! You not yourself this morning. What happened between them that upset you so?'

'They was talking about America. Archie was telling him he could get a good job over there and about all the things he could do if ... if....' Clara broke down afresh.

'If what?' The neighbours' alarm had free rein now.

'I don't know.... I don't know. Why you asking me? You must ask Roddy.' Clara·ran inside.

The fear defined itself and it deadened their hearts.

Overnight the spell of enchantment had been lifted from the dolly house. Clara's happiness burned up and vanished. Life changed. Her girlish giggle – like the morning and evening kiss – fell into neglect. They stopped going to the pictures. There were no more walks with the children around the Queen's Park Savannah on Sunday afternoons; no more coconuts. Old joys had soured. The break in the pattern of their lives had been abrupt and radical. Roderick was sullen and hostile. Often he was late home from work, provided no explanations and refused to eat the dinner Clara had cooked. Nightly the neighbours listened to Clara crying. At weekends Roderick paced the yard and his sabots clicked.

Then the shouting began.

'How you expect me to stay like this? A man must have some ambition in this life. Otherwise he might as well be dead. I never wanted to stay a sanitary inspector all my life. It have so many things a man can be in this world if only he put his mind to it. I have to take my chances where I find them.'

'And what about me?' Clara replied, shouting too. 'What about my chances? Where will I find my chances? You just can't leave me like that. A man with a wife and three children just can't up and go whenever he feel like it.'

'You said once upon a time that you would want whatever would make me happy.'

'But not this, Roddy. I can't let you do this thing to me. I can't.'

Roderick shifted from anger to entreaty. 'It will be for only two – or three years at the most. Why you can't give me that? Why you have to be so selfish?'

'You calling *me* selfish.' Clara laughed bitterly. 'That's a good one.'

'I'm a young man, Clara. I have a good brain. I can feel it beating inside my head. I don't want to let it dry up and rot from idleness. That would be a crime.'

'What about me?' Clara persisted. 'What you want to do to me is also a crime. I'm young too. I only have twenty-three years. What you expect me to do while you in America improving yourself?'

He embraced her. 'You have to be patient. It's not for ever. When I come back we'll still be young. There'll be time for everything then.'

'There won't be time for nothing,' she said. 'You don't love me any more.' She extracted herself from his embrace – so warm yet already so distant! 'You tired of me. I let you down. That's why you want to go and leave me.' She raised her voice. 'You want . . . you want all those white chicks!' She began to whimper but would not let him touch her.

Roderick groaned and cursed.

She loved him. Why could he not understand that simple thing? Beyond that there was nothing more to say; beyond him there was nothing left to desire. If she was fond of her children it was because she saw scattered bits and pieces of him in them. Her maternal pride had no greater satisfaction than to hear somebody say that one of the children looked 'just like Roderick'. It was through him that she loved them; through them that she celebrated her love for him. Her fondness did not root itself directly. Perhaps that was wrong. But she could not help it. Her passion was like a consuming, fiery wind. She questioned neither its origin nor its purpose: it was sufficient unto itself.

Clara remembered the night he had asked her to marry him. They had gone to the Trade Fair because Roderick wished to see the engineering exhibits. Every day on her way to and from school she had been passing the site near the harbour which had been selected for the fair-ground. They had set off at dusk to join the jostling queues. The fair-ground glowed and shimmered in the dark like an outpouring of incandescent gas. It seemed to hover weightlessly in the air; transparent and crystalline. Clara gazed in ecstasy at the floating towers, domes and cupolas whose curves were sinuously defined against the black sky by the electric glare. The multicoloured, foaming plumes of the fountain arched in rods of pencil-thin spray. Flags flapped and fluttered from tall white poles. Clara was afraid to take her eyes off it, fearful that the wraith might disintegrate and vanish. Somewhere a band gusted into life amid a steady thumping of drums and the crash of cymbals. A twinkling glass globe revolved above the entrance.

Inside they could not hear themselves talk. All around them voices hummed with wonder and admiration like telegraph wires. Each booth, tent and gaudy pavilion sent forth its own tributaries of sound to swell the main stream. They strolled slowly down the central promenade lined with cardboard palaces decked with tinsel and strings of coloured bulbs. They crossed an artificial lake by a tiny footbridge. Clara leaned against the railing and stared at the dark leaves of the water-lilies. Real fire shot from the chimneys of a miniature oil-refinery. The colours were intoxicating, transfiguring ordinary objects into subtle but harmless mysteries. Fire would not be hot enough to burn. Water would not be deep enough to drown. A fall from the tallest tower would not hurt. It was a dream of unblemished joy and happiness. Clara's head swam pleasantly. As they approached the fountain, the stinging spray blew into their faces. She sat on the rim of the basin and dangled her feet in the cool water; while Roderick wandered off to study the exposed engine of a tractor revolving on a pedestal.

The fair-ground resolved itself into a rapturous blur. She had a vague recollection of standing in a steaming tent and peering between sweating shoulders at the antics of a performing monkey; of biting into an ice-cream the coldness of which hurt her teeth; of the crunch and slip of gravel underfoot; of wet, shining grass; of trampled mud. High above the floating towers, domes and cupolas she could always see the foaming plumes of the fountain. No object or moment of time was distinct from another. The former were all one and the latter all simultaneous.

They stood by the picket fence enclosing the ferris-wheel. The rims and spokes were strung with coloured bulbs. Clara watched it go round, listening to the clatter of its engine and the screams and laughter of those riding on it. Every few minutes it halted its revolutions and disgorged some of its giddy cargo while those with tickets rushed and scrambled for the empty seats.

'I would like a ride,' she said.

They bought their tickets and waited. When it stopped they dashed into the enclosure and climbed into a swaying cabin. They started to rise. A cool current of air fanned her face and the lights of the fair-ground spread out far below. At the top she had a glimpse of the ships in the harbour and those anchored farther out to sea. The harbour and the ships sank out of sight and the lights of the fair-ground rose up to meet them.

Suddenly she was terrified. She shut her eyes and grasped Roderick's hand. The sound of the engine grew louder; then faded. They were rising again. She opened her eyes and closed them immediately. The cool air played on her cheeks. Her stomach heaved. Roderick was speaking close to her ear but she could not hear what he was saying because of her giddiness and the screams and laughter ringing about her. She could no longer tell whether they were going up or down; standing still or going round. The cabin seemed to pitch and toss in every conceivable direction. It plunged into interminable headlong dives and then shot upwards as if it had been loosed of its moorings and catapulted into space. She was screaming. 'Don't let go of me! Don't let go of me!' It was a senseless, nightmarish chaos. She was aware of Roderick's warm breath on her ear. He was saying something to her. Having soared upwards to infinity, the cabin was hurtling downwards in one of its interminable dives when, quite unexpectedly, the vicious motion was arrested. Their journey had ended. But the sensation of falling into bottomless blackness persisted. She stumbled from the enclosure, her head spinning, hardly able to draw breath.

Roderick caught her. 'What's the matter, Clara?'

'Don't let go of me! Don't let go of me!' Gradually, she grew calmer. 'I was so frightened up there. So frightened.'

'It's all right now,' he said. He seemed mildly impatient. 'Didn't you hear what I was saying to you on the ferris-wheel?'

She shook her head.

'I was saying we should get married. What do you feel about that?'

There was trouble when she returned home late that night.

'You been with that man?' her mother asked.

'Yes.' Clara was defiant.

Her mother hit her.

'You won't be able to do that much longer,' Clara said. 'We going to get married.'

'Over my dead body, you little. . . .'

'You can't prevent us.' And then, seeing that her mother was about to strike her again, Clara told a lie. 'Because I having a baby for him.' As if to prove the truth of her assertion, Clara vomited: it was not difficult; her stomach still heaved.

Now Roderick was letting go of her; and the senseless nightmarish chaos of that evening was closing in again. 'Let him go,' the neighbours counselled. 'Let him get it out of his system.'

'He will never come back to me,' Clara said.

'The man love you. He bound to come back.'

'If I let him go,' Clara said, 'if I let him do this thing to me, I will never see him again.'

'Listen to us, doux-doux. You shouldn't take on so. We women somehow always seem to need less than men to be happy. You have to give a man his head from time to time. Otherwise. . . .' They gestured wearily.

'I will never see him again,' Clara said. 'And, even if I do, what difference will that make? It will still be like not seeing him.'

The neighbours did not understand. They were startled by the odd conviction with which she spoke. 'How you mean, Mistress Clara? When the man come back to you as he bound to do. . . .'

'I not sure myself what I mean,' Clara said. 'But it's something I feel deep down in my bones.'

'Shush. You talking nonsense, Mistress Clara. The man basodee about you. Crazy!' Nevertheless, she frightened them.

'It won't make no difference,' Clara repeated.

They stared hopelessly at her.

The neighbours did not care to apportion blame. Life alone could be blamed; the process of living. They grieved for them both.

In the seventh year of his marriage, Roderick Dawson, driven forward by the brain he could feel beating so warmly within his head, resigned his job as sanitary inspector with the borough council and, leaving behind him a wife and three children, departed for America. The possibilities of the house had been realised after a fashion: it served as security for the loan required to pay his passage.

Clara did not cry – as she had done more or less without interruption during the days preceding his departure. The time for tears was past: the hurt was too deep.

To survive, Clara took in washing. Her clients were some of the more well-to-do families in the district. She had gone from door to door peddling her services at a price undercutting the majority of her rivals in the trade. Commissions, as a result, had been plentiful. She washed on Mondays, Tuesdays and Wednesdays; and did the ironing on Thursdays, Fridays and Saturdays. On Sundays the various consignments were packed neatly into cardboard boxes and delivered. The work for the following week was collected at the same time. Paulette was her mother's chief assistant in these labours: she it was who did the fetching and the carrying, skilfully balancing the boxes on her head.

Clara did not trade gossip with the neighbours over the fence. She had discarded frivolity: her energies were consumed by her work. The neighbours saw her bent over the washtub, concentratedly scrubbing and wringing; and afterwards pegging the sodden clothes out on the washlines, the soap-stained wooden clips clenched between her teeth. She was remote. Roderick was never mentioned – except by the children. 'When is Pappa coming back?' they would ask. Clara would generally respond to their enquiries with a more dogged application to whatever she happened to be doing. Sometimes she slapped them hard on the mouth. Her silence was like a denial of his existence; a denial of the past; a denial, even, of grief.

Once a week the postman brought the envelope with the red, white and blue border. Ignoring the children's clamour, she would tear open the envelope, cursorily skim her eyes over the written sheets and then squash it into her bosom. Roderick wrote with undiminishing enthusiasm about America – his letters were like effusions from someone on holiday. He was having a busy time. By day he worked in a meat-packing plant; by night he took a course in mechanical engineering.

'How is he getting on?' the neighbours would ask.

Clara never replied. They would have preferred to hear her rail and curse: almost anything would have been preferable to her impenetrable silence about him.

And there was something else about which she would say nothing: the regular visits of Reuben the preacher.

Horatio Reuben was an assiduous saviour of lost souls: they were, in a manner of speaking, his stock-in-trade; his reason for living. With unflagging zeal, he scoured the city in search of his quarry. For months, one of the chief topics of conversation on the street had been Clara. The merits and demerits of her case were still being zestfully discussed and dissected when Reuben surfaced on one of his periodic tours of inspection.

'Is not we you should be trying to save,' he was told. 'You should go and preach instead to the young lady up the road who husband leave her just like that and went off gallivanting to America.'

Reuben's appetite was whetted. 'Which lady?'

They launched into the details of the story. Reuben did not wait for them to finish. He recalled Roderick's violent reception and the blasphemies he had uttered. Reuben was not unaccustomed to being met with a certain amount of rudeness and hostility. In his type of work he recognised it was unavoidable (there was much sin in the world) and he made allowances for it. Up to a point, they were part of the challenge of the job. Roderick had overstepped those limits. Reuben could not think of his threats and blasphemies without flinching. As he walked quickly up the street, the memory only rankled but also angered him afresh. However, Reuben indulged this luxury: had he not been harshly dealt with?

Clara was pegging clothes out on the washlines when he arrived. She did not recognise him immediately.

'What you want?' She did not stop what she was doing.

Reuben smiled. 'Have you forgotten me, Mrs Dawson?'

Clara frowned suspiciously at him. 'How you know my name?'

Reuben approached to within a few feet of her. 'The last time I called, your husband was somewhat . . . somewhat abusive.'

Clara squinted at him. Then recognition dawned. 'Why! It's the preacher.'

Reuben tilted his head graciously. 'The very same. The name is Horatio Reuben – in case you have forgotten.'

'I don't have time to waste, Mr Reuben. I'm a busy woman.' She indicated the dripping clothes strung out on the washlines. 'I have to work hard to keep my children bellies full.'

'I won't take up too much of your time.' He waved sympathetically at the washlines. 'I appreciate how hard you have to work. But no one should ever be too busy to hear the Word of God.'

'The Word of God isn't going to help me keep my children bellies full, Mr Reuben.' She moved away from him towards the washtub.

'I have heard about your tragedy.' Reuben's voice planed downwards. 'I am here to bring you comfort, peace of mind and repose.'

Reuben sang rather than spoke. Comfort. Peace of mind. Repose. They were like hymns. His words touched the core of her grief, reawakening it from its hibernation. Suddenly she wanted to cry out her despair to him. She restrained herself.

'Go from my yard, Mr Reuben. Neither you nor anybody else can help me.' Clara drew a wet hand across her forehead. She was giddy.

'But that is why I am here – to help you.'

'Please go from my yard. Please.'

Reuben grasped her arm firmly. 'Let me take you inside. You don't look too well. Perhaps you should lie down.'

She tried to push him away. 'It's nothing. Only a little giddiness. It will pass away.'

'All things will pass away,' Reuben said. 'Even this grief.' He took firmer hold of her arm. 'Let me take you inside.' He was adamant and Clara too weak to resist.

He led her to the house, guiding her up the front steps. Clara, refusing to lie down, slumped into the rocking-chair. Reuben sat beside her, resting his briefcase on the floor. He rubbed his bony hands and looked solemnly at her.

'Suffering is our common human lot.' He crossed his legs. 'We can only be saved by obedience to the Word of God.'

Clara's mouth drooped. 'Why did your God make me suffer so much?'

'He's not only my God, Mrs Dawson. He's your God too. Thy people shall be my people, and thy God my God.' Reuben stood up, shoulders stooped. He was gigantic in the small room. 'Our sufferings are sent to us as a trial; a test of our faith. Your . . . your husband, (Reuben's lips curled in involuntary distaste), was sent to try *you*. Why? That I cannot say. The Lord moves in mysterious ways. But know that the greater our suffering in this world, the greater shall be our reward in the next.'

'I don't care about the next world,' Clara said. She raised her head and scanned the towering figure looming above her.

Reuben sighed. He sat down beside her again. 'I see you are one of those who believe only in the things of Caesar. That is the source of all evil and misery. Free yourself of that attachment. Cleanse yourself of an unworthy desire for a. . . .'

'For a what?' Clara asked.

Reuben checked himself. He pulled a handkerchief from his pocket and dabbed his face with it.

Clara's eyes were fixed on him.

'The flesh must be mortified – it must be denied – if the soul is to be saved.' Reuben jumped up from the chair. He was very excited. 'Let me help you cure yourself of this disease. For make no mistake. That is exactly what it is. A disease!' Reuben was standing over her like the very incarnation of the God he claimed to represent. 'The source of your suffering is attachment. In this case, attachment to . . . to a most ungodly man. . . .'

'My husband,' Clara said. 'My husband. My husband. My husband.'

'Your – husband.' The use of the word seemed to require effort. 'But still, for all that, a mere mortal. Attachment is a weakness of the flesh. Mortify the flesh and kill attachment. When attachment dies, so does suffering. They are two sides of the same coin.' Reuben spoke with hypnotic, catechistical authority. Clara felt herself sinking into it.

She looked away from the stooping, gigantic figure. His words were not easy to follow. But that hardly mattered: their message, the promise they held out, was clear enough. To be rid of this pain! With this strange man's assistance it might be cured. She was prepared to try any remedy.

'Do you have a Bible?' Reuben glanced around the room. Before Clara could answer he smiled and said: 'A stupid question. Pardon me. A man like that would not have been likely to keep such a thing in his house.' He opened his briefcase. 'I shall give you mine.' He placed on her lap a leather-bound volume stamped in gold. 'Now I shall leave you. I have no wish to take up any more of your precious time.' He locked the briefcase. 'But I shall come again. Soon.' He bowed and went out.

Reuben began coming to the house every Sunday – Clara's day of relative rest. They would remain closeted together for as much as two hours during which time the children were banished to the yard. What went on inside the little room no one knew for certain: their voices never rose above a whisper and the curtains were kept tightly drawn.

These visits perturbed the neighbours. They were sufficiently familiar with Roderick's hatred for 'idle preachers' to be amazed at his wife's behaviour: his lessons must have had even less effect than they had imagined. But, more than that, they did not like Reuben himself. The sessions with him seemed to debilitate Clara. She would emerge from them pale and preoccupied; indifferent to the needs of the children and to what was going on around her. It was as though Reuben had been feeding on her in the interval; siphoning off her vital juices into himself.

'You should stop seeing that man, Mistress Clara. Drive him from your yard.'

'Mr Reuben is a great comfort to me,' Clara replied.

'He no good for you,' they insisted. 'He only going to make matters worse for you in the long run.'

Clara looked at them dismally. 'Let me be the judge of that.'

'What about Roderick? You know he don't like people like that.' They watched her closely: to mention Roderick's name was a calculated risk.

'Roderick! Roderick!' Clara jeered. 'Who is this Roderick you and everybody else always talking about? What he have to do with anything?' Her face was made ugly by the warring anguish and rage distorting its features.

Nevertheless, it pleased the neighbours that they had managed to stimulate a response of some kind.

'He is your husband,' they said. 'The man you love.'

Clara blocked her ears.

'What are you going to do when he come back?'

'Who tell you he coming back?'

'Who tell you he *not* coming back?' they countered.

Clara turned from them.

'Like you don't want him to come back?'

'Why can't you leave me alone?' Clara cried softly. 'Why?'

The postman steered his bicycle to the kerb, tinkling the bell on the handlebar. Excited shouts rose from behind the wooden fence and the raggedly dressed children charged through the gate and surrounded him, grabbing at the mailbag slung across his shoulders. The postman parried goodnaturedly.

'What is this at all! I don't have no letter address to any of you.' Laughing, he slid from the saddle. 'Where's your mother? Is she I have a letter for.'

The neighbours leaned out of their windows and watched.

'And I don't have no letter for any of you either,' the postman said, looking up at them and laughing in the same goodnatured manner.

'Letter for you, Mamma,' the children shouted. 'Letter from Pappa.'

Clara came from the side of the house, walking slowly towards the postman. Her arms, from the elbows down, were covered with soapsuds. Strands of tangled hair formed black, interlocking veins on a forehead moistened by sweat. The postman surrendered the airmail envelope whose distinctive red, white and blue border the children had come to know so well. He looked at her – as did the neighbours who now leaned farther out of their windows – with an air of vague expectancy; as if the letter were common property and its contents to be divulged there and then. Clara turned away and walked quickly to the house. The children ran after her.

'Get away from me!' Her arms flailed out.

She went inside and sat down on the rocking-chair. She tore open the envelope. Her eyes skimmed over the sheets of paper. Abruptly, she crumpled them into a ball. She rose from the rocking-chair and stared distractedly around the room. Going to the jalousied window she looked out at the road, her back to the clamouring children.

'What Pappa say?' They mobbed her.

Their mother did not answer. She gazed out at the broken, yellow day.

'Did Pappa say when he was coming home?'

'Keep away from me! Keep away from me!' Still holding the crumpled ball of the letter, she ran out of the room. Dodging the wash-lines, she stalked barefooted across the muddy yard to the washtub.

Clara thrust the letter into her bosom and plunged her arms up to the elbows in the grey, soapy water.

Clara was not prepared for the announcement in Roderick's letter. She had stubbornly closed her mind to the possibility of his return and its implications for her. To think about it would have served no purpose; made no difference. Her burned-up happiness was beyond recapture. Reuben had told her it was an ensnarement: he had given her a whole new vocabulary. The things of Caesar, her attachment to a piece of mere mortal flesh – these had been the cause of her suffering and misery. Her 'happiness' had always been an illusion. He had taught her a bitter knowledge; but, despite his constant assurances, it had given birth only to bitterer despair. Try as she might, Clara could not shake off that despair. At every step it lay in wait for her. Roderick's return would intensify her sickness. It was not possible to re-embark on that voyage. That was asking too much. The ship was broken in two. But memory would not be stilled; and the renunciation Reuben demanded (why did everyone have their own demands?) was not possible either. That also was asking too much of her. The heavenly spaces were inhuman; terrifying. She would never be at home in them.

Intermittently, for one or two hours at a stretch, Clara would feel she had come close to the state Reuben desired of her. Her other life dimmed to insignificance and eased its grip on her. She saw Roderick as a kind of mirage and Reuben's God – she could never separate Reuben from his God – was very near. She had only to reach out and she could embrace Him. But these interludes were short-lived. Reuben's God would recede from her and be swallowed up in the darkness. Then it was He who seemed a mirage and mere mortal flesh was all that there was or ever could be.

Her distraction was complete by the time Reuben arrived on his Sunday visit. Immediately he walked into the room, Clara thrust the letter at him. Her face was drawn and sallow and her hands trembled. Reuben looked curiously at her, read the letter calmly and returned it to her. He sat down and crossed his knees. Idly swinging his free leg, he smiled at her.

'What I going to do, Mr Reuben?' Clara stuffed the letter into her bosom from force of habit.

'You should know the answer to that by now,' Reuben replied equably. 'The Lord is testing you.'

'What is the answer, Mr Reuben? You must tell me.'

Reuben raised his eyebrows.

'I don't know what to do.' Clara wrung her hands. 'I been so confused. I don't feel I know anything any more.'

Reuben's earlier assurance faltered. His smile faded. He uncrossed his legs. 'Do you mean to say that even now – even now! – you will allow yourself to be tempted and led astray?' Reuben levelled a black finger at her.

Clara lowered her head. 'I wish you would understand, Mr Reuben. . . .'

'Understand what?' Reuben spoke with gathering fury. 'That you haven't learnt your lesson? That you wish to be ensnared yet again? That you wish. . . .'

'No!' Clara blocked her ears. 'But. . . .'

'But what?'

'I not sure that I have the strength, Mr Reuben.'

Reuben was silent.

Clara got up from the rocking-chair and went to the window.

'The Devil drives,' Reuben muttered.

She came away from the window and subsided on the floor close to his chair. 'So you won't help me, Mr Reuben?'

'I can't help you if you refuse to help yourself.' Reuben was cold.

She began to weep.

Reuben shut his eyes to her tears. 'Have you prayed?'

'Day and night.'

'And?'

'It didn't help.'

'Then you must pray some more.'

Clara stared desperately at him.

'At the first test you trip and stumble.' Reuben waved his arms angrily. 'And for what? For *who*? A blasphemer! All this for a man who insulted God's servant. My efforts have been wasted on you. Wasted!' He was shouting now and jerking his arms wildly.

Clara suddenly sprang up from the floor. 'You understand nothing! Nothing!' She was shouting too. 'You're just like the rest of them.'

'I understand all too well,' Reuben replied, becoming calm again and smiling sardonically at her.

'No. You don't understand a thing! You don't care what happens to me. All you can think of is how you wasted your efforts. That was what *he* thought as well when I let him down.' Clara circled round him, brushing her tangled hair away from her face. Her tears flowed freely. 'He use almost the exact words to me that first morning you come here and give me the magazine. Almost the exact words.'

'Do not compare me with that . . . that. . . .' For once Reuben was at a loss for the apt phrase.

'I'll compare you with who I like. At bottom you and he are just the same. You both have. . . .' She circled round him. 'Yes! That's it. You both have *ideas*.' She seized with despairing triumph on the word. 'Wherever I turn it's only ideas, ideas, ideas. But what about me?' She gazed at him frenziedly. 'Why is it I have no ideas like you and he, Mr Reuben?'

'I've warned you before not to compare me with that son of Satan.'

The leather-bound Bible he had given her lay on a tiny side-table next to the rocking-chair. Clara reached down, picked it up and hurled it at him with all her strength. Reuben dodged successfully. He uttered a nervous laugh as he bent down to retrieve it.

'I shall pray for you,' he said.

'I don't want your prayers. They're no good to me. No good at all. Now take your Bible and go. I never want to see your face here again. Get out of my sight!' She pointed at the door.

'Is that your final word?'

'That is my final word.'

Reuben departed.

After he had gone, Clara collapsed into the rocking-chair. She kicked it into motion. Her shining forehead puckered. She fished out the letter from her bosom and clasped it in her palms. Bars of sunlight and shadow, thrown from the jalousied windows, patterned the bare, dusty floorboards. The rocking-chair – which had long since lost its glitter and acquired the decrepit appearance of the other furniture – creaked back and forth in rhythmic sequence. The ring she was wearing flared when it caught the sun. Her face moved from shadow into light and then into shadow once more.

Clara disappeared from view. The neighbours were reluctant to intervene. They had already given all the solace they could. There was nothing more they could do. They took charge of the children who – abandoned by their mother – maundered about the yard unwashed and unfed. Clara seemed to notice neither their presence nor their absence. She noticed nothing. Hour after hour, with scarcely a twitch of a muscle, she sat on the rocking-chair, her hands resting flat on her lap. When she could no longer bear to be still, she got up and stared at the road. Roderick's letter, forgotten, lay undisturbed where it had fallen on the floor hours before.

Then came the evening of the second day when Paulette, sent by the neighbours to check on her mother, fled screaming from the little room and tumbled down the steps into the yard. The neighbours did not pause to question the hysterical child but shook her aside and dashed into the room. Clara was sprawled across the bed, her fingers clawing the bedclothes. She was drained of colour. A metal container had spilt its contents on the floor.

'The rat poison!'

The dose was not fatal. The doctors at the General Hospital pumped her stomach out. Every day the neighbours took it in turn to go with the children and visit her.

'You should have let me die,' she said to them.

'Foolish, foolish, doux-doux,' they chided. 'What a way to talk. You have so much to live for and you want to die.'

'I have nothing to live for.' She was unmoved; unrepentant. Her hollow eyes stared out at them from a pinched, ravaged face.

One afternoon they said: 'Look. We bring a present for you. All the way from America.'

Roderick, dressed in a smart brown suit and wearing a gaily coloured tie, bent down to kiss her. She shrank away from him.

'But doux-doux . . . doux-doux. . . .'

Roderick placed the bunch of red carnations he had brought her on the bedside table.

Clara, her head sunk into the pillow, watched him impassively. Neither spoke.

The neighbours were afraid to look at them; afraid especially to look at *her*. Those brown eyes were shorn of their bridal innocence. It was not easy to decode the message they carried. Her ordeal did not betray itself on the surface: it had been pushed back out of sight and buried deep in their brown depths. Yet it was plain that that ordeal lived on within her. It was flesh of her flesh. She was suffused by it. Desolation was like a curtain drawn between her and the world. Those eyes proclaimed her isolation; proclaimed that what she had been through could never be adequately told. She was a traveller who, unaccompanied, had undertaken a bizarre and dreadful journey across a strange land.

'What happened?' Roderick said to the neighbours when they were on their way back home. He was bewildered. 'How. . . .'

'You men don't know anything about we women. It might take less to make us happy. But it have some things. . . .' They clucked their tongues. 'Better not to talk about it. It was a terrible thing to have to witness. Terrible! So the less said the better.'

To the neighbours, Clara seemed possessed of a knowledge surpassing theirs. She was no longer a child. But she had paid an inordinate price for the privilege. Their present and future silence would be part of their respect; part of their homage.

To Roderick, who had stared at her in speechless astonishment, there seemed to be no bridge existing between Clara and himself. That bridge had been washed away along with much else. When? How? But he would never know. She could never tell him because they spoke in different tongues and there was no one to translate.

Mr Sookhoo and the Carol Singers

Mr Sookhoo, a short, fat man with a pot belly and a bushy, black moustache, drove the only truck in the village. He carried anything people would pay him to carry: furniture, sand, gravel; and, when the village headmaster asked, he took the schoolchildren on excursions to the beach, sugar-cane factories and oil refineries. It was a way of life that Mr Sookhoo found entirely to his liking: he was his own boss.

He was rocking slowly on his veranda, scraping thoughtfully at his teeth with a toothpick, when his wife appeared through the doorway.

'Eh, man. For the past two days all you doing is sitting here and rocking. Mr Ali tired ask you to carry that gravel to Port of Spain for him. What's more, he pay you for it already.'

'Ali could wait.' Mr Sookhoo continued to pick his teeth. 'So you been wondering what I been doing these past two days, eh?' He tossed the toothpick over the veranda rail and Mrs Sookhoo followed its flight with interest. 'All you could see was me rocking. But there was something else I was doing. Somthing invisible.' He smiled slyly at her. 'I was *thinking.*'

'Thinking!' Mrs Sookhoo weighed the significance of this remark. It worried her. 'Be careful, man. I sure it not good for you.'

Mr Sookhoo laughed scornfully. 'Now and then a man have to do a bit of thinking. Otherwise . . .' Losing the thread of his argument, he shrugged.

'I still think you should deliver that gravel to Mr Ali.'

'Ali could go to hell.' Mr Sookhoo expanded his chest.

'But what get into you so all of a sudden, man? I know all this thinking wasn't good for you.'

Mr Sookhoo waved a finger at her. 'I just been working out a master plan. Tell me – how many days it have till Christmas?'

Mrs Sookhoo frowned. 'The radio say it have about twenty-seven or so shopping days to go.'

'Right!' Mr Sookhoo gazed fiercely at her. 'Christmas is coming and the geese is getting fat. Time to put a penny in the old man hat.' He took another toothpick from his pocket. 'Believe me when I tell you the geese is really going to be fat this year. And it going to have so

many pennies in the old man hat by Boxing Day that you will bawl
when you see them.'

Mrs Sookhoo could not disguise her alarm. 'What get into you so
sudden, man?'

'Tell me,' he went on, scraping vigorously at his teeth, 'tell me how
much children it have in the school?'

'Twenty, thirty . . .'

'To be on the safe side, let me say it have twenty-five. Twenty-five
divide by five is five. Agree?' Mr Sookhoo tossed the toothpick over
the veranda rail and, as before, his wife followed its flight with
interest. He got up from the rocking-chair and leaned against the rail,
staring up at the sky. 'So that if I divide them up into five groups and
say each time they sing they get a little dollar or so . . .'

'What you intending to do, man? You sure is legal?'

He ignored her. '. . . and say each group sing about ten time a night
for twenty or so nights . . .' Here the magnitude of his calculations so
affected Mr Sookhoo that he let out a prolonged whistle, slapped his
stomach and spat on a rose-bush. 'Of course I'll have to take the cost of
the gasoline into account.' A shadow crossed his face. 'Still . . .'

'You going to land in jail, Sookhoo.'

'Chut, woman! People like hearing little children sing. Once you
could organise it properly, it have a lot of money in it. All this carol
singing need is organisation.'

'You forgetting one thing.'

'What?' Mr Sookhoo asked sharply.

'You is a Hindu.'

He laughed. 'Who is to know that in Port of Spain? It have
hundreds of Christians out there who look just like me. Like you
never hear of the Reverend Hari Lal Singh?'

'I still don't like it. And another thing. All them children you does
see singing carol singing for charity.'

'That is what they would like people like you and me to believe. All
that money they does collect going straight into their own pocket.
Charity!' Mr Sookhoo spat disdainfully on the rose-bush and went
inside.

Mr Sookhoo changed into his best suit and left the house pursued by
his wife's anxious enquiries. He walked the half-mile to the village
school with a quick, firm step.

Mr Archibald, the headmaster, stared at him suspiciously from behind the pile of copybooks he was correcting. He was well aware that Mr Sookhoo grossly overcharged him for the school's excursions.

'Good afternoon, Head. How is life with you these days?' Mr Sookhoo hummed under his breath.

'As usual.' Mr Archibald was guarded. 'I think I know that tune you're humming', he said. 'Christmas is coming and the geese are getting fat. Time to . . .'

'First time I hear of that one, Head. You wouldn't imagine how sometimes I does regret not having a education. It must be a great thing.'

Mr Archibald looked doubtfully at him. 'I suppose you have a reason for coming to see me, Mr Sookhoo?'

Mr Sookhoo leaned his elbows confidentially on the desk. 'I'll come straight to the point, Head. They asking me to organise a charity.'

Mr Archibald dried his forehead with a handkerchief, a symptom of his incredulity. 'They asking *you* to organise a charity, Mr Sookhoo? Who asking you to organise a charity?'

'The Deaf, Dumb and Blind Institute. They want me to help organise a little carol singing for them.'

'I never knew such an Institute existed.'

'Is a new thing.'

'Ah. But why *you*, Mr Sookhoo? Not that I want to be rude, but to be frank . . .'

Mr Sookhoo smiled gallantly. 'I not offended, Head. I know that my life – up until now that is – hasn't been exactly perfect. Like most men I have a few faults . . .'

'A few!'

Mr Sookhoo laughed. 'I don't know how to say this, Head – it going to sound funny coming from a man like me – but, all the same, I think I finally see the light.'

'What light?'

'Head! How you mean "what light"? That don't sound nice coming from a man like you, a man of education.'

Mr Archibald's vanity was touched. 'Sorry, Mr Sookhoo. But, as you yourself said, coming from a man like you . . .'

'Sooner or later a man have to set his mind on higher things,' Mr Sookhoo intervened solemnly.

'That is something nobody can teach us, Mr Sookhoo.' Mr Archibald's eyes swept vaguely across the ceiling. Then they hardened, assuming a more businesslike expression. 'But why *you*, Mr Sookhoo?

That is what I still don't understand. Even accepting that you have seen the . . . the light, it's very odd that the Deaf, Dumb and Blind Institute should ask you to . . .'

'Transport, Head. Transport.' And he added hastily: 'Don't think I is the only one. I only in charge of one area, you understand. This is a big operation they have plan.'

Mr Archibald nodded. 'Where do I come into it?'

Mr Sookhoo leaned closer to him. 'Not you so much as your pupils. This is a chance for them to help out a worthy cause by singing a few carols. My truck is at their disposal. Don't worry – is I who going to be paying for the gasoline.'

Mr Archibald stared at him. 'I really don't know what to say, Mr Sookhoo. Your generosity is overwhelming.' He fluttered the handkerchief before his face.

Mr Sookhoo grinned broadly. 'You teach them to sing a few carol and I take them to Port of Spain in the truck free of charge. That's a deal.' He held out his hand.

'Your generosity is overwhelming, Mr Sookhoo.'

'Is because I see the light,' Mr Sookhoo said.

It took Mr Archibald a week to teach his pupils a repertoire of six carols. Mr Sookhoo went to the school every afternoon to listen to them practise. Standing at the back of the classroom, he would shout encouragingly at them. 'That's the way, kiddies. Remember it's a worthy cause you singing for.'

Mr Archibald, beaming, would swing his baton (in fact a whip) with renewed vigour.

The first expedition into Port of Spain was a gay affair. Mr Sookhoo polished his truck and drove to the school. Freshly washed and dressed in white, the children looked convincing. Mr Archibald provided them with candles. 'I felt it was the least I could do considering you giving the gasoline,' he explained to Mr Sookhoo. They drove to one of the richer suburbs of the city and Mr Sookhoo parked his truck discreetly in a narrow side-street. He gathered the children about him, dividing them into groups of five.

'It have two things I must tell you about,' he said when he had finished. 'First and most important – don't mention my name to nobody . . .'

'Why?'

Mr Sookhoo glowered at the questioner, a small, earnest boy.

'Because I is a modest kind of person, that's why. If they ask you who send you say is the Deaf, Dumb and Blind Institute. And if they say they never hear of that before, tell them is a new thing just open up. You understand?' The children nodded confusedly. 'Second. Try to get a dollar each time you sing. When they pay you, stop. What would be the point in singing more after that, eh?' Mr Sookhoo giggled. The earnest boy gazed sternly at him. Mr Sookhoo, catching his eye, turned away in discomfort. The groups dispersed and, fetching a deep sigh, he took a toothpick from his pocket and scratched contentedly at his front teeth.

The choirs met with immoderate success. Their renditions were listened to attentively and no one gave them less than a dollar. In all, Mr Sookhoo collected just over forty dollars. He was jubilant.

'Good work.'

'Mr Sookhoo . . .' the earnest boy began.

'Later, sonny, later.'

'Have a look at that, woman.' Mr Sookhoo displayed the night's takings to his wife. 'Forty dollars in hard cash. And how? By using the brains God give me. By thinking. That's how.'

'Some people does call it embezzling. They bound to find out sooner or later what you doing.'

'How they go find out?' Mr Sookhoo folded the notes and put them in his pocket.

Success stimulated ambition. 'We going to start earlier and finish later,' he informed the children the next day. The choirs were not quite as gay as they had been the night before, but they set about their task without complaint. That night Mr Sookhoo collected fifty-five dollars. He could hardly contain himself, counting the notes again and again. 'Orgainisation was all it needed,' he said to himself.

'Mr Sookhoo . . .'

'Later, sonny, later.'

Mr Sookhoo prospered for a whole week. He had collected over three hundred dollars. And there were still many shopping days to Christmas. And there were still several suburbs waiting to be plundered. His eyes glittered. 'You going to end up in jail, Sookhoo,' his wife warned. He laughed and continued his calculations.

Early one morning Mr Archibald came to see him.

'How things going, Mr Sookhoo?'

'As well as could be expected in the circumstances, Head.'

'You not collecting enough?'

'Is a hard business, Head. These rich people tight, tight with they money.'

Mr Archibald dried his forehead with a handkerchief. 'You know Horace?'

'Which one is Horace?' Mr Sookhoo's heart sank.

'A thin little boy. He say that you working them down to the ground and that you collecting one hell of a lot of money.'

'I always thought he was a trouble-maker.'

'That boy is my brightest pupil, Mr Sookhoo. He's going to go far.'

'They is the worst kind.' Mr Sookhoo spat on the rose-bush.

Mr Archibald cleared his throat. 'You sure you being honest and above board with me, Mr Sookhoo? I mean this Institute really exist, not so?'

Mr Sookhoo gave the headmaster a pained look. 'Head! Head! How you could say a thing like that to me? A man of your education to boot!'

'Just put my mind at rest, Mr Sookhoo. You really see the light?' Mr Archibald spoke in a whisper.

Mr Sookhoo rested a comforting hand on the headmaster's shoulder. 'Honest to God, Head. I really see the light.'

Mr Archibald relaxed. He was anxious to believe Mr Sookhoo. 'These children working real hard,' he said. 'You could buy them a little sweet drink and ice-cream every day. I'm sure the Institute wouldn't mind.'

'Anything you say, Head. But I'll have to tell the Institute about it.'

'I could do that for you. I don't want them to think you're cheating them.'

'Don't bother yourself, Head. They trust me.'

Mr Archibald smiled and left the house.

The following night – it was the second week of their carolling – Mr Sookhoo took the children to the Trinidad Dairies. He bought them a Coca-cola each. When they had finished Mr Sookhoo got up to go.

'You forgetting something,' Horace said.

Mr Sookhoo instinctively felt for his wallet. His hand caressed the square lump. 'What it is I forgetting, Mr Know-All?'

The children gathered in an expectant circle.

'Mr Archibald tell you to buy ice-cream for we.'

Mr Sookhoo scowled. 'They don't sell ice-cream here.'

Horace appealed to the other children for support.

'I just see somebody buy a ice-cream,' one of them said.

'Well, I say they don't sell ice-cream here. And therefore they don't. You understand?'

'I know for a fact they does sell ice-cream here,' Horace insisted. 'To tell you the truth, I believe you trying to cheat we, Mr Sookhoo. I believe you keeping all that money we been getting for yourself.' Horace pouted insolently.

For a moment Mr Sookhoo hesitated, resisting the temptation to slap Horace. Finally he said: 'You little sonofabitch!'

'All you hear what he call me? You hear?' Looking greatly aggrieved, Horace walked away from the bar.

'I feel like letting that sonofabitch find his own way home.' Unhappily, he could read no sympathy on the faces of the choir.

Mr Archibald had a visitor.

'I come to ask a favour of you, Headmaster.'

'I will do anything in my power to help you, sir,' Mr Archibald replied primly.

'I'm involved in charity work . . .'

'I myself have been having a little experience of that.'

'Have you? Well, I was wondering if your pupils would care to sing carols for my charity. We choose certain schools each year . . .'

Mr Archibald smiled sympathetically. 'I'm afraid we're already booked up this year. I'm sorry.'

'I understand. As I always say at times like these, one charity is as good as another. The unfortunate, no matter what their affliction, are always to be succoured.'

For some seconds both men savoured their goodness.

'Incidentally, Headmaster – and I hope you don't mind my asking you . . .'

'Not at all, sir. I have no secrets.'

'What charity are your pupils singing for?'

'The Deaf, Dumb and Blind Institute. I believe it's a new thing just opened up a few months ago.'

His visitor started. There was a long silence while they looked at each other.

'That's very strange, Headmaster. You see, I work for something called the Blind Institute. But the Deaf, Dumb *and* Blind Institute . . .

luckily I have a list of accredited charities here with me.' He took a pamphlet from his pocket and scanned it.

'I feel quite faint.' Mr Archibald fluttered his handkerchief.

'Pardon me for saying so, Headmaster, but I think you've been taken for a ride.'

'I really do feel quite faint.'

Trinidad is a small island in a small world.

When Mr Ali saw the group of children led by Horace coming confidently up the path towards him and singing 'Silent Night', he lost his temper.

'Stop that blasted racket this minute!'

The choir stuttered into silence, their candles guttering in the wind. Loose gravel shifted under their feet. It had been their rudest welcome to date.

'Tell me who it is send you to disturb my peace.'

'Is the Deaf, Dumb and Blind Institute what send we.'

'The Deaf, Dumb and Blind Institute, eh! Try me with another one.'

'Is a new thing. Just open up these last few months,' one of the children ventured timidly. He looked round for Horace, their acknowledged leader. But Horace had detached himself from the group and stood to one side, lost in contemplation.

'You have any identification?' Mr Ali was very threatening.

The child cringed. 'Ask Horace over there. He will know.'

Mr Ali strode over to Horace. 'Tell me who send you,' he shouted. 'And remember no lies, if you not careful I'll skin the whole lot of you alive.'

Horace smirked. 'Is Mr Sookhoo who send we.'

'Mr Sookhoo! He have a moustache and big belly?'

Horace nodded.

'And he does drive a truck?'

'He park just down the road waiting for we to come back.'

'And what about this so-called Institute? It have any truth in that?'

'Mr Sookhoo make that up.' Horace's smirk intensified.

'What a tricky bugger, eh! So that's why he wasn't delivering my gravel. Come and show me where Mr Sookhoo is, Horace. I have a little outstanding business to settle with him.'

Horace, abandoning his candle, skipped eagerly down the path, followed by Mr Ali and the nonplussed choir.

Mr Sookhoo was sitting in his truck, sucking a toothpick and occasionally looking at his watch. A notebook lay open on his lap covered
with scrawled calculations. The confused sound of children's voices
reached him. 'How come they so early tonight?' he wondered, peering
into the rear-view mirror. He stiffened. The toothpick hung limp
between his teeth.

'Mr Sookhoo! I so glad I manage to catch up with you at last. I been
longing to have a chat with you.' Mr Ali's voice floated sweetly on the
night air.

'Believe me when I say you still have a lot of catching up to do,' Mr
Sookhoo muttered. He flung the toothpick out of the window. The
engine stammered into life and the truck lurched away from the curb,
gathering speed.

'Don't think you getting away this time, Mr Sookhoo.'

'Mr Sookhoo! Mr Sookhoo! Wait for we! Wait for we!'

The cries of the choir faded behind him, drowned by the noise of
the engine.

'Woman, bring your clothes quick! I think we have to go away from
here for a while. Things hotting up.' Mr Sookhoo raced up the steps to
the veranda and stood there catching his breath.

'Good evening, Mr Sookhoo.' Two large policemen came strolling
casually through the sitting-room door, flourishing torches.

Mr Sookhoo clutched at his heart. However, he recovered himself
quickly. 'Why is you, sergeant.'

Mr Archibald trailed behind them, accompanied by his visitor. Mrs
Sookhoo, her cheeks wet with tears, brought up the rear.

'Man . . . man,' she moaned.

Mr Sookhoo paid her no attention. 'Why, Head – you here too. And
I see you bring a friend with you as well.'

'You deceived me, Mr Sookhoo. A most cruel deception.'

Mr Sookhoo gestured resignedly.

'I really thought you had seen the light, Mr Sookhoo.' Mr Archibald seemed on the verge of tears.

The sergeant produced a notebook and licked the tip of his pencil.
'Mr Sookhoo will see a lot of lights in jail,' he said quietly and started
to write.

Mrs Sookhoo moaned louder.

'This gentleman,' the sergeant went on, indicating Mr Archibald's
visitor, 'is from the Blind Insitute. Show him your card, Mr Harris.'

Mr Harris showed Mr Sookhoo his card.

He refused to look at it. 'I know all them tricks,' Mr Sookhoo said. 'Ask him how much money he does make out of it. Go on. Ask him.'

Mr Harris flushed. 'I get paid a salary for the work I do, Mr Sookhoo. Legally. Just because I work for charity doesn't mean I can live on air.'

'Living on air my arse! You see the expensive clothes he wearing? I could tell you where he get the money to buy all that.'

'This is to add insult to injury,' Mr Harris said.

'I should warn you, Mr Sookhoo, that everything you say will be taken down in evidence against you.' The sergeant scribbled energetically.

A sleek motor-car stopped outside the gate. Horace and Mr Ali entered out of breath.

'Ali! Like is a party we having here tonight.'

'I not in a party mood, Mr Sookhoo. I come for all that money I pay you to deliver my gravel.'

'What gravel is this?' the sergeant asked interestedly.

Mr Ali outlined his grievances.

'The plot thickens,' the sergeant said.

'Man, remember how I did tell you all this thinking would be bad for you. Remember . . .'

'Go and do something useful, woman. Bring me a toothpick.'

Horice sidled up to Mr Archibald. He tugged at his trousers. 'He didn't buy we any ice-cream either. And you should have hear how he insult me when I remind him.'

'Don't worry, Horace. Mr Sookhoo is going to get what he deserves.' Mr Archibald patted Horace.

'I think you should expel that boy from your school, Head. He's a born sonofabitch.' Mr Sookhoo spat on the rose-bush.

'You hear the kind of thing he does call me?' Horace exlaimed aggrievedly.

The sergeant closed his notebook. 'You better come to the station with us, Mr Sookhoo. You could make your statement there – for what it's worth.'

Sandwiched between the two policemen, Mr Sookhoo was escorted to the waiting car. He waved to the small crowd that had assembled on the pavement.

'Don't say I never warn you, Sookhoo.'

Mr Sookhoo smiled at his wife. 'You didn't bring me that tooth-pick.' He laughed.

The car drove off.

'The Good Lord is just. Isn't he, Horace?' Mr Archibald curled an affectionate arm around the boy.

'Yes.' Horace grinned and thought with delight of the ice-cream Mr Archibald had promised to buy him.

The Father, the Son and the Holy Ghost

Flea looked at the dark, pinched face and the tiny shrivelled legs, like twigs, kicking in the air. Carmen lay beside the child, her skin shining, and watched him with exhausted eyes which yet were vaguely questioning and pensive.

Flea, a short and wiry man, with closely cropped, curling black hair and arms tattooed with big-bosomed mermaids, shook his head sorrowfully and sighed. 'So, this is what God decide to do to me,' he said. He gazed at the child, his face wrinkling with dismay. It started to scream. 'I wonder what God expect a poor sailor like me to do with this one. Another hungry mouth to feed.' He lifted his woe-struck eyes up to the ceiling and let them rest there.

Carmen laughed. 'I don't see what God have to do with all this, Flea. I could see your true feelings as plain as daylight in your eyes. I don't know why you does always be pretending to have children all over the place. You should be thankful for even having one, instead of rolling your eyes up like that.'

Flea's features having composed themselves, his gaze returned to the screaming child. 'What you mean "pretending"? I is a sailor now, you know. Not some stupid carpenter. Don't forget that. Things very different out on the high seas. The sea does change a man. A sailor is a lot different from other people.' His gaze roamed up the wall and his eyes contracted thoughfully. 'In a way,' he said, 'we is really wicked men. Take my captain, for instance. He have a child in nearly every port in the West Indies. He was telling me just the other day that Spanish women is the worst of all, and I think I agree with him. You yourself have a little Spanish blood, not so?' Carmen nodded. 'You must know for yourself what I mean then. I wouldn't tell you a lie.'

'I must say, I never know you to tell the truth, Flea. Sailor indeed! You only been working on them boats for six months now, so I don't see how you could have any other children, unless they does fall down out of the sky.' Carmen giggled. 'I bet you never even went as far as Jamaica.'

'What you mean I never even went as far as Jamaica? I been further. To Cuba. Havana. That's how I come to know about Spanish women.' He sucked in his breath. 'They know how to do things over there,' he said. 'A man don't stand a chance with them.' Carmen laughed.

'You trying to make me jealous, Flea?'

Flea felt ashamed of himself and resentful. He knew Carmen to be an ultra-cool and experienced woman of the world, so absolutely sure of herself as to be incapable of any paltry feeling like jealousy. It had put her far beyond him and it made him powerless before her. He was aware that beyond this was a long dead love, a passion played out in the shadows of her youth, full of romance and heartache. Such at any rate was the story. But Carmen never talked about it. It may have been an invention, perpetuated by Carmen for her own secret purposes.

Flea was silent for a time. Then he said, 'And I been to Jamaica twice as a matter of fact. You could ask the captain, if you doubt me.'

'I wouldn't trust what your so-called captain say either. If anything, he sound like an even bigger liar than you.'

The child continued to scream.

'And anyway,' Flea added, 'is more than six months since I went to sea. Is nearly a whole year since I stop working in old Ramchand sawmill.' He scratched the tip of his nose. 'You think the child hungry?' he asked, peering at it with sudden concern.

Carmen lifted the child off the sheets without ceremony and unbuttoning her bodice, brought its lips to the almost black nipples of her breast. It fell to with a contented gurgle. Flea watched her. She was a good-looking woman. Her face was round and full and she had big, dark eyes and a fine, straight nose. She radiated health. Flea remembered what Felix, his predecessor in Carmen's affections, had said about her. 'That woman have the biggest thighs I ever see. Big like lampposts. But soft, man, much softer. That Carmen is a real thoroughbred. You can't beat the Spanish blood in a woman.' Felix had carved languid patterns in the air as he spoke. It was then that Flea, who had never seen her, fell hopelessly in love with Carmen.

At that time both he and Felix had been working in old Ramchand's sawmill. Carmen cooked for the Ramchands and Felix, who in his capacity as foreman had access to the old man's house, had made such good use of his time there that a child had resulted from these visits. When the sawmill had started to run into serious difficulties (from its inception it had been threatened with disaster), old Ramchand had taken to having his lunch brought to the office, in the belief that a more prolonged physical presence there would, in some mysterious way, halt the slide to chaos. Punctually at one o'clock Carmen would appear, a bright, flowered scarf fluttering on her head, bearing the little white enamel containers wrapped in napkins. To Flea, she was an apparition of pure delight risen freshly each day from the sawdust. Day after day Flea had watched her flitting, light as a butterfly, among the piles of timber and the ugly, growling heaps of machinery. From afar he had gazed at those thighs, big as lampposts, and in imagination explored their yielding softnesses. His chance for closer acquaintance came one day when Felix was absent on business. He got into conversation with her and offered to share his lunch. Flea exerted all his charm. Perhaps it was the hopelessness of his passion; perhaps it was the absurdity of his ambition; perhaps Carmen was touched by his simplicity; it is impossible to say, but whatever it was an intimacy of sorts was established. Unfortunately it was not long after this that the sawmill had gone out of business and Flea, having listened long to Carmen extolling the masculinity of sailors, had taken reluctant leave of his mistress and gone to sea in the guise of a ship's carpenter.

For a moment, thinking of these adventures, his eyes filled with pride and he traced with a finger the outline of the mermaid imprinted on his left arm. Then, a worried frown distorted his features.

'You see much of Felix while I was away?'

Carmen shifted the baby's head. 'On and off. But not since the baby born though.' The child sucked noisily.

He leaned over Carmen and peered closely at the child's face. 'You sure this child is mine, Carmen? I don't find it resemble me all that much. It look more like Felix if you ask me.'

Carmen raised her head interestedly. 'You really find it resemble Felix?' she asked, scrutinising the child's face with a curiosity greater than she normally allowed herself.

Flea shrugged. 'I think it have his nose.'

Carmen giggled. 'So, it have Felix nose. I wonder who else it resemble?' Her giggle changed into a high-pitched laugh. The child having had its fill, had fallen asleep, its lips stained with milk. Carmen rested it gently beside her and buttoned her bodice.

'What you laughing at? What it is you find so funny, eh? Sailors like me don't stand much for that kind of behaviour, you know. You think I was sending you all that money to support another man child?'

'Don't get on such a high horse, Flea. I just find it funny that you should say he have a nose like Felix. That's all. Come to think of it, I never really notice Felix nose at all when I was going with him. What it like?' Carmen choked on her laughter.

Flea cursed under his breath, striding up and down the narrow room, examining with displeasure its furnishings.

'Anyway,' Carmen went on, brushing a tear away from the corner of her eye, 'since when twenty dollars is a lot of money?'

'Is twenty dollars more than you deserve. I don't believe that child is mine. The nose give it away. You would think that the baby would at least have my nose . . .' Flea gestured futilely.

'You right. Is Felix child.'

Flea turned pale.

'I only joking,' Carmen said soothingly. 'The child is yours, Flea. Yours.'

'You sure you not fooling me?'

'I wouldn't do a thing like that, Flea. I already have one child by Felix, as you well know. So, what I want another one by him for?'

Flea relaxed. Carmen's logic, though dismal, was convincing and, above all, Flea wanted to believe her. Nevertheless, the thought that had been nagging him ever since he had entered the room returned.

'Where you get all this fancy furniture from? Flea pointed at a dresser, obviously new, with swing mirrors.

'I buy it secondhand,' Carmen replied, glancing carelessly at it.

'It look brand new to me. And I recognise the workmanship as well. You can't fool me so easy.'

'After the business collapse, old Ramchand was selling off all kind of thing dirt cheap.'

Flea looked doubtfully at her. 'I don't see Mistress Ramchand allowing he to do that. She's a real tigress when it come to money. She refuse to pay me for the last two weeks I work in the sawmill. Say they didn't have any money. I had a lot of dealings with she in my time.'

'All the same,' Carmen insisted stubbornly, 'old Ramchand sell me that dirt cheap. It was a kind of favour.' She smiled, 'When you going away next?'

'It depend on what happening to the child. We got to think about that.'

'We?'

'What you mean "we"?'

'You think I is a millionaire or something, Flea? I didn't keep the child I make for Felix. So why should I keep the child I make for you, eh?' She might have been a potter talking about his pots.

'And so, you expect me to keep the child?'

'You could always send it to the Belmont Orphanage.'

Flea was glum. He scratched the tip of his nose. 'I think that would be a wrong kinda thing to do. After all, the child is mine, not so?' He looked searchingly at Carmen.

'You think is the Holy Ghost who came in here one night?'

Flea could not suppress a smile. 'Don't worry, Carmen. I know the child is mine,' he said. He walked across the room to the window and looked out. The yard was black and muddy. Some ducks were fishing in the turbid pools of water. He smiled. Paternity sat lightly on his shoulders. A lifelong ambition had been realised. Not only had he a child but, what was even better, it was illegitimate. There could be no doubt about it now: he was a true sailor, one of a gallant fraternity much admired by Carmen, and Felix and the rest could no longer laugh at him. However, Flea's love for the child was only notional. The idea of paternity was all that appealed to him. For the rest, his son was an encumbrance. He saw that clearly. Flea was aware of someone staring at him. A woman was walking past below the window and craning her neck at him. When he caught her eye she smiled familiarly. That smile disturbed Flea and he came away from the window.

'Why that bitch laughing at me?'

'Who?'

'That bitch who does live next door to you.'

'Go and ask she. Not me.' Carmen's eyes gazed with unabashed serenity at him.

He brightened. 'You could go back to work with old Ramchand. That will give you enough money to keep the child.'

'But didn't I tell you they fire me? The moment Mrs Ramchand see my belly swelling up with another baby, she order me out of the house. Without so much as a by-your-leave. She didn't pay me either.'

'Why don't you give it away to somebody then?'

Maternal pride stirred fitfully in Carmen's breast. 'But what you think it is, man? You think it was a sack of flour or potatoes I was carrying in my belly for nine months? Try and remember that is your child as much as mine. I wonder how you does treat all them other children you claim to have all over the place.' Her lips formed into a smile, half-mocking.

'Hear she talk now! Who was just saying to give it away to the Belmont Orphanage?'

'I was only making a joke.'

'I tell you what,' Flea said, 'why don't you give it to the Ramchands?'

A curious look seeped over Carmen's face when Flea said this, but she remained silent, as if following a quite separate train of thought. Much of this escaped Flea's notice. 'You remember how I used to break my back working in that rundown sawmill? They owe me something for all those years' faithful service. Old Ramchand used to underpay me like crazy, but I never complain once. Mind you, it wasn't him to blame. He have a kind heart. I mean, take that dresser he sell you so cheap, I bet Mistress Ramchand would have rather dead than do that. She have him under she thumb. You must know yourself how she does insult him in front of total strangers. I tell you, sometimes I used to blush for the poor man.' Flea lowered his voice confidentially. 'You know why she never had any children by him?' The dreamy look had not yet left Carmen's face. 'Because she find him too black and ugly. That's why. Poor fella. Nobody want a child more than he. You could take my word for that. A man need some comfort in his old age.' Flea stopped and studied the sleeping child. 'He need this boy more than we. After all, in nearly every port from Port of Spain to Kingston I have two or three children calling me daddy . . .' Flea raised his eyes to the ceiling, swept along to such an extent by this wave of sentiment that he had actually come to accept the altruism of his motives. A tear rose to his eyes.

Carmen, roused from her reverie, laughed, though the curious expression had not entirely left her face. 'You should have been an actor, man. You would have put the whole of Hollywood to shame. None of them could ever have hoped to compete with you.'

The following day Carmen went to see Flea. He had spent an uneasy night, greatly troubled by his conscience. His sentiment had shifted its ground. Flea had come to believe that he had a profound love for the child. Carmen, her flowered scarf fluttering, settled like a butterfly on his bed.

'I been thinking about what you was saying yesterday, Flea.'

Flea was glum. 'What about?'

'About giving the child to the Ramchands. I think is a good idea.' Carmen twiddled the buttons on her blouse.

'I change my mind about that,' Flea replied. 'I think is a wrong kinda thing to do.'

'But you is a sailor, Flea. You going to be away for months on end. You call that being a father?'

'I don't have to be a sailor. I could set up as a carpenter.'

'You is not a true sailor at all. I disappointed in you.' Carmen untied her scarf and shook out her hair. It settled, a dark, restless mass, on her shoulders. 'All the sailors I know . . .'

'But . . .' Flea's despondency deepened.

'And you have all your other children to think about,' Carmen said.

Flea cast a despairing glance at her. 'I like this child the best, Carmen.'

'I thought you was feeling so sorry for old Ramchand.'

'Ramchand could look after himself.'

'All the sailors I know is generous, carefree men. Devils!' Carmen's eyes flashed. 'Wicked men, as you yourself tell me. You is not a true sailor at all, Flea, a mouse not a man.'

'But . . .'

'No buts. Be brave. Be generous. Be a sailor! If you think I going to waste my life living with you and looking after this child, you have another think coming.'

'You mean to say you will walk out on me just like that?'

Carmen played with her scarf. 'It wouldn't be the first time I do something like that, Flea.'

Flea thought of those thighs, big as lampposts, walking inexorably away from him and his heart ached.

'You sure the Holy Ghost had nothing to do with this child, Carmen?'

Carmen gave one of her high-pitched laughs, but she did not answer his question.

'The child is mine, not so, Carmen?'

'Stop asking stupid questions and go and see old Ramchand.' She began winding the scarf about her head.

'Why me? Is you who want to give them the child. Not me.'

'The child is yours too, Flea. You must accept some of the responsibility. And anyway, I don't feel like meeting Mrs Ramchand. She tell me she would call the police if I ever set foot in that house again.'

Mrs Ramchand was a thin, fine-boned woman. The structure of her face was delicate: the high cheekbones, the bright almond-shaped eyes, the flawless olive complexion. Only one thing could be said to detract from her looks: her narrow pinched lips which she always kept tightly pressed together. Even when she smiled (a rare occurrence) this rigidity was apparent, lending her face an air of profound insincerity. Mrs Ramchand was not a likeable woman. Flea's information was correct. Mrs Ramchand despised her husband. As Felix had once said to Flea, 'She hate the very dirt old Ramchand does walk on.' She admired two things to the exclusion of all else: wealth and fairness of complexion. Unfortunately, one of the first lessons that life had taught her was that these two things did not invariably go together. Mr Ramchand was a compromise. He was rich but at the same time dark and inescapably ugly. This dissonance had provided Mr Ramchand with a fertile source of metaphysical meditation and formed the theme of all her lamentations. Compromises are never inspiring and from the first day of their marriage Mr Ramchand had found himself the object of his wife's never-ending scorn. He had gone the way of all compromises. She had, as Flea said, refused to bear him any children. In front of guests she would say, 'The reason why we don't have any children is simple. You ever see a man uglier than my husband? Look and see for yourself.' She would then give a guided tour of her husband's infirmities. Mr Ramchand would shrink into himself and submit to the silent scrutiny of the assembled company, usually his wife's relatives.

When Flea presented himself, Mrs Ramchand examined him scornfully from head to foot. Having satisfied herself, she pursed her lips and stared at him.

'Is your husband I come to see, Mistress Ramchand.'

'He not home, Flea. He gone to Port of Spain to waste some more of my money. You could talk to me. What concern him also concern me.'

Flea shifted uncomfortably from foot to foot and gazed distrustfully at her. 'Well . . .'

'Time is money, Flea. At least my time is.'

'But is your husband I come to speak to, Mistress Ramchand. I'll come another day.' Flea started to move towards the door.

'You won't come another day, Flea. You not going to leave this place till you tell me what it is you come for.' She darted ahead of him and blocked the door. Her agility unnerved Flea. 'Now,' she said, 'you going to tell me what kind of underhand business you and that scoundrel trying to cook up behind my back.' Flea was silent. 'Tell me!' she shouted suddenly. Flea cringed. 'You and Hari planning some mischief together? I thought these last few months he was looking all kind of secretive and worried. Jumping at the slightest sound, looking at me out of the corner of he eye. The both of you figuring out some new way to throw more of my money down the drain? Eh? Tell me.' Although Mrs Ramchand had come to her husband with no personal fortune, she had fallen, without effort, into the habit of thinking of her husband's wealth as entirely her own, free to dispose of as she saw fit – normally to her relatives.

'It have nothing to do with what you say. You remember Carmen?'

'You think I could ever forget that prostitute my husband bring here to cook? I surprise she didn't poison me. The way that bitch used to look at me, laughing at me behind my back . . .'

Flea chose to ignore these remarks. 'You know she was . . .'

'I know, I know. You would think being a prostitute she would know how to take care and avoid that kind of thing. But stupid people is stupid people, I suppose.'

Flea drew himself up to his full height, which made him look slightly ridiculous. Realising this, he lowered himself to his customary hunched stance. 'I would not have you speaking of my Carmen in that way, Mistress Ramchand. I would have you know . . .'

'Your Carmen, Mr Flea?' Mrs Ramchand's nostrils twitched scornfully. 'You mean she was going with you too? You mean you let she fool a sensible man like you?'

'I would have you know, Mistress Ramchand, that my Carmen is . . .'

'Your Carmen! Your Carmen was leading you round the place by the nose.' Mrs Ramchand was pitying.

'Nobody could ever lead me round by the nose, Mistress Ramchand . . .' Flea paused, his confidence checked. 'That nose . . .' he said, half to himself.

'What nose you talking about, Mr Flea?'

'Nose? Did I say something about a nose?'

'That's what I thought. That woman making you take leave of your senses.'

'I must have been thinking about something else, Mistress Ramchand. I have a lot on my mind these days. What I wanted to say was . . .' He stopped and looked about him. He heard Felix's languid voice. 'Thighs big as lampposts. But soft, man, much softer.' His heart ached.

'I don't have all day to stand up here talking to you, Mr Flea. I not an idler like my husband. Say what you have to say. And if Madame Carmen send you here to ask me to take she back, you shouldn't waste your breath. Once I make up my mind even God – note that – even God won't make me change it. He could fall down on his knees and beg, but even He won't make me change it. So now you know the kind of woman you dealing with.' Mrs Ramchand had put such energy into this declaration of faith that droplets of sweat appeared on her upper lip.

Flea drew a deep breath. 'Is nothing like that,' he assured her. Mrs Ramchand was unable to hide her disappointment. She wiped the droplets away with the sleeve of her dress.

'Well?'

'What I wanted to say was that I am the father of that child.'

'You, Flea? But how you could be sure about a thing like that? Especially with someone like Madame Carmen.'

'I sure. That child is mine. It certainly wasn't the Holy Ghost.' Flea could not suppress the worried smile that accompanied this declaration.

'What?' Mrs Ramchand, leaving the doorway, approached Flea and thrust her face close up to his. It was one of her favourite tricks with Mr Ramchand. 'What the Holy Ghost have to do with all this?'

Flea withdrew further into the depths of the room. 'That's the whole point, Mistress Ramchand. The Holy Ghost have nothing to do with it at all.'

'You don't sound too sure to me, Flea.' Mrs Ramchand clapped her palms against her hips and laughed loudly. Flea's poise crumbled altogether.

'What you laughing at so, Mistress Ramchand?'

'You must excuse me, Flea.' Mrs Ramchand quickly recovered herself. 'But with someone like Madame Carmen I wouldn't rule the Holy Ghost out of the picture.' She spluttered into fresh laughter. It was not often that the world afforded Mrs Ramchand such pleasure.

'I tell you the child is mine, Mistress Ramchand. Why would I lie about a thing like that? I don't stand to gain anything from doing that. The child have all my features.'

'All right. All right. So you think you is the father of the child. What that have to do with me?'

'We was wondering if you would like to keep the child.'

'What! You sure I hear you right the first time, Flea?'

'Is the least you could do for me. Since Carmen get fired, she hardly have a penny to spend on sheself, much less on the child. Is you who responsible for that. And don't forget how hard I used to work for you down at the sawmill.'

'You mean how hard you used to work at cheating me. Robbing me right, left and centre. If you had the chance you would have run away with the whole place, lock stock and barrel.'

'I never rob anybody,' Flea replied with glum defiance. 'I is an honest man and I used to do an honest day's work. In fact you didn't pay me for the last two weeks, but I not the sort of man to remind you of that. I not even asking for it.'

Mrs Ramchand snorted. 'And what you think you doing now? Praying in church? And what about you? You have a job, not so?'

'Sailors don't get pay much, Mistress Ramchand. Anyway, I have a lot of other children to look after already.'

'You?' Mrs Ramchand brought the full weight of her scorn to bear on Flea. 'You have other children? Don't give me that one, Flea. What woman go like you?' She laughed as before, her palms resting on her hips.

At that moment, Mr Ramchand came into the room. He was a short, very dark man and, although he had a disproportionately large, moon-shaped face, his eyes were little more than bloodshot slits. His nose was flat and spreading, as if it had been melted by the heat and later congealed into its present shape, and his nostrils were shaped like cavernous triangles, dark caves out of which peeped clotted strands of greying hair. Flea's face brightened. However, when he saw Flea, Mr Ramchand stumbled in astonishment, his face clouding over. With one eye on his wife, he retreated back to the doorway.

Mrs Ramchand glanced disdainfully at him. 'Don't run away, Hari. It was you who Flea come to see in the first place.'

'Me?'

'I think you should know what Flea come here to ask. You remember that child the cook was having?'

'Cook? What cook?' Mr Ramchand asked in a soft, debilitated whisper.

'Don't tell me you don't remember Madame Carmen, Hari. That prostitute you yourself bring here to work for we.'

'Oh, Carmen. Yes. I remember she.' Mr Ramchand's voice crackled from the doorway. He avoided looking at Flea who was staring intently at him and wrinkling his brows.

'Well, Flea say he is the father.'

Mr Ramchand jumped and stammered something.

'Speak up, Hari. I can't hear what you saying.'

'Nothing. Nothing.'

'Stop wheezing like that then. Mind you,' Mrs Ramchand went on, 'I don't believe for a moment that he is the real father.'

Mr Ramchand retreated out into the passage. He uttered a shrill laugh and fell silent.

'I is the father, Mr Ramchand,' Flea said.

'Come into the room, Hari. I not going to bite you this morning.' Mrs Ramchand tittered.

Mr Ramchand shambled hesitantly into the room.

'What we would like to find out,' Mrs Ramchand said, 'is the name of the Holy Ghost.'

Mr Ramchand seemed to shrink into himself.

'Anyway, that is neither here nor there.' She looked at her husband. 'The point is that Flea is asking me to keep a black and ugly child in my house. You ever hear more?'

'The child not so black and ugly as you think, Mistress Ramchand.' Flea felt the nagging pull of paternal pride.

"It not?' Mr Ramchand's agitation had lessened.

'What you think it is, Mr Ramchand? Carmen have a lot of Spanish blood in she.'

That seemed to please Mr Ramchand. He rubbed his palms together and smiled.

'I don't see what you have to be smiling at, Hari. Whether Carmen have Spanish blood or not is nothing to do with you. So I don't see what you grinning all over your face for. I sure the child is a lot prettier than you.'

The smile faded from Mr Ramchand's face, though he appeared less perturbed than usual by this rebuke.

'What sex is this child, Flea?'

'That's the best part of the whole business, Mistress Ramchand. It a boy. Boy-children is a lot less trouble than girl-children. You take my word. For instance, in Puerto Rico . . .'

Mrs Ramchand signalled him to be silent. 'I don't want to hear about your so-called children in Puerto Rico, Flea. So you say the child not bad-looking?'

'It resemble me, Mistress Ramchand. It have all my features.'

Mr Ramchand looked strangely at Flea.

'You is not the best looking of men, Flea. In fact, to be frank with you, I could think of only one man who is uglier than you and we all know who that is.'

Flea's pride was too heavily involved for him to bestow any sympathy on Mr Ramchand. 'I never said I was the handsomest of men, Mistress Ramchand.' He pouted sullenly, scratching the tip of his nose.

Mrs Ramchand turned to her husband. 'What you think of the idea, Hari?'

Mr Ramchand cleared his throat. 'I don't think is such a bad idea. Is up to you of course, but I feel we bound to need somebody to look after we in we old age.' Mr Ramchand's agitation had returned with all its previous force and his voice trembled and crackled as he spoke.

'You could bring him up here as a kind of houseboy,' Flea added encouragingly, if not eagerly.

'A houseboy,' Mrs Ramchand considered. Servility, in any of its forms, invariably appealed to her. It was what she understood best and now it exercised a kind of magical influence over her. 'All right, Flea,' she said with a show of reluctance, 'you bring the child and I'll have a look at it.'

Flea brought the child the next day and Mrs Ramchand looked at it.

'What you think of it?' Flea asked.

Mrs Ramchand, turning the child over as if it were roasting on a spit, clucked her tongue distastefully.

'This child is ugly like sin, Flea. In fact, it might be even uglier than that. And it so black too. I never see such a black child in all my born days. It almost as black as Hari. You ever see such a black child, Hari?'

Mr Ramchand glanced quickly at the child and said nothing. His eyes, after a sleepless night, were like red cracks.

Flea pouted. 'It have hundreds of children in Africa a lot blacker than he, Mistress Ramchand. You don't have to take it if you don't like it. Nobody forcing you.'

'Don't be hasty, Flea. It not all that black. Houseboys don't have to be pretty.' And, as Flea was leaving, she called after him. 'What you say about all them really black people in Africa, it have any truth in that?'

'I only see them in pictures,' Flea said. 'But from what I can see there some of them black like coal.'

'Like coal!' Mrs Ramchand was astounded.

She looked at her acquisition and shook her head sadly.

'Come on, Flea. I haven't seen you smile for a whole week. Woman troubles? Have some more rum. That will make you happy.' Felix, tilting the bottle with an unsteady hand, poured some rum into Flea's glass. 'Drink that up, man, and tell Felix what on your mind. Rum is the best medicine for woman troubles. When you have enough experience of that kind of thing, you will agree with old Felix.'

Flea frowned morosely at the rum and drank it down in one gulp, drying his lips with the back of his hand. 'I have enough experience already,' Flea said.

'Don't fool yourself, man. If you was really experienced, like me, you wouldn't let what a woman say trouble you. Ignore them and after a while they go come running to you.'

'When you love a woman,' Flea said, staring balefully at the bottle of rum, 'it hard to behave like that. And anyway, the woman I thinking of would never come running to anybody.'

'Is Carmen you talking about?'

'Who else?'

Felix grinned. 'You letting she bother you?'

Flea looked up in surprise. 'I never hear you speak like that about she before.'

'You will learn in time, Flea. It have a million women like Carmen in this world.' Felix snapped his fingers.

'When you fall in love, you will see things in a different light.'

Felix laughed. 'Till that time come,' he replied and snapped his fingers again. He leaned back in his chair and gazed up at the rows of glittering bottles behind the bar. A silver chain gleamed through his shirt and a gold identity bracelet glittered loosely on his wrist. He wore a wide-brimmed hat which was set firmly on his head. Felix was dressed in the height of fashion.

For a while, they were silent. Then, with an abrupt nervous movement of his whole body, Flea said, 'Turn your face up to the light, Felix.'

'Why? Like you take up painting these days, Flea?'

'Turn your face to the light. I just want to see something.'

Felix turned his face towards the light, striking a comical pose as he did so. Flea studied the upturned face. He shook his head sorrowfully. Felix laughed.

'Satisfied now?'

Flea nodded and poured himself some more rum.

'What's the matter with you, man? Tell Felix. We is old friends.'

'The Holy Ghost is the matter with me.'

'The Holy Ghost? Like you turning religious, Flea?'

'Is only a joke.' Flea, smiling mournfully, tore away the label from the rum-bottle and rolled it into a ball. 'Tell me something, Felix, Carmen have any other men?'

'Hundreds of them. Carmen know how to butter she bread.'

'I don't mean that. I know lots of them does hang around she like flies. I mean this other man who she does never talk about.'

Felix was thoughtful. 'To tell you the truth, Flea, I don't believe that man ever exist.'

'But she had a child by him, not so?'

'So they say. They say he used to be a sailor. One night in a storm he fall overboard and drown.'

'Who say that?'

'People.'

They looked solemnly at each other.

'And how is Carmen baby, Flea?'

'It fine. It fine,' Flea replied, shaking the rum in his glass.

'You wouldn't believe this, Flea. But, you know, I haven't been to see she since the child born. I too smart for that kind of thing.'

'I don't see why you should have to go and see she. Is not your problem.'

Felix' solemnity vanished. He laughed happily. 'I glad to see you learning fast. Hit and run. That's the way to do it. Still, I'll go and see she and the child one of these days.'

'It don't have much to see,' Flea said. He blinked nervously several times and rubbed his stomach.

'What you mean it don't have much to see?' Felix, fingering his silver chain, narrowed his eyes suspiciously. It was a trick he had picked up from a gambler in a popular Western.

'It belong to the Ramchands now. It going to be their house-boy when it grow up.'

Felix leapt from his chair. The customers looked up in alarm.

'Let me hear you repeat what you just say, Flea. My ears must be fooling me.'

Flea was calm, resigned almost to this latest development. 'I say I give it to the Ramchands. It going to be their houseboy when it grow up.'

Felix swooped down suddenly and lifted the table. The bottle of rum rolled off and clattered on the floor. However, it did not shatter. The rum flowed in a brown stream over the tiled floor.

'Come on, Flea. Stand up and fight like a man.' Flea remained sitting. He scratched the tip of his nose. Felix turned away from him in disgust and addressed the customers. 'You hear what this man gone and do? He gone and give my child – note what I say – he gone and give *my* child away to strangers. And for what, I ask you? So that he could get a good education? So that one day he could become a doctor or lawyer? Nothing like that. He going to become their houseboy when he grow up. Imagine that! If it was his child I wouldn't mind, though that would be bad enough. But imagine giving another man child away to become a houseboy. Just like that.' Felix snapped his fingers. 'Tell me if I don't have the right to smash his face in for him. Tell me!' Felix swung his clenched fists through the air. Although he showed all the outward signs of uncontrollable fury, he made no move to carry out his threat, remaining frozen in the dramatic pose he had assumed at the start. Flea watched him impassively.

'Is my child,' he said softly, speaking into his glass. 'I have a right to do with it as I like.'

'You hear him? You hear him? You ever hear such shamelessness in your born days? His child! As if he could ever have a child. Women does scream and run and hide when they see him.'

The customers laughed. One or two of them came closer, to get a better view.

'Fight! Fight!' The murmur spread round the bar. More of the customers left their tables and crowded round the combatants, urging them on. The barman watched worriedly from behind the counter. 'I won't have nobody fighting in here,' he shouted. 'As it is the police already threaten to close we down and I not going to lose my job for any sons of bitches like you two. I got my wife and family to think about. You hear that?' He lifted the lid of the counter and came quickly towards them. 'Go outside and fight on the pavement if you bitches have to fight. But if you make another false move in here, I'll get the police on to you. I'll call the police.'

'Don't worry, Mister,' Felix said, grateful for any excuse. 'I won't be the cause of you losing your job. I have nothing against you and your family. I go fix this sonofabitch somewhere else.'

The barman returned muttering to the bar.

Felix rested his hands on the table and glowered at Flea. 'That child is my child, Flea. You hear that? Is my child. I is the man who Carmen really love. She would lick my boots for me if I was to give she the chance. What you think was happening when you was spending all the time gallivanting around the place in some boat or the other? You think Carmen went and join a nunnery because of you? Is me she love. Is me. You can take my word for that. Come with me. Let we go and see she now and ask who is the child true father. Come.' Felix attempted to grab Flea by the elbow. Flea pushed him away.

'You lying, Felix. You fooling yourself if you think is you Carmen really love. Is my child. It have all my features except maybe for the nose.' Flea's voice rose hardly above a whisper.

'And I could tell you who that nose belong to, Flea. It belong to me. That is my nose you was seeing.' Felix thumped his chest.

'You never even seen the child. So how you know that?' Flea's confidence was returning. 'The child nose not shaped like yours at all. This child have a flat and spreading nose.'

'All baby have nose like that. Come. Let we go and ask Carmen who is the child true father. Like you frighten of the truth, Flea?'

Flea got up slowly and walked unsteadily out of the bar. Felix once again addressed the company. 'Come with us, gentlemen. You will be the judges of the case. Come and see for yourselves.' Felix, accompanied by some six or seven men who had taken up his invitation, followed Flea out of the bar. There was much good-natured laughter and speculation on the way to Carmen's room. Felix was in high spirits.

Carmen was brushing her freshly washed hair when they arrived outside her door.

'Watch me, fellas,' Felix said. He pushed his way past Flea and walked boldly into the room, surveying the furnishings with a pro-prietorial air. He went up to the startled Carmen and even as she had begun to protest at this invasion, folded his arms around her waist and kissed her on the nape of the neck. She pushed him away roughly. Felix stumbled into the middle of the room and stood there grinning with just a hint of sheepishness.

'You are drunk, Felix.' She looked at the men crowding the doorway. 'Who is all these people you bring here with you? Who tell you you could come barging into my room with all these riff-raff, eh? Eh?' Carmen lowered at the mob. Flea came into the room, his face set and tight.

'You too, Flea,' Carmen said, pouncing on him. She sniffed his breath. 'And smelling like a rum factory as well. I wouldn't have expected this kind of behaviour from you.'

'I have nothing to do with all this, Carmen. Believe me.' Flea crossed his heart. 'Is Felix you must hold responsible. Is he who invite all these people here.'

Carmen turned on Felix. 'Well, Mr Big Mouth, what you want?'

Felix was embarrassed by his reception. 'Is really Flea fault,' he said. 'None of this would have happened if it wasn't for Flea.'

'I don't know which of you to believe. You are two of the biggest liars in the whole of Port of Spain.'

One of the mob started to clap. 'Some woman.'

'That's right,' Carmen shouted. 'And if the pack of you don't leave my room this minute, I go "some woman" you all right.'

'That is what we want you to do, darling.'

Maidenly modesty had not entirely deserted Carmen. She blushed and in order to hide her confusion, rounded again on Felix. He fingered his chain haplessly. 'Well, Mr Big Mouth, you haven't answered me as yet. I want to know why you bring all this riff-raff to my door.'

'I go be frank with you, Carmen. This miserable man Flea is going about all over the place claiming that he is the father of your child. I want you to tell these gentlemen the truth. I want them to hear that I is the father of that child from your own lips.'

Carmen reddened and her eyes, laden with accusation, gazed at Flea. 'So, Flea, after all the kindness I show you, this is how you paying me back. Spreading my name all over Port of Spain, trying to shame me. I should have known better than to trust a man like you.'

'You see what I mean, gentlemen . . .'

'Shut up, Felix. I going to deal with you in a minute. Now, Mr Flea, tell me what you been saying.'

Flea scratched the tip of his nose. 'I ain't been saying nothing bad about you, Carmen. In fact is Felix here who been saying really bad things about you. He say it have a million woman like you in this world and that you dying to lick his boots for him, only he wouldn't let you . . .'

'He lying! He lying!' Felix screamed. 'I didn't say nothing like that.'

'Shut up, Felix. Go on, Flea. Tell me what else Mr Felix was saying about me.'

'He was saying that the best policy with women was to hit them and run . . .'

'He lying! He lying. I didn't say nothing like that.'

'I tell you to shut up, Felix. Go on, Flea.'

'It don't have much more to say, Carmen. Except that I wouldn't say nasty things about the woman I love with all my heart and soul . . .'

Carmen blushed. There were cries of derision from the doorway. Flea paused in confusion and traced with a finger the outline of the mermaid on his left arm.

'So, Mr Felix. It have a million woman like me in this world. You does hit them and run, eh! Well, let me show you what hit and run really is.' She raised the hairbrush. Felix cowered, shielding his face with his hands. The hairbrush landed with a solid thump on his shoulders. Felix danced out of the way. Carmen ran after him, hitting out with the hairbrush, her hands flailing wildly in all directions. 'This is what I call hit and run,' she panted in his wake. 'This is what I call hit and run.' The crowd cheered and chorused encouragement. Felix flitted about the room. 'Flea was lying, Carmen. Flea was lying.' Finally, out of breath, Carmen gave up the chase.

There were whistles and more clapping from the doorway. A man in a red jersey ran into the room and before Carmen had a chance to realise what was happening, shook her hand and ran out again.

'That's the way. Give it to him good.'

'Some woman.'

Carmen sought in vain to disguise her pleasure at these compliments.

Felix, having to some extent regained his composure, though keeping well out of Carmen's reach, said with a show of his former bravado, 'Now you have had your fun, Carmen, tell these gentlemen who is the real father of the child.'

'But what the hell you think it is, Felix?' She lunged at him with the hairbrush. Felix dodged successfully. Tired out by her exertions, she decided to confine herself to abuse. 'What the hell you take me for, eh? You think I is some common kind of market woman? Well, you have another think coming if you think that. You think I have no morals? And why the hell you bring all these people here for, eh? Eh? You think is a circus I running? Well, let me tell you something, Mr Hit and Run. If you think is a circus I running here, you is the chief clown . . .'

The mob could hardly contain itself. There was further whistling and clapping. The man in the red jersey turned a somersault.

'What a woman!'

'Give it to him real good! That's the way.'

'Get out of here, you hooligans. Get out! Otherwise I'll get the police on to you. This is molestation.'

'She know a lot of big words too,' the man in the red jersey said.

Carmen flung the hairbrush at them. They scattered as it crashed against the wall, but soon regrouped, though at a more discreet distance. The mob was cowed, though the man in the red jersey did manage a forced laugh.

'You refusing to tell these gentlemen who the real father of that child is, Carmen?'

'Like you haven't learnt your lesson as yet, Felix. You more stubborn than a mule.' Carmen advanced threateningly on him. 'Get out of here, Felix. I warning you. Don't provoke me. Take these people with you and go from here.'

Felix dashed to the doorway and squeezed himself in amongst the mob. 'Come, gentlemen. Since she playing stubborn, we'll go and do the next best thing. We'll go and have a look at the child itself. To Mr Ramchand, gentlemen.'

There were cries of approval from the doorway.

'Felix! What the hell you think you doing?'

But Felix pretended not to hear her. The procession filed out of the house, Felix at its head. Flea and Carmen looked at each other.

'Carmen . . .'

Carmen waved him away irritably. She picked up her scarf from the dresser, holding it lightly between her fingers, as if undecided about what she must do next.

'But Carmen . . .'

'No time for talk now, Flea.' Carmen hurriedly changed her bodice. Flea angled his head discreetly.

'You playing the gentleman too late in the day,' Carmen said. The scarf had fallen on the floor. Flea picked it up and handed it to her. 'No time for that,' she said, flinging it on the bed, where it settled gently in a yellow heap; and without even looking at herself in the mirror, she ran out of the room.

Flea laboured after her, clutching, for some strange reason, the hairbrush. 'Carmen . . .'

Carmen tossed her head impatiently and ran on in front of him, her hair streaming behind her. 'I tell you already that this is not the time for questions, Flea.' She said something else, but her words were carried away by the wind. Gathering up her skirt, she quickened her pace.

They caught the procession about a hundred yards from the Ramchands' house. The mob had grown. Felix had taken off his shirt which he was now using as a flag. His back shone with sweat and the silver chain glinted in the bright sunlight. He was singing loudly, skipping out from time to time into the middle of the road and dancing. The Ramchands, attracted by the noise, came out on the veranda. When Felix rudely pushed open the front gate, Mrs Ramchand screamed at the top of her voice and boldly advanced down the path to intercept him.

'This is private property. I order you to leave this minute.' She came up to Felix and thrust her face under his chin. Mr Ramchand watched from the verandah. Felix stopped singing and draped his shirt over his arm. Carmen and Flea, breathing heavily, stood next to him. The mob, its enthusiasm checked for the moment, formed an untidy circle around them.

'We come to see the child, Mistress Ramchand,' Felix said.

'What business is that of yours, Mr Felix? I not going to answer one question till you ask these louts to leave my yard. Otherwise, I'll call the police. Hari, go and bring the police.'

'To get the police he'll have to get past all these people, Mistress Ramchand.'

'You threatening me, Mr Felix?' Mrs Ramchand pressed her lips together.

Mr Ramchand, who was leaning as if mesmerised over the veranda rail, remained where he was. His eyes were fixed on Carmen.

'These gentlemen,' Felix began.

'Louts, Felix,' Mrs Ramchand interrupted him. She counted. 'To be exact,' she said, with an air of triumph, 'you have twelve louts here with you and one prostitute.' She smiled pleasantly at Carmen.

'I will not have you insult my Carmen in front of all these strangers, Mistress Ramchand,' Flea said.

Carmen rested an arm lightly on his shoulders. 'Don't worry, Flea. Insults don't bother me.'

Mrs Ramchand's face contracted into a sour smile. 'Get these louts and prostitutes out of my yard this instant, Mr Felix. Or I'll make Hari go and call the police. Hari, go and bring the police.' She gave her husband one of her withering looks, but Mr Ramchand seemed not to notice. Carmen engrossed all his attention.

'These gentlemen,' Felix said, 'will leave your yard the minute you show us the child. Isn't that so, gentlemen?'

'That's right, Mistress Ramchand,' the gentlemen chorused. 'We will leave your yard the minute you show we the child.'

The man in the red jersey bowed low from the waist.

'Stop playing the fool, Sammy,' Felix said.

Mrs Ramchand hesitated. 'And what so important about the child all of a sudden, Felix? I never see people make so much fuss over such a black and ugly baby. Though Flea was telling me the other day that it have people in Africa blacker than coal.'

'Flea, as you must know by now, Mistress Ramchand, is a born liar. Still, forgetting that, whether the child ugly or pretty don't matter. The point is that I is the real father of that child. Not that sonofabitch liar Flea.' Felix spat.

'But I thought you and he was good friends, Felix.'

'Not after what happen today, Mistress Ramchand.'

'That sound to me like the pot calling the kettle black,' Mrs Ramchand replied. This witticism pleased her and her lips compressed themselves into a smile. 'Then, you is the father of this child? But Flea swear to me on his bended knees that he was the father of the child.'

Felix laughed. 'Flea, as I told you just now, Mistress Ramchand, is one of the biggest liars to ever walk the face of this earth. A man like he doesn't hold anything sacred . . .'

Flea started to protest, but Carmen again rested a restraining hand on his shoulder.

'He would sell his old grandmother for five cents,' Felix went on smoothly as if reading a prepared speech, 'if he wanted a packet of chewing gum. A man like he does stop at nothing to get what he want. You yourself know how he used to behave down at the sawmill, always hanging round the cash-box and that kind of thing. But his greatest crime, for which one day he'll fry in hell, was to give away another man child to become a houseboy.' Felix lowered his head. 'I could forgive him all the rest,' he concluded, 'but I can't forgive him that.'

'Hear! Hear!' Sympathetic growls circulated among the mob.

'I, not Flea, is the true father of that child. These gentlemen here will be the judges. A child must resemble his father, not so, Mistress Ramchand?'

Mr Ramchand, looking dazed, sank down on a rocker. Carmen stared at Felix.

'So, Felix, you is the Holy Ghost?'

Felix laughed. 'Ah. Now I understand what Flea was talking about this morning. Yes, Mistress Ramchand. I suppose I is the Holy Ghost.'

'But the child is our property now, Mr Felix. You shouldn't be so careless about things like that. Say I refuse to give it back to you. What you go do then?'

'Then it will be a police matter, Mistress Ramchand. They call it kidnapping. Is one of the most serious crimes you could commit. You are keeping my son, my own flesh and blood, under false pretences. In some countries they does hang you for that, you know. And I not joking either.'

Mrs. Ramchand blanched.

'Don't get me wrong,' Felix continued. 'After we settle this matter we could come to some little arrangement about the child. But I'm not exaggerating about this kidnapping business, Mistress Ramchand. Just last week I think it was, they hang somebody in New York – or they put him in the gas chamber, I can't remember which – for kidnapping a little boy, the son of some millionaire or the other. You must have read the case in the newspapers. I think they was going to make him a houseboy as a matter of fact.' Felix fingered his chain.

'Bring the child, Hari. You hear what Felix say? I sure you wouldn't want them to hang you for such a black and ugly child.' While she regarded her husband's fortune as entirely her own, she took good care to see that his misfortune remained entirely his.

Mr Ramchand appeared not to hear. He dried his forehead with a handkerchief and looked around wildly. Carmen too was distracted. Flea twiddled the hairbrush and stared down at the ground.

'Like you deaf or something, Hari? I say to bring the child. Is enough as it is being the wife of a ugly man like you. You want to make me the wife of a criminal on top of all that?'

The mob laughed.

'They does hang you for taking people children away from them, you know, Hari. You yourself must have hear what Felix say.'

Mr Ramchand disappeared into the house. There was an excited buzz of conversation among the mob. Mr Ramchand took his time. When he returned to the veranda with the baby wrapped in a blanket, the slits of his eyes were almost invisible among the folds of his face. He cradled the child in his arms, hugging it close to his chest. It was screaming. Carmen ran up to him and took it. Mr Ramchand sank as he had done before into the rocking-chair and mopped his brow with a handkerchief.

'I must say I don't think this child resemble you all that much, Felix. Maybe you is not the Holy Ghost after all.' Mrs Ramchand giggled.

'We will soon see about that, Mistress Ramchand. Gentlemen! Compare the features of this child with mine. It's a little darker, I grant you that, and maybe the nose is a little flatter than mine. But then, every baby that was ever born in this world have a nose like that. Apart from that though, it's a mirror image of me, not so?'

Flea remembered something. His face puckered and raising his head slowly, he gazed first at Felix, then at Mr Ramchand. His eyes shone.

'I know who it is the child resemble the most,' he declared suddenly. Everybody looked at him in surprise. The mob's chatter died away. Carmen bit her lower lip. 'And is not Felix either. That nose, all those features belong to ...'

'Flea,' Carmen said, 'stop shouting like that. You frightening your son. That is no way for a father to behave.' She cooed to the child and kissed it.

Flea stuttered into silence, twirling the brush. Mr Ramchand was drying his forehead furiously.

'You lying,' Felix shouted. 'That's the second time today somebody decide to tell a lie against me. I is the father. These gentlemen will support me.'

'You is not the father, Felix,' Carmen replied calmly, still cooing to the child. She felt it was her turn to harangue the mob. 'You want to tell me, gentlemen, that I don't know who the father of my own child is?'

The mob grunted approvingly. The man in the red jersey performed another of his somersaults and skipped excitedly around the yard.

'She right. She must be right. All woman must know who the true father of their child is.'

Mr Ramchand got up from the rocker and stood at the top of the veranda steps.

'Anyway,' Felix said, 'the child you give me is a hell of a lot prettier than the child you give he. I never thought a woman like you could make such an ugly baby.'

Carmen shrugged. 'In that case, you have nothing to quarrel about then.'

Felix fell silent.

Several of the mob came up and shook Flea by the hand and slapped him heartily on the back. Flea grinned weakly at them and twirled the hairbrush.

'You can't trust these sailors an inch,' one of them said. 'Real devils when it come to the women.'

Carmen walked up the path to Mr Ramchand. He came down the steps to meet her. Without a word, she handed him the child. Mr Ramchand took it without a word and, cradling it close to his chest, disappeared into the house.

'As it is,' Felix was saying, 'apart from this child I have by Carmen, I have more than enough of them to call me daddy nearly all over Trinidad. So ...' He looked towards the heavens and gestured hopelessly.

'We must celebrate this,' the man in the red jersey said. 'I always thought Felix had a big mouth. Still, I glad everything turn out right in the end.'

'Yes,' Flea said, 'everybody happy now. Even Mistress Ramchand.'

'Come on, Flea. I can't stand here waiting for you all day.' Carmen held out her hand to him. Flea clasped it gently. And they went, without further ado, out into the street.

The Tenant

Pankar the jeweller was a well-known and respected figure, admired as much for his technical and artistic skill as for his honesty. This was no mean achievement. Jewellers as a class were under constant suspicion of cheating their customers, or if not, of harbouring the intent to do so. This attitude was not confined to what was supposed to happen in their workshops. It extended to their everyday lives as well. The jeweller was a marked man, never more than one step away from abuse or arrest.

Pankar was determined to avoid this. Given to calculation, he had catalogued what he considered to be his colleagues' shortcomings. For a start, they were too friendly. This did not inspire trust. Therefore, Pankar was austere and distant, taking charge of his customers' gold with the greatest reluctance. Secondly, they were too democratic: they accepted everybody's custom. This also did not inspire trust. Therefore, Pankar only did work for people of a certain class. Finally, he disliked the gaiety and opulence of their shops. Pankar's shop was small and dark. All anyone could see were the instruments of his trade and Pankar, dressed in soiled overalls, seated at a cluttered table, peering through his magnifying glass. He was a great success.

He had been the aberration in his family. Among them there had never been a hint of artistic inclinations, and Pankar himself had shown no early signs of possessing any spectacular gifts. He had run away from school when he was fourteen and gone to live with an aunt who had quarrelled with the family. She was a mild woman, and being slightly afraid of Pankar, she let him have his way. He smoked and drank and seduced the girls in the neighbourhood. Between these bouts of dissipation he was moody and silent and confessed to having a religious vocation. He talked with priests and for a time flirted with the idea of becoming a Roman Catholic. They gave him numerous pamphlets which he read carefully. But eventually his more worldly energies reasserted themselves and Pankar put away the pamphlets and behaved as before. This time, however, he added a refinement: he joined a gang which specialised in breaking windows and petty theft. He was caught and sent to a detention centre for three months. There, the religious urge reasserted itself, accompanied by an intense, a morbid, interest in his abilities. He questioned one of the social workers closely.

'You feel I have a talent for anything?'

'Everybody have a talent for something.'

This answer did not satisfy Pankar.

'You don't understand me. I mean a special talent, a . . . a gift.'

'Who can say? You got to put your hand at something before you can know whether you have a gift.'

'And you think if I try my hand I'll find something?'

'Determination can move mountains.' She examined his hands. 'You have delicate fingers. You ever think of taking up jewellery?'

Pankar was inspired. It seemed to him that this was the revelation he had been waiting for. When he was released from the detention centre, she found him a job as apprentice to a famous jeweller in Port of Spain. He learned quickly. 'It's a gift from God,' he told the social worker. She was impressed and advised him to set up on his own. 'They will come running after you, once they know. You'll be a rich man in no time.' 'It's not money I after,' Pankar replied, 'but before I do anything like that I must find a wife. I want a nice simple girl. The uglier she is, the better.' In two months he found one. Dulcie was overwhelmed by Pankar; she was simple; and above all, she was ugly.

Pankar's asceticism infected his other activities. He lived, with monastic devotion to his trade, in a tiny room above the shop, which he shared with his wife. She was a thin, querulous woman, whose two pregnancies had ended in miscarriage. Pankar, cushioned by his asceticism, quickly recovered from these initial failures. He even derived some consolation from them.

'You know,' he said to his wife one day, 'sometimes I does think it's a blessing in disguise that we don't have any children to bother we. To do the kind of work I does do you need to be a sort of priest, lock away from the world and temptation. It's a kind of religion really.'

Dulcie was not moved by this declaration of faith. She hated the tiny room, with its narrow bed, unadorned wooden tables and enamel cups and plates.

'Look at it this way,' she replied, 'I don't know anything about being a priest, but I want to say this. You have all this money you save up which you don't do nothing with, with the result that the two of we living like a set of church mice. You not living like a priest, you living like a miser.'

'You in too much of a hurry, Dulcie. Buying a house is not like spitting, you know. It's an investment and you got to make sure it's a sound commercial proposition.'

'Well you better hurry up then. I sure if it wasn't for this damn place I wouldn't be so sick all the time and we could have . . .'

'Calm yourself, Dulcie. The room have nothing to do with all that. I don't think God wanted you to have children. Just have some patience and remember I making this sacrifice for your sake, not mine.'

But Pankar was not to be hurried, even when making a sacrifice. As in everything else, he was strict and methodical. He went to see nearly all the houses that were advertised in the newspapers, but there was invariably something the matter with them.

Then he was told about a house for sale on the Western Main Road, a most unlikely place to seek the religious life, but Pankar seemed not to mind that fact. At that moment, commercial considerations were uppermost in his mind, and it sounded promising. The prices in the area were rising steadily and the house itself, though not grand, was decent and spacious. There was only one drawback. It shared a communal yard and water supply with two sets of tenants, occupying two barrack-like rooms to the rear. He took Dulcie to see it. She was appalled, not by the house, but by her future neighbours.

'What kind of people you bringing me to live with, Pankar?'

'You does worry too much, Dulcie. I'll have them out of here in no time. You wait and see.'

They moved in.

Their neighbours were the Smithers, a cowering family of Grenadians, who lived in one room with their three children, and Mrs Eugenie Radix, who lived alone. Pankar's optimism was not entirely unfounded. He had sufficient money to hope to buy them out. The Smithers were easy. They jumped at Pankar's offer and left within weeks. Mrs Radix, however, was intractable. Dulcie claimed to know this would be so from the moment she first set eyes on her.

Eugenie Radix was a tall, dark woman of half-Indian, half-Negro extraction. She was about forty, the possessor of a ponderous bosom, thick, full lips, and long black hair which fell in uncontrolled curls down her back. It was not obvious how she earned her living. During the day, she wandered through the yard, dressed in a loose smock, torn in places, a bucket propped against her hip, singing to herself.

She was proof against all Pankar's persuasions and blandishments.

'I don't hold it against you, mind, but it go take more than the offer of a few extra dollars to get me out of here. Anyway, what harm you think an old woman like me could do to you?'

'It's not me that worried,' Pankar confessed, 'it's the wife. She nervous, you know.'

'What, she think I want to eat she?'

'I wouldn't be surprised.' Pankar laughed. They were sitting in her room, surrounded by pots and pans and old Chinese calendars. The air was sweet and oppressive, burdened with the odour of stale incense. Mrs Radix had one book in the room, the Bible, which was well thumbed. The cover had been torn away. The kettle steamed in the coal-pot. She was making him tea.

'You believe in dreams?' she asked suddenly, as she was pouring the boiling water into the tea-pot.

He was taken aback by the question. 'Well, I never really think about it.'

'You know, is a strange thing, but I had a dream the other night which tell me that the two of you was moving in here. I could have describe you before I ever set eyes on you, tall, a little grey hair, fair.' Mrs Radix opened her eyes wide in amusement. Pankar sipped his tea slowly. The subject had aroused his interest.

'You does interpret dreams, then?'

Mrs Radix giggled. 'You trying to find out my secrets, eh? I go tell you one thing though, the people around here believe I is some kind of a devil woman. They believe I does work obeah and black magic.' She grinned happily at him.

'You does interpret dreams?' Pankar was insistent, ignoring these other disclosures.

'Like you really interested in that. Why, you been having funny dreams of late?'

He gazed at her over the rim of the tea-cup. 'Well, I don't know if you could call them funny . . .'

'Come, let me see your palms.' She held his extended palm and studied it, frowning and running her fingers along the lines.

'You see something bad?'

'No, no. Nothing like that,' Mrs Radix reassured him. 'You have a long life line and your heart line strong, very strong.' She shook her head. 'Still, all is not plain sailing. You have to have your troubles like the rest of us.'

'I going to have a bad sickness?'

Mrs Radix smiled. 'You turning as white as a sheet.' That seemed to please her. 'No. No sickness. But tell me your dream.'

Pankar described his dream. Mrs Radix, her eyes exploring the features of his face, nodded from time to time. When he had finished, she said, 'Well, the water is a good sign and the way you was crying mean you will be happy. Dreams is a funny thing. They does say exactly the opposite of what they want to say. If you dream you sad, it mean you going to be happy; if you dream you happy, it mean you going to be sad. Is a mystery really, but that's the way it is. It need someone who is a expert to tell you what they mean exactly.' Pankar listened eagerly, his face tight and serious. 'If you ever have any more dreams like that you must come and see me. I'll tell you exactly what they mean.'

Pankar's dreams obsessed him after this meeting. On waking up in the morning, he turned them over in his mind, trying to unlock the secrets which, he suspected, lurked in every minor detail. Invariably, he failed and was driven back to the superior knowledge and guidance of Mrs Radix. She never failed him. To have to live through a day, unsure of what it held in store for him, a prey to fallibility, gradually assumed the dimensions of a dreadful punishment. Dulcie looked on, disturbed, disapproving, envious.

Dulcie's relationship with Mrs Radix, taking a different path, developed more slowly.

'She's a prostitute, I tell you,' she said to Pankar, when they had been living there for a week. 'You see how she clothes tear to show she belly? I really don't know what kind of gutter people you bring me to live with.'

'Do you know what a prostitute is, Dulcie? You ever see any men visiting here?'

'Where does she get she money from then? Don't tell me she does shake if off the plum-tree. The only thing I ever see she shaking is she backside.'

'She might be married for all you know and separated from she husband. That kind of thing does happen, you know.'

Dulcie winced. 'Huh! Could you ever see any man marrying she? Still, you never know. All you men is the same.'

Pankar was silent. He appeared to be thinking about something else.

Mrs Radix, despite Dulcie's efforts to get rid of her, was friendly and open towards her; even, one might be tempted to say, anxious to please. When she came to fill her bucket at the tap, she beamed good-naturedly at Dulcie who would be watching her sourly from the kitchen window. One day she stepped up to the window, the empty bucket rattling on her hip.

'I been wanting to talk to you for a long time, but I was frighten to think you might feel I was interfering, but I want you to know that I truly glad and thankful that those other people sell the house to you and move out of here.' She paused, as if to see what effect this implicit declaration of good will would have on her listener. Duclie stared, still sour, her eyes full of mistrust. 'They was so unpleasant to me,' Mrs Radix went on, ignoring her hostility. 'Well, he wife was anyway.' There was another pause.

'Why?' Dulcie was unable to resist asking. She had vowed not to encourage Mrs Radix in conversation.

Mrs Radix laughed, happy to gain a response. 'You may well ask, my dear.' Dulcie winced. 'She get the idea into she head that I was trying to take she husband away from she.' Mrs Radix grinned pleasantly at Dulcie, inviting her to savour the improbability of the accusation. 'Imagine that, my dear! As if an ugly old woman like me could take away anybody husband from them.' Dulcie gazed indecisively at her. Perhaps Mrs Radix was mocking her. She smiled weakly.

'Yes . . . well, I better go and cook the food now. Pankar go be coming back from work soon and he go lose he temper if the food not cook.'

'You don't have to tell me, my dear. All these men does behave just like spoil children. I know that even without having a husband. My brother used to be just like that. He was a real little baby, just like Pankar.'

Dulcie moved away from the window, and Mrs Radix, singing, went to fill her bucket.

'You know,' Dulcie reported to Pankar that evening, 'that woman had the bold face to come up and talk to me this afternoon.'

'What wrong with that?' Pankar, never a great eater, toyed with the food on his enamel plate. It was one of the things Dulcie held against him.

'She was telling me about some confusion she had with the people who used to live here before we.' Pankar made circles in the rice with his spoon. 'The wife thought she was trying to take away she husband.' Pankar looked up. 'And another thing. She was calling you Pankar, as if she is your equal.'

He shrugged. 'What wrong with that? You want she to come and kiss my feet?'

'I wish you would eat the food I does cook for you.' She stared irritably at the circles of rice, and getting up suddenly, went out of the kitchen.

Mrs Radix courted Dulcie with a rising fervour. There was a plum-tree growing near her room, whose fecundity was the marvel of the neighbourhood. She claimed sole rights over it and allowed no one to pick the plums, which when in season hung in thick yellow clusters from the branches. She had warned them about this on the very first day. 'Is I who plant that tree and I doesn't let anyone, man, woman or child, touch it without my permission.' Nevertheless, Mrs Radix did not hoard her fruit. One day she appeared with a basinful of over-ripe plums outside the kitchen window and offered them to Dulcie.

'For you,' she said. Dulcie accepted the gift, but again she complained to Pankar about Mrs Radix's effrontery.

'I don't know who it is give she the idea that she own that plum-tree. Is our property, not so?'

'Why don't you just eat the plums and keep quiet, eh?'

Another day Mrs Radix leaned confidentially against the window sill. 'Call me Eugenie,' she said, 'Friends shouldn't call each other by their second name.'

When she told Pankar about this latest overture, he replied, 'You say that the other woman thought she was taking away she husband from she? It look more like the other way round to me. Soon I go have to start worrying that she taking away my wife from me.'

She looked at the circles he had carved in his rice. 'I really wish you would eat the food I does cook for you.'

But, despite herself, she had begun to warm towards Mrs Radix.

'Those plums were real nice, Eugenie.'

'I glad you like them, Dulcie. I chose them especially for you.'

For several weeks the friendship blossomed. Dulcie discovered in Mrs Radix unsuspected virtues and talents and in return she received buckets of plums and had her dreams unravelled. Mrs Radix promised prosperity, happiness, good fortune, and here and there, for good measure, a minor tragedy was mixed in. Any thoughts Dulcie might have entertained about getting rid of her were submerged in the seductive atmosphere of their friendship and the mutual exchange of confidences through the kitchen window.

*

Unfortunately, Mrs Radix had not confessed all. The initial revelation occurred one evening, when Dulcie saw her friend clad in a long white preacher's gown, a candle in her hand, a garland of red hibiscus on her neck, walking, as in a dream, through the yard, intoning a chant whose words she could not understand. Dulcie choked on the greeting that had already formed on her lips and ran softly out of the kitchen. There was a full moon and the yard was bathed in a blue light that washed over the roofs of the neighbouring houses. She followed Mrs Radix to her room, which was lit by rows of candles. An improvised altar, draped with a piece of gold cloth, had been erected at the top of the steps. It was bedecked with brass images of animals and Christ on the Cross and hung with hibiscus and oleander. Mrs Radix bowed low before the altar and prostrated herself, uttering low, ecstatic moans and lifting her hands towards the bright sky. Dulcie, mesmerised, followed her every movement, then abruptly turning away, she ran, through the contorted shadows of the plum-tree, back to the house.

The doubts which she had only so recently stilled assailed her anew, their former animosity exaggerated, but now, in addition, edged with a superstitious fear. Dulcie lived through all the agitations of a lover betrayed. 'If she had only tell me before,' she kept repeating to herself, 'it wouldn't have been so bad. But she had to be underhand about it, and there I was telling she everything about myself and Pankar. All we troubles and everything.'

Some days went by before she had the courage to describe to Pankar the events she had been witness to.

'That woman,' she concluded, 'if you could call she a woman, that is, is a witch, not a prostitute.'

'I glad you make up your mind at last. But you never know. She might be both.'

'Eh?'

Pankar grinned at her.

'Well, I don't claim to know, but whatever she is I don't like it. I always thought there was something fishy about she and since you don't want to move she out of here . . .'

'What give you that idea, Dulcie?' he seemed genuinely interested in her answer.

'I haven't seen you doing anything about it. You always going there telling she what you dream, asking she for advice, sucking up . . .'

'You is a fine one to talk.'

'If you want she to stay why don't you out with it and say so?'

Pankar winked at her. 'Okay. You right. I do want she to stay.'

'I don't like those kind of jokes.' She knew he was not joking. The prospect of losing Mrs Radix alarmed her probably as much as it did him, and aware that nothing she said could alter the situation, she felt free to continue the attack. It was soothing exercise and helped her to believe that she could defy and in defying, exorcise the evil influence.

'I don't see what so difficult in getting she out of here. Somebody else would have had she out of here in two twos.'

'She have a lease on the place, Dulcie. You can't fight a lease. Anyway, what harm she do you? She's a very religious woman, that's all.'

'Bring out a writ, then. Forget the lease.'

'A writ?' Pankar was amused. 'Do you know what a writ is?'

'Writ! Lease! You only making excuses. Let we build a fence then, since we so powerless.'

'You want to deliberately insult she or something? But what she do to you that you want to behave so? The trouble with people like you is once you don't understand or appreciate something, you does begin to get on a high horse and condemn. It's sheer ignorance and jealousy.'

'Me jealous of she? Huh! You must be crazy. What it is she have that I got to be jealous? Tell me.' Dulcie was unable to hide her distress. She watched, frustrated, perplexed, as Pankar traced curious patterns in the rice. 'Jealous! Me! I remember when we had first come here you was running your mouth all over the place about how quick you would have she out of here. Now all of a sudden . . .' She stopped speaking and bent low over his plate. 'What you drawing there?' Pankar scrubbed out the patterns. 'She working she magic on you, you know. She go have you in she power soon. "Imagine an ugly old woman like me taking away somebody husband",' she mimicked Mrs Radix. 'She good-looking, too, eh? Big bust, not so?' Dulcie extended her arms.

'You have a dirty mind, Dulcie.'

Dulcie laughed bitterly, and thought of her own pitiful underdeveloped breasts.

Mrs Radix stayed locked in her room an entire week. On the third day Pankar went to visit her. His knock had not been answered, and he was about to go away when Mrs Radix opened the door. She invited him in. The windows had been shuttered and the room was lit by a single candle burning feebly on the dresser. Crushed flowers littered the floor. Mrs Radix sat on the bed. She seemed thinner and her hair was even more tousled than usual. There were black rings under her eyes. They looked as if they had been painted on.

'I suppose you been wondering what happening to me.'

Pankar did not answer. He studied the confusion in the room.

'You ever hear about the Rosicrucians?'

'A little bit.' One of the Catholic pamphlets had mentioned them in passing.

'Well, is partly that and partly Baptist. The powers I have is something I was born with.'

Vague religious sentiment stirred in Pankar.

'You mean the Spirit does take you sometimes?'

'It does take me every full moon, as you see for yourself.'

'And so you always in contact with It?'

Mrs Radix nodded. 'It does guide me all the time.' She waved her arms. 'Come and sit on the bed by me. You too far away.' Pankar sat next to her. 'The Spirit does exhaust me and sometimes I does have to stay in my room like this for days.'

'One time I wanted to become a Catholic. I used to go and talk to all them priest in the church.'

Mrs Radix pressed her lips tightly together and frowned. 'Catholic no good. I used to think like that myself one time, but in the end the Spirit tell me that wasn't for me. One day the Spirit going to call on me to serve Him all the time and when that day come I going to leave this place and go somewhere very far away, like a pilgrim. But that day ain't come as yet. That is why I was telling you it would take more than a few dollars to get me out of here.' Mrs Radix laughed. 'Don't look so embarrassed. I know it wasn't your fault. Catholic not for you, Pankar. You is different kind of man. The Spirit tell me that.'

'It really say so?'

Mrs Radix sprawled full length on the bed. 'You mustn't ask so much question. It does get angry when you do that.' She raised her hand and rested her palm on his neck. 'This is the only true way. You got to do what the Spirit mean for you to do.' She drew his face down to hers. Her skin smelled of flowers and stale incense. 'I glad Dulcie like the plums I give she.' The rings under her eyes disappeared into her wrinkles as she smiled up at him and drew his face yet closer.

Dulcie watched impatiently for signs of Mrs Radix's reappearance. She was envious of the privileges accorded Pankar and was several times tempted to go and knock on her door. But it was not pride alone that dissuaded her; she relished her resentment and the pain it caused her, and in proportion as she did this, so much sweeter by contrast were her visions of the ultimate reconciliation.

The morning she emerged, Mrs Radix walked slowly through the yard, gently swinging the bucket from her hips. She smiled pleasantly at Dulcie, who was staring at her from the kitchen window. However, Eugenie, instead of stopping to talk, went straight to the pipe and started to fill her bucket. Dulcie closed the window with a bang. Mrs Radix filled the bucket and returned to her room. Dulcie was devastated by the coolness of her reaction. Whatever she had been hoping for, Eugenie, clearly, was not prepared to give it. She set about planning her defences.

Since she was not allowed to build a wall, she decided to make a garden. She would retaliate by magnifying her presence. The soil was not particularly fertile; it was hard and yellow, but with application and the liberal use of fertilisers, she succeeded in coaxing from it roses, hibiscus, oleander, canna lilies and lime and orange trees. Soon, Mrs Radix was blotted from view by the flowers and trees. Even Pankar was pleased. He said it improved the value of the property. Duclie worked in the garden in the afternoons. She had bought a watering-can and a set of garden tools. She hoed and raked and weeded, and every evening at six she watered the flower beds. Mrs Radix renewed her overtures of friendship.

'I don't think you planting the hibiscus right, Dulcie. It look as if it need some more manure.'

Dulcie scraped away at the soil, not answering. Nevertheless, she was flattered by these attentions. Mrs Radix modified her approach.

'But the canna lilies looking really nice, though, together with all them other trees you plant. I think you have a hand for gardening. I been peeping at you these last few months and I feel sure about it. What do they call people who good at growing things?' Mrs Radix puckered her brows. Dulcie gazed up at her, flushed with excitement. Eugenie had been 'peeping' at her!

'Ah yes, Green fingers. I read that in the paper the other day. You have green fingers.'

Dulcie blushed. 'You only joking with me.'

Mrs Radix shook her head. 'You know me better than that, Dulcie.'

Dulcie flushed again. 'You really think so?'

'I won't answer until you call me Eugenie.' Mrs Radix frowned pettishly at her.

'You really think so, Eugenie?'

'Yes, man. Not everybody could do what you do.'

'All it need is a little effort, really. But you know people don't like to apply themselves to anything these days.'

'Is strange that you should say that. Me and Pankar was talking about that kinda thing the other day. He was saying a jeweller have to be a kind of priest, but that most people don't appreciate that. But I was saying that all three of us was at bottom like that. You is a gardener, he making jewel and I praying and making contact with my god. Same thing really, eh? We all have that one thing in common – doing the thing we have to do.'

It was still and extremely hot in the yard. Only an occasional car on the Western Main Road disturbed the mid-afternoon silence. Through a gap in the wooden fence Dulcie saw across the neighbouring yard into a side street, empty and silent. A small, dry wind shook the leaves of the lime and orange-trees and ruffled Mrs Radix's thin white smock and strands of tangled hair. Lulled by the heat, the old resentment stirred fitfully in Dulcie. Her desire to please and be accepted by this woman was wounding and offensive to her sensibilities. It was, she knew, a one-way traffic with very little return. Yet, instinctively, she had come to recognise the power, the attractions, wielded by Mrs Radix. Unfortunately recognition had come too long after surrender for it to matter. Perhaps it would have made no difference in the first place. Recognition merely served to emphasise the inequalities, the essential hopelessness and pointlessness of the battle. And a battle it was, for Mrs Radix commanded not the affections, but something more elemental: the pull, inexorable, irresistible, exerted by the strong on the weak. Dulcie had found herself competing, not with her, but with Pankar. Logic had been reversed, and husband and wife had been transformed into rivals struggling each with the other to become the first object of their tenant's concern. Painfully she imagined their conversations and pictured the intimacies she exchanged with him in the privacy of her room. Pankar had nearly been right after all. Given the opportunity, Eugenie would have taken her away from him.

She half-listened to what Mrs Radix was saying and to the sounds of her smock flapping in the wind.

'Do you want some flowers, Eugenie?'

'I wasn't suggesting . . . but that would be nice. I could use them in the room.'

Dulcie recalled the performance of that strange rite, the altar draped with gold cloth, the garlands of hibiscus and oleander draping the necks of those idols. She felt that her offer made her part of what she suspected was a blasphemy, the work of the devil. It was her initiation, her token of good faith. Heavy with guilt and discomfort, she gathered and presented a bunch of her favourite flowers to Mrs Radix. After that, whenever Mrs Radix asked she got the flowers she wanted.

The strange rites went on, more frequently than before. On moonlit nights the same solitary procession through the yard would be repeated, and Dulcie would watch the glimmer of the candles through the trees. She could never escape a feeling of acute discomfort when she remembered that it was her own flowers that dangled from the necks of the idols and decorated the altar at the top of the steps. But Mrs Radix was always so charming the next day, and Dulcie invariably overcame her scruples. They became friends again, and it was Mrs Radix who carried her into the house and put her to bed the day she fainted in the garden.

Dulcie's pregnancy shocked everyone. Pankar paled when she told him.

'But how come you having a baby all of a sudden?'

'You should know.'

He was silent.

'What's the matter with you, Pankar? You looking as if you see a ghost. Have I kill priest or something? I thought you would be . . .' But Dulcie failed to convince even herself.

'Calm yourself, Dulcie, it's only the shock. You know how.'

That night he went to see Mrs Radix.

Pankar worked hard, returning from the shop later than usual. He insisted on sleeping in a separate room.

'After what happen I got to purify myself,' he explained to Dulcie. 'To do the kind of work I want to do you need to be clean in mind and body.'

She detected the voice of Mrs Radix in all that he said, but she was afraid to question him.

'Don't talk like that, Pankar. It does make me frighten.'

'That's only because you ignorant of these matters.'

Dulcie bowed her head. Even at second hand, Mrs Radix could not be denied.

The only furniture Pankar would allow in his room was a bed and a chair. He removed all the pictures (photographs of friends and family) and in their place hung a crucifix he had made himself. The floor he scrubbed white.

'Purity,' he said. 'Purity.'

It had been a bad month for Dulcie. She had been vomiting every day and in spite of her pregnancy she looked strangely worn and emaciated. They were having dinner when Pankar took a small, very ornate box out of his pocket.

'I got something to show you, Dulcie.'

'What?' She was listless, playing with her food. Pankar, on the other hand, had of late developed an appetite. With an exaggerated delicacy and caution, he opened the lid of the box and taking out a gold amulet, laid it flat on the palm of his hand. The light from the naked electric bulb reflected sharply off it.

'Bring it closer, Pankar. I can't see.'

'No, no. You come here.' And she had to lean close over him to see what it was.

'Do you know what that is, Dulcie?'

It had been delicately carved. In the centre there was a picture of Christ on the Cross surrounded by the signs of the zodiac.

'No.' She looked ill and pregnant. She drew away quickly. 'What you doing, Pankar? What you showing me that for?'

'It's an amulet. You know what they use for?'

She shook her head.

'It's a charm. It does bring good luck.' He held it up to the light. 'It take me a long time to make this and it's all for you.'

She raised herself heavily from the chair, and never taking her eyes off him, backed slowly to the window.

'I don't want that thing, Pankar. You dealing with obeah and I is a clean-living woman. Give it to Eugenie. She would know what to do with it.'

'Eugenie? But it's not she who making a baby, Dulcie.'

They were both standing near the window now. A white figure swirled through the darkness outside, bucket rattling.

'What you trying to do to me, Pankar? What has that witch done to you?'

They heard the tap running, the water drumming into the bucket. She tried to drag the amulet from his hands. 'Come, come, man. Give that thing to me and let me throw it in the dustbin where it belong. Give that . . .' Her voice trailed away. The tap went silent and this time the white figure lurched ponderously through the darkness. Dulcie, clutching at her stomach, stumbled out of the kitchen. Pankar laughed softly.

Dulcie painted white crosses on all the doors of the house. Every morning she prayed in the nearby Roman Catholic church and before going to bed she recited novenas. When Mrs Radix came to ask for flowers she refused. Eugenie was not offended.

'I see you putting crosses on all your doors. But why for, Dulcie? I never know you was a Christian.'

'You should know the answer to that.'

'Me?'

'Yes. You and he. Your innocent face doesn't fool me.'

'But what's the matter with you, Dulcie? What get into you so suddenly?'

'Don't put my name in your mouth.'

Mrs Radix was distressed. She eyed Dulcie disconsolately. 'You know what I think? You too old to be having a baby. People always say that when you over forty and making a baby you in for trouble. The Lord knows why, but that's the way it is. You should have take the amulet that Pankar spend so much time making for you, but . . .' Mrs Radix waved her arms resignedly and gazed at Dulcie's swollen stomach, pitying, regretful. Dulcie felt the spell descending. She walked away and from her bedroom window saw Mrs Radix cutting flowers. She sank wearily on the bed and closed her eyes.

Dulcie was too ill to look after the house, and it was Mrs Radix who cleaned and did the cooking. She wandered freely about the rooms in her torn smock, dusting the furniture and singing softly to herself. At night she and Pankar rocked on the veranda, marvelling at the number of cars that went by on the Western Main Road. 'This area getting busier and busier,' Pankar murmured admiringly. 'Prices sure to be rising.' Later on in the evening when the traffic had lessened, he discussed his dreams with her. Sometimes they spent the night in her room. Dulcie had confined herself to her bedroom. She ate little of the food Mrs Radix brought and left outside the door, convinced they were planning to poison her. Too weak to move around, she spend much of the time lying flat on her back, staring up at the ceiling, listening to the flutter of the bats roosting in the eaves.

The baby was born deformed. Some of its toes were missing and it could not cry properly. The day after it had been born Pankar came into the bedroom. During the previous month he had visited her only once or twice a week. Mrs Radix she saw not at all. Dulcie, haggard and yellow, was feeding the baby. Pankar studied them.

'A fine son, he said. 'You should be proud and thankful to God.'

The baby sucked at its mother's breast with difficulty.

'Let me hold it.' He approached the bed and leaning over, attempted to shift the baby's head from her breast.

She stayed his hand roughly. 'You leave the child alone.'

'It's my child, too, Dulcie.'

'Your child! That's the best joke I hear for a long time.' She twisted the baby's face away from the nipple. It tried to cry but could not. 'Look at that, Pankar. That's your work and that woman's as well.'

'You shouldn't speak of Eugenie in that tone, Dulcie. She was only trying to help you, but you was too obstinate. If you had listen to what she was saying in the first place, all this wouldn't have happened.' He pointed at the baby's deformed feet. She raised herself from the bed, fixing the baby in her arms.

'Stop torturing me, Pankar. It's you and she who make this child come out like this and you know that.'

'You don't know what you saying, Dulcie.'

'It's you and that . . . prostitute you bring inside the house to live with you. Obeah and amulets. "Look, Dulcie, I make this amulet specially for you!" ' She mimicked his voice.

'You don't know what it is you mocking, Dulcie. Control yourself.'

'Control myself! What do you take me for, Pankar? A whore like she, taking away other people husbands? A obeah woman?' Dulcie's voice rose to a scream. Mrs Radix came running and stood in the doorway. 'Well, I not nobody's whore, you hear, and I not nobody's witch either. I is a decent self-respecting woman, not a shameless whore!'

Pankar laughed. Her face contorted.

'I'll show the two of you how to laugh.' She raised the child.

'Dulcie!'

'Don't touch me. I not pure enough for you. Remember?'

Pankar grabbed at the baby. But he was too late and Dulcie too agile. The child fell with a thud and lay wriggling on the floor. Its mouth writhed soundlessly in its tiny pinched face.

'Well, you not laughing?' She was crying. 'I thought you and Angel Gabriel over there would be grinning on both sides of your face.'

Mrs Radix patted Pankar on the shoulder. 'Come, come, is best to leave she to sheself. A long time ago I was telling she that people as old as she shouldn't be making babies. It does do strange things to you.'

Dulcie stiffened. For an instant she seemed poised to fly at Mrs Radix, but only for an instant. Almost immediately, the tautness slackened, and remembering what she had done, she looked down at the baby, squirming at her feet. She bent down and, picking up the child, she collapsed limply on the bed with it, at the same time peering anxiously at its agitated features. The next day, taking the baby with her, she left the house.

After Dulcie had gone, Mrs Radix moved in. 'Somebody got to look after him,' she told the neighbours. They did not believe her, but were afraid to say so, afraid, in fact, of what she might take it into her head to do to them. Her powers had been sufficiently displayed to silence any criticism. Pankar worked harder than ever, and was unusually friendly to everyone. They did not trust him, although, in his case, they were less afraid to say so. Nevertheless, they were cautious, anxious not to offend Mrs Radix.

Pankar renovated the shop. It was no longer dark and crowded and there were many pieces of glittering jewellery under glass, showing the old artistic and technical skill. He even employed a pretty secretary. Yet, some of his former clients withdrew their custom. Despite this, Pankar smiled and appeared to prosper. He bought a car, repainted the house, and in place of the garlands of hibiscus and oleander Mrs Radix wore necklaces of an intricate and occult design. Then he was accused of adulterating a client's gold and taken to court.

Pankar was brave in his own defence, supported no doubt by the presence of Eugenie among the audience. He explained to the magistrate that he was a man of God, that his talents as a jeweller were dedicated to the service of the spirits (at this point Mrs Radix gazed benignly at him and fingered the necklace she was wearing), that the gold he had 'appropriated' would do more for the soul of the 'donor' than any rings or bracelets he might have made for him. The magistrate was not convinced. Pankar had to pay a heavy fine and in the ensuing scandal he was forced to close his shop. The neighbours were appalled by what they considered the magistrate's foolhardiness. He had flouted Mrs Radix. Doom must surely follow. They sat back and awaited the catastrophe. Nothing happened. On the contrary, the magistrate was mentioned in the New Year Honours List and commended for 'services rendered to the noble cause of justice'.

'Somebody really got to look after him now,' Mrs Radix said.

Pankar continued to do occasional work for the faithful, those people whose admiration for his genius had only been augmented by the recent events. But most of his time he spent in the garden. He added to the fruit and flowers Dulcie had planted, introducing carnations and bougainvillaea, anthurium lilies and frangipani, and was no less assiduous than his wife had been in the application of fertilisers. As a result, the garden flourished.

Pankar was disturbed. He had had an extraordinary dream which woke him up in the middle of the night. Together with some friends of his childhood he had been driving along a narrow road carved out of the sides of a precipitous cliff. Below them stretched a bare, treeless plain, lit by a sun made peculiar by the extreme yellowness of its light. Bordering this plain was another mountain, squat and table-topped, with a covering of green on the surface of its plateau. Its slopes were scarred by a constellation of black holes, entrances to caves running under the plateau, and numerous sand-filled craters. Magically, they were transported across the arid plain and found themselves standing outside the entrance to one of the caverns. He entered the cave. Inside was a thick, grey darkness, and in the centre of the floor he saw that a turgid, oily pool of water had been gouged out among the rocks. Near the edge of the pool was a platform of smoother rock. He dived, fully clothed, off the platform. At the bottom of the pool he found discs of a greyish, glutinous substance. They were threatening, malevolent. He swam quickly back to the surface. For a time he lay on the platform, powerless to move. The whole atmosphere of the cave, dank, dark, exhaled disease. His friends laughed at him. Their laughter grew louder, more hysterical. He struggled, trying to raise himself off the rock, but his body refused to obey. The laughter around him swelled. He cried out.

It was then he had woken up, shivering and frightened.

'What happen? What frighten you so?' Eugenie gripped his arm.

'Nothing, nothing. Don't worry.'

'You had a bad dream?'

'I tell you is nothing.'

Pankar, afraid to sleep, remained awake until day-break, listening to the bats scurrying in the eaves.

The next morning he worked in the garden. Eugenie, leaning against the fence, watched him.

'I think you have a hand for gardening, you know.' Pankar was weeding the anthurium patch.

'Don't come telling me I have green fingers, Eugenie.'

He studied the sun-darkened face with the thick, full lips, hovering above him. They both laughed, but without any enthusiasm.

'We must not joke about that. It might bring bad luck.'

He stared at her, the laughter drained from his face. She frowned and he resumed his weeding.

'You behaving very odd, you know. Since last night.'

'I need rest. I tired.'

Mrs Radix raised her eyebrows sceptically.

'Tell me what it is you dream last night.'

'I tell you I didn't dream anything.'

'Well, you don't have to bite me. I only trying to help.'

Pankar laughed. 'I feel I hear that somewhere before.'

'Watch what you saying.' Mrs Radix raised her voice.

Pankar straightened himself abruptly.

'I not taking any orders from you, Eugenie. Mind how you speak to me.'

He spoke softly, as if he were gently reasoning with her.

'And who is you to give me orders, eh?' She stood before him, belligerent, uncompromising. 'Ask yourself who it is teach you all you know. That scrawny woman with no breast at all who you used to call your wife?'

'Mind how you speak of Dulcie.' He too raised his voice.

She laughed, loud and scornful. 'Hear him talk now.' She seemed to be addressing not him, but the neighbourhood. 'Why don't you go back to she, since you like she so much? Why don't you go back, eh? I won't try and stop you. Go on. Give it a try. Go back to she!'

He walked away from her.

'You going?'

'Yes.'

'For good?'

Pankar did not answer. He quickened his pace. Eugenie's laughter was soon lost among the roar of the traffic on the Western Main Road.

Pankar walked a long time. He followed the side streets down to the Quevedo Avenue and continued down some more until he came to the waste land near the docks. There was no shelter from the sun here. Only a thin scrub vegetation grew on the poor soil, recently reclaimed from the sea. He walked slowly through the knee-high grass to the sea wall. The smaller ships, those that trafficked among the islands, docked here. He sat down on the sea wall. Apart from himself, it was deserted. Two schooners, small, dirty ships, were anchored near the pier, about a mile away. The warehouses were empty. Pankar closed his eyes and listened to the water lapping against the stones and, as it penetrated the crevices, the small sucking sounds it made. Cold shivers ran down his back, despite the heat. He dozed from time to time, waking with a start. A large ship gradually disappeared over the horizon. The tide rose, and the water, licking at the stones, crept up the wall. The sun spread out across the water. It grew cooler and darker. He fell asleep.

Someone was shining a light on him. It was a policeman. He regarded Pankar with mild curiosity.

'What going on with you, mister? You drunk?'

Pankar shook his head.

'You sick? If you stay here like this you bound to catch cold.' The policeman bent down to take a closer look at him.

'You don't look too good to me, mister. Why don't you go home?'

Pankar stood up.

'All kinds of funny people does come here in the night. Couples, you know. I does use my torch light to flush them out. For a moment I thought . . .' The policeman licked his lips. 'You don't look well to me at all. Come on, go home.' He patted him encouragingly on the shoulder. Pankar stepped off the wall.

'You going home?'

'Yes.'

'If you do these kind of things too often, you go worry your wife to death, not so? Think about that, man.'

Pankar, stumbling through the grass, laughed, and waved the policeman good night.

Eugenie was preparing dinner when Pankar arrived.

'You just in time,' she shouted as he was coming up the steps. 'I had made up my mind to eat it all if you wasn't back by seven o'clock.' Pankar sprawled on the bed and stared at the floor.

'You looking as if you dog tired. A little food go do you good. Like

you take a really long walk?' She studied his face. His eyes were
bloodshot. She smiled. 'Anyway you come back in time for your food
and that's the main thing.' She served him the food. Pankar rested the
plate on his knee.

'Eugenie . . .' Pankar made circles in his rice.

'What?'

Pankar scratched his head. 'You know, I had such a funny dream
last night . . .'

'Tell me,' Mrs Radix said.

Lack of Sleep

Last night I dreamt of my own death. From my window, I saw a hearse parked outside the front door and, though I was far from being dead, it was evident it had come for me. Mrs Maundy, dressed in black, was calling out impatiently from the front steps and anxiously scanning the empty street. She urged me to hurry while there was no one about and reminded me that to keep the hearse waiting was an expensive business. Typical. 'I'm not ready,' I cried out to her. 'Send it away. I'm not ready to die as yet.' Most dreams fade the moment you wake up but this one remains fresh in my mind.

It is several days now since I have been able to get a good night's rest and I am at my wits' end. How cruel it is to have to get out of bed so early in the morning and be forced to crouch in front of the electric fire waiting for Mrs Maundy to come and clean the room. If only she would let me sleep a bit longer the nightmares, I am sure, would disappear of their own accord. What a delightful thing sleep is! That hour or two of rest I am able to snatch towards morning is much too vital to be interrupted and squandered so recklessly. But that, needless to say, is precisely what happens to me.

The effects of all this have not been altogether lost on Mrs Maundy. She is an observant woman. However, she won't let herself be affected by me. Not her. She doesn't like the smallest inconvenience. Mrs Maundy never swerves from the letter of the law as laid down by herself. That, by her book, is a crime. About three days ago she said to me, 'You'd better watch yourself. You're much too jumpy for my liking. It makes me nervous when old people get like that. You should go for a long walk. Use up all that excess energy you have.' I replied that my jumpiness, as she chose to call it, had nothing to do with excess energy but was due, purely and simply, to lack of sleep. 'Huh!' she retorted.

The trouble is that my room, being at the top of the house, is the first to be cleaned in the morning. Mrs Maundy firmly believes it is easier for her to work downwards rather than upwards. Certainly it may be easier for her. I don't deny that. Nevertheless, at my age you would have expected her to show a little more consideration. But no.

She wakes me – me! – while she allows Herbert, that dreadful son of hers, to go on sleeping peacefully on the first floor. 'Is this fair?' I asked. She stared at me scornfully. 'Herbert is a working man,' she replied. 'What work do *you* have to do?' I had no wish to drag Herbert further into the argument. That, I suspected, was dangerous ground. And not only because I feared to antagonise his mother. Above all, I felt it would not be wise to get on the wrong side of Herbert Maundy. Yet Mrs Maundy regards herself as the soul of kindness. I have listened to her working herself into a fine froth over the treatment of those she is fond of describing as 'our senior citizens.' I can't square it with the way she treats me. But that is Mrs Maundy all over.

Risking her wrath, I reminded her of the avowed concern and suggested – as politely as I could – that right under her very nose was a golden opportunity to display it by working upwards for a bit ('to tide me over this difficult patch' was how I put it) instead of downwards and so giving me a few extra minutes of precious rest. She did not take at all kindly to the suggestion and, for a moment, I thought she was going to lose her temper and shout at me – as she does to the other tenants now and again. That would have been hard to take. If there is one thing I am unable to tolerate, it's people shouting at me. When that happens a kind of raging black cloud seems to envelop me. Thankfully, she didn't shout. 'Are you trying to teach me my own job?' she asked frigidly. I let the matter drop. The Day of Judgment would find her working downwards and not upwards.

Yesterday morning she again said, 'You're altogether too jittery for my liking. It makes me nervous. If you don't want to go for a walk then go to the cinema. See a nice film. Or read a book. I don't care what you do – within limits, of course. Only, for God's sake, stop being so jittery. I don't want you dying off on my hands in the middle of the night.'

Dying off on her hands in the middle of the night! How could she bring herself to speak to me like that? You don't say that sort of thing to a man in my position. It's insensitive. Downright insensitive. As if I could help it if I died. Recently I have noticed that Mrs Maundy has fallen into the habit of taunting me about death. It has become one of those perverse games she likes to play with me. She always manages to introduce the subject into our conversations nowadays. She enjoys observing the effect it has on me. 'I can see you don't care to talk about it,' she would remark sententiously, 'but all the same you should prepare yourself for it. Get yourself into the right frame of mind. It's no good pretending you're going to live forever.'

She treats death as if it was something unnatural and obscene. I remember what happened when Mr Maundy died. For some days none of the other tenants was aware that he had died and if I had been out at work like the rest of them, I don't suppose I would have known either. We hadn't even been told he was ill. Everything was hushed up. It was in the middle of the afternoon when there was hardly anyone about on the street I saw the hearse drive up to the front door and wondered who it could be for. There was a solitary wreath on the coffin. Two hours later, having, as you might say, disposed of the body, she was back, stern and white-faced. By evening she appeared to be perfectly recovered. I expect it will be like that when I die. No crowd of mourners. No tears. Perhaps not even a solitary wreath.

Keeping as calm as I could, I assured her I was merely suffering from lack of sleep. My jitteriness, my jumpiness, whatever it pleased her to call it, had nothing to do with dying and would she be so kind as to refrain in the future from making such callous remarks. 'Believe me,' I said, 'the last thing I would want to do is die on *your* hands in the middle of the night.' However, Mrs Maundy doesn't recognise sarcasm. It's a blind spot with her.

But enough of this. I have no desire to dwell on this subject. It depresses me.

I offered to do without the privilege of having my room cleaned every morning. Not that it is a privilege. Strictly speaking, it is my right and her duty. I pay an extra ten shillings a week to have it done. This fact doesn't prevent Mrs Maundy from behaving as if it were an imposition I personally inflict on her and from which she gains no advantage. That too is Mrs Maundy all over. She rejected my proposal out of hand, saying she had yet to meet an old person who knew what cleanliness meant. 'Not that I am blaming the little dears,' she meandered on in that sickening, sugary way of hers. 'All the same, you must admit old folk do tend to let themselves go to pieces. I hear too many stories about your sort passing over and the body not being discovered for days.' She shook her head and smiled. 'I can't afford to take any chances.' She giggled. 'In any case you pay for having your room cleaned and I don't want it to be said of me I cheat anybody out of their fair due.' 'Ah, Mrs Maundy,' I was on the point of replying, 'you cheat me out of my fair due of sleep and, what's more, you enjoy doing it.' Naturally I held my peace. 'Now, now. None of your cheek.' She squinted slyly at me and wagged a finger in my face. 'Cheek?' I was puzzled. She laughed. 'If by any chance you're planning to worm your way out of paying the little extra. . . . I've been in this business long enough to know all the little tricks and schemes you tenants can get up to.'

I protested. Ignoring her unsavoury reference to bodies not discovered for days, I insisted that I was not planning to worm my way out of anything. The extra ten shillings a week I paid for having my room cleaned was a trifling consideration compared to the precious sleep I was losing. I was perfectly willing to sacrifice it. To waive my right and relieve her of an onerous duty. 'An old man like you,' she said, 'with nothing to do all day but sit up there and stare out of your window – and, let me add, with the sunniest room in the whole house – and you object to getting up a little early. That is the only sacrifice I want you to make.' I was sorely tempted to answer her thus: 'Thank you for mentioning that. Don't forget on top of everything else you charge me an extra five shillings because it is the sunniest room in the house. It's a bit much to make a profit out of that sort of thing. But since you make a profit out of it you should learn a lesson from the sun. It works its way *upward* in the morning. Take note of that. Upward. Not downward.' I restrained myself. A long speech would have exhausted me. And, as I have already remarked, Mrs Maundy is impervious to sarcasm. Anyway, she had such a queer expression. I was puzzled. It was almost as if I had spoken my thoughts out aloud. 'I'm only jittery because I don't get enough sleep,' I said. 'Nonsense,' she replied, moving to the door and continuing to look at me with that queer expression. 'Old people don't need much sleep. Everybody knows that.' There the matter rested. How can you fight such blind obstinacy? It was the closest she and I had ever come to having an open disagreement. Which just goes to show how bad things are with me. How can she say that old people do not need much sleep? That is a lie. A fabrication.

But no! I must control myself. I must be calm. My nerves really are in shreds. I jump at the slightest sounds. Sometimes I forget what I am doing. My thoughts wander disconnectedly and inconclusively. Most worrying of all, I find I cannot say for certain whether I have actually done or said something or simply imagined myself doing or saying it. Are these the infirmities of old age? Or do they herald the onset of a

horror I dare not think about too much? Not merely death – though
that is horror enough. But I refuse to think about it. Not now. It has
all become so confusing for me of late. My dreams can seem so real, so
compellingly vivid. On the other hand, what I do when I am awake
can assume all the fantastic, disjointed qualities of dreams. What a
torture it is. Frequently I have seen Mrs Maundy stop and stare at me
with that queer expression. 'What is it?' I ask anxiously. 'What are
you looking at me like that for?'

One incident in particular obsesses me. To tell the truth, it is that
which has reduced me to my present state. I had gone to the pub on
the corner. Often I go there at lunch-time for an hour or two. I find it
a nice change from my room and it relaxes me to see different faces
and listen to the chatter of different voices. Opening the front door
and walking down the steps helps to remind me that my room is the
habitation of a free man and not the cell of a man imprisoned. Mrs
Maundy doesn't approve of these excursions, though she herself
isn't above the occasional pint. 'Wasting all your money on beer,'
she would say, wagging her finger in my face. 'But just you wait.
One day I shall be told you have no money left to pay the rent and
then, I suppose, you will expect to live off my charity. You old
people!' As if I would ever allow myself to live off her charity. That
would be a fate worse than death. Still, I don't let her prevent me. A
man must stick up for himself. And the fact that Mrs Maundy dis-
approves adds a keen edge to my pleasure. It may even be the whole
pleasure.

I was sitting at my usual table in the saloon bar staring at the
whirling patterns traced on the coloured glass of the windows when I
suddenly became aware of someone standing in front of me. I had
noticed this lady many times before without paying more than a
cursory attention to her. She was one of the fixtures of the pub. An
explosive cascade of bright red hair foamed down to her shoulders. It
had doubtless been dyed or bleached to that striking colour. Her lips
were usually daubed with some gaudy preparation not always in
harmony with the painted eyebrows. To me she was virtually an
extension of the coloured glass. I looked at one as I looked at the other.
She was not very pretty. Flesh running to seed prematurely, bruised
by indulgence. She glowed with a dull, cosmetic sheen. Perched on a
bar-stool, she would survey the regulars with a kind of defiant but
inviting lewdness. When she was bored, she preened and ogled herself
in the mirror behind the bar. She drank a great deal. All of this I

noticed because it was impossible not to. But, beyond that, I never paid her too much attention. Not until now.

'How about buying me a drink, grandfather?' She pushed up her hair and stared into the mirror. 'I'm skint this morning.' Without invitation, she sat down next to me.

The regulars were amused. 'Watch out! She's expensive, that one.'

I was so astonished – and embarrassed – by this focusing of the pub's attention on myself, I didn't know where to look.

'Don't pay any attention to them, grandfather.' She put a blue-veined hand on my coat-sleeve and stroked it gently. 'They're just jealous of you.'

I couldn't remember when last somebody had stroked me like that. My skin tingled. How soothing it was. How soothing to be stroked so gently. 'Buy me a drink, grandfather.' I must have implied assent by some subtle, surrendering motion because she immediately turned towards the bar. 'A whisky and soda, Fred. Double.' The barman gazed enquiringly at me. I must confess I blanched when I heard the order. But while she stroked me like that and while wave upon wave of stale, body-scented sweetness washed over me, I could do nothing else. Her presence encompassed me. The barman, receiving no sign to the contrary from me, shrugged and went away to pour the drink. The regulars shook their heads sadly but it was as if they did so from a receding distance.

'What's your name?' I asked.

'You can call me Sally if you like. Call me anything. Whatever takes your fancy.' She turned again to the bar. 'Hurry up with that drink, Fred. I'm parched.' Fred brought the drink himself. 'Now that is what I call real service.' Sally grinned up at him but he did not smile back. His face was blank. In one gulp she finished the drink, screwing up her face. She ordered another. This time Fred did not even look at me.

'I will call you Sally,' I said. 'I like the name.'

Sally laughed. Fred brought the second drink. She drank it as she had drunk the previous one.

'I like how you stroke my arm, Sally,' I said.

'Do you now, grandfather?' She stroked me now with the merest hint of roughness. 'Then you can buy me another drink.'

'I'm not sure I can afford it, Sally. There's the rent, you see. . . .'

She took her hand away abruptly. The painted mask was hard and closed against me.

'Don't be like that, Sally.' I did not want my skin to stop tingling. It was like ceasing to exist.

'Then buy me another, grandfather.'

There was no alternative. I was powerless, a victim of my craving for existence. For life. I ordered a drink for her and one for myself. Money flowed out of my wallet. After the fourth drink she said, 'That's better. Now I feel human again.'

'So do I, Sally,' I said. 'You make me feel human again.'

Sally tittered. Her moist fingers lifted my coat-sleeve. She stroked my bare skin. Then it was I had my inspiration. It came to me in a flash. Just like that. Perhaps the drink had something to do with it. I began to chuckle to myself. I was thinking of Mrs Maundy. What an apt revenge it would be to take a woman like this back to her respectable lodging-house, to inject into its astringent smells these waves of stale, body-scented sweetness. I was trying to picture Mrs Maundy's face as her nose picked up the corrupting trail of vapour. Imagine. This woman! In Mrs Maundy's house. I nearly strangled on my laughter.

'What's up, grandfather? Are you drunk?'

'I have an idea, Sally.' I brought my laughter under control. 'Why don't you come back to my room with me? It's not far.'

'Hey!' Sally exclaimed. 'Hey!'

'Not for long,' I coaxed.

'If you buy me a bottle of wine, grandfather,' Sally said. 'Anything for a bottle of wine.'

On the way out I bought a bottle of wine. Blank-faced Fred wrapped it in a sheet of brown paper. I tucked the bottle under my arm. As we walked back to the house Sally whistled and sang, which caused people to look at us curiously and disapprovingly. I believe she too was a little drunk after all those whiskies. But I was past caring. And whenever I thought of this woman desecrating Mrs Maundy's house, I laughed out loud.

I quietened Sally when we reached the area railings. The house watched us in stony silence. I unlocked the front door as quietly as I could and peeped in. The hall was gloomy and empty. I started at the sight of some white envelopes strewn on the red carpet. Steadying my jangled nerves, I signalled for Sally to follow me. She crept in, a hand clapped over her mouth to stifle her giggles. I stooped to pick up the envelopes, then changed my mind. What was the point? No letters ever came for me. I led Sally up the lightless stairs to my room at the top of the house. She settled herself on the bed. Now she had come I wasn't sure what to do with her. She seemed more than ever a garish apparition. Reclining on my bed, she was as startling as the envelopes strewn on the hallway carpet. Somehow my idea didn't seem so funny any more. I was frightened.

'Hey, grandfather. What's up with you? You look as if you've seen a ghost. Uncork the wine. Let's drink each other's good health.'

'Yes,' I said, striving to shut out the fear. 'The wine ... the wine. . . .'

We drank the wine, clinking glasses. It was cheap, rough stuff and it made me sleepy.

'Come, grandfather. Come and sit beside me.' She patted the bed and heaved herself over to the wall. Where she had lain the sheets were warm and scented. I nestled my head in the folds of her fleshy shoulders. She smelled of decaying roses. Her lips brushed the nape of my neck. Her presence encompassed me.

'There is something I must know, Sally.'

'What is that, grandfather?'

'Are you real, Sally? Or do I dream you?'

Sally laughed. 'Poor grandfather.' She eased herself from me and sat up. 'Does it matter?'

'No,' I said after a while. 'Perhaps it doesn't.' And, truly, it didn't seem to matter. Not just then anyway.

'Nothing matters,' Sally said.

I watched her like a child and it was like a child that I took into my mouth the speckled, ivory breast she proffered.

'Oh, Sally! I'm so old, so desolate and so frightened I won't be able to pay my rent.'

'You and your rent.' She wrenched her breast from my mouth.

I groped blindly for it.

'You've had enough, grandfather.' She clambered out of the bed and crossed to the wash-basin. She peered into the shaving mirror, pushing up her red hair and adjusting her clothes. Her hair flamed in the ugly glare flooding in from the window.

'Don't go so soon, Sally. Stay a while longer.'

Sally laughed. She came back to the bed. 'I won't be going until you pay the five pounds you owe me, grandfather.' She held out her hand.

I was dumbfounded. 'For what, Sally?' Why do I owe you five pounds?'

'For the use of my beautiful body,' Sally said.

'But I don't have five pounds to give you, Sally,' I said. 'If I do I won't have anything left to pay the rent with. You have no idea what Mrs Maundy can be like when it comes to that.'

'Pay up, grandfather.' The mask was hard again. Closed against me.

I gave her my last five pounds. 'You are heartless, Sally,' I said. 'You have no pity for an old man.'

'No,' she said. 'I have no pity.'

I listened to her footsteps fading down the stairs. From my window I watched the pitiless lady walk quickly up the street.

This is how things stand with me at present. Therein lies the source of my sleeplessness and my nightmares. Today Mrs Maundy will expect me to hand over the rent. She will not ask for it directly. She never does. 'It makes it all so crude and mercenary,' she says. Nevertheless, she will be expecting it. A week in advance to be paid on Friday. That, despite her mock delicacy, is one of the laws from which she never swerves. And I have nothing to give her. My consolation is that I may have imagined the whole thing. Dreamt it. But, if that is the case, then where has the money disappeared to? I can't even lay hands on my wallet. It has vanished. I have looked on top of the wardrobe. Under the bed. I have crawled, scraping my knees, combing every inch of the floor. I have searched high and low for it. It is slowly driving me mad. Possibly I am already mad. Yes, that is the word. That is the thought I dare not think.

Because even if Sally belonged to one of my dreams it is only the mad who dream so vividly. Oh pitiless lady, did I invent you? Did I spin you out of my longings? Maybe, as you suggested, it doesn't really matter. For, imaginary or real, and pitiless as you were, I still yearn to lay my head on your sweet-smelling breast and sleep, like a child forever. My life ebbs for lack of you, Sally. When I think of how you stroked me and how my skin tingled, I want to scream and scream and scream. . . .

No! No! I must stop travelling round in this despairing circle. That is the recipe for madness. I refuse to work myself up into a frenzy as I crouch here like a supplicant, vainly holding out my clammy, freezing hands in front of the electric fire.

This desire to scream scares me. The man who lives in the house opposite, he screams. Like me, he has a room on the top floor. But facing north as it does, the sun rarely shines into it. Mrs Maundy constantly threatens to have them – whoever 'they' might be – 'cart him away.' I often wonder where they take such people and what they do with them. She would not hesitate to let 'them' cart me away if I began to scream like him. Therefore I mustn't. I must be sensible and control myself. 'He shouldn't be allowed to upset decent people,' she says, 'screaming and carrying on the way he does. It's a disgrace. Mind, I'm not saying I'm not sorry for him and all that. He served his King and country in two world wars. But that is no excuse for upsetting decent people. He should be locked away for his own good.' Locked away for his own good! Such is the extent of Mrs Maundy's gratitude to a man 'who served his King and country in two world wars.' She told me he had been a prisoner of the Japanese during the last war. The experience had driven him insane. He stands for hours at that window of his jumping up and down like a jack-in-the-box and screaming until he is hoarse. 'You yellow bastards! You yellow bastards!' Terrible phantoms must patrol the darkened spaces of that deranged mind. What a lot of madness there is in this city. It's quite appalling.

My head is aching. It's horribly cold and damp in this room despite the fire. Mrs Maundy will be here any minute, rattling her keys like a jailer. Yes. Here she comes, predictable as some infernal clockwork. How I loathe the slow, heavy, martyred tread with which she climbs the stairs. Like doom itself. She could move with greater speed if she cared to. There is nothing to prevent her. She is always boasting about the fine state of her health.

She enters, as is her wont, without knocking. I have successfully conquered the irritation which this used to cause me. She leans in the doorway, leering at me. 'What a smell! You would think I hadn't cleaned this room for days. You could at least draw the curtains and get some light in here.' She crinkles her nose. 'Poof! What a smell.'

'Does it smell like roses?' I ask, half-eagerly, half-fearfully.

'Roses indeed!' She giggles. 'Rotting roses maybe.' She shakes her head at me. 'And there you are grumbling about me cleaning it for you.'

'It's not that I grumble about,' I say. 'It's. . . .'

'I know. I know. You're a lazy old man.' She pulls the curtains. The light dazzles me. I close my smarting eyes. 'It snowed during the night, did you know?' I open my eyes. The roofs are white with it. The gardens are white with it. The pavements are white with it. I am oddly thrilled at the thought of all that whiteness blanketing the city. 'I hate snow in the town.' Mrs Maundy's voice breaks rudely into my reverie and scatters it. 'Out in the country, though, it's very beautiful. Nothing to beat our English countryside is what I always say.'

That's Mrs Maundy all over. Giving her opinions about everything. She bristles with opinions. Who gives a damn about what she thinks of the snow in town or country? She probably never set foot in the country in her entire, godforsaken life. Now she is staring at me with that queer expression again. 'What is it?' I ask. 'What are you looking at me like that for?'

'You're a funny one,' she says. 'And getting funnier every day by the looks of it.'

'How do you mean, "funny"?'

'Oh nothing, nothing,' she replies hastily. 'It all comes out in the wash, I expect.' She considers me wisely.

'Listen, Mrs Maundy,' I say with sudden decision, 'there is something I have to tell you.'

She props herself against the broom and stares at me interestedly.

But my courage declines as rapidly as it had arisen. 'Another time,' I say, glancing evasively about the room. 'When you are less busy.' Thankfully, she does not press me. My cowardice disgusts me. I begin afresh. 'It's to do with . . . with. . . .'

'With what?' She eyes me with visibly intensifying interest.

'Nothing,' I say. 'It's not all that important anyway.'

She wags a finger at me. 'You have something weighing on your conscience. I can tell that a mile off. Out with it!'

'Later,' I say, 'at breakfast.'

'You old people are so secretive.' She busies herself with the cleaning. I go to the window and look out at the snow-covered street. In my mind's eye I see the pitiless Sally walking quickly up it.

I have my breakfast in the poky little dining-room, covered with flowery paper, on the ground floor. As I descend the stairs the smell of brewing coffee drifts up to meet me. I collect my newspaper from the table in the hall and shuffle into the dining-room, pretending to be absorbed in the headlines. I don't look at the other tenants who all have their heads bent low over their plates. We never greet each other. That is the established practice in this house. I slide as noiselessly as possible into my chair. Herbert Maundy sits next to me. He is a dour, unfriendly man. I don't recall ever having seen him smile. Once or twice I have met him on the street and he betrayed not the smallest sign of recognition. Mrs Maundy describes her son as a 'working man.' But what Herbert Maundy works at is a mystery to me. Even his mother is reticent about it. All I know is that he leaves the house on a bicycle which, when it is not in use, he keeps carefully covered with a sheet of canvas. However, it is not the unresolved mystery of Herbert's employment which disturbs me. It is his eyes. They are of a mesmeric blue-grey colour – the colour you sometimes see in a thundery sky. Lifeless and yet threatening. Cold eyes unwarmed by any human sympathy. He never seems to be seeing what is directly in front of him. Those eyes, unbending, inflexible, see only what they choose to see. They have the glazed expression of the blind. But Herbert Maundy is not blind. That is why he frightens me. He invades my nightmares, presiding over them like the Angel of Death. And he frightens not only me, I suspect. I have observed that his mother watches him warily and never speaks a rough or even mildly scolding word to him.

Mrs Maundy is talking about the snow – though to no one in particular. She brings me a tiny glass of orange juice and a rack with three thin slices of cold toast.

'How would you like your eggs this morning, dear?' She invariably calls me 'dear' when the other tenants are within earshot.

'Scrambled,' I say, without holding out any great hopes.

'If *you* had to scrub the pots and pans you wouldn't want scrambled eggs, you old dear.' She twists my ear playfully. 'Why don't you have some nice fried eggs instead? I have two keeping warm in the oven and it would be such a waste. . . .'

I nod resignedly, giving in to her blackmail. She brings me the two rubbery fried eggs. This is another of the perverse games she likes to play with me. Dangling non-existent choices. She leaves me and starts to fuss around Herbert.

'Is your egg right for you, Herbert dear?'

Herbert is having boiled eggs. For some reason he always has his eggs done differently from the rest of us.

'Yes, mother. They're just right.'

'Some more toast?'

'No, thank you, mother. I have quite enough.' Herbert slurps his coffee noisily. He is a messy eater. Mrs Maundy doesn't dare complain when he spills things. But if I do I never hear the end of it.

I cannot concentrate on my newspaper this morning. For distraction I turn to the pair of ragged budgerigars perched in their cage on top of a dark-stained chest of drawers. Like those of us sitting at the table, they pay no attention to each other. Passion has long been killed in them. They resemble waxen images. Unfortunate things. You should be wheeling freely through the African jungles – or wherever it is you come from. What a fate for you to have fallen into the clutches of Mrs Maundy. You should not have let her imprison you like this. I lift my gaze to the photograph of the fluffy white Persian cat hanging on the wall above the cage. The dead blue eyes stare back at me. I am reminded of Herbert and look away. The budgerigars are motionless in their cage. They will probably die soon. Just as well. But how cruel that they should die in captivity. Perhaps you are dreaming of the warmth and freedom of your tropical home. What an indignity for you to die in a cage. Ironically, Mrs Maundy proclaims herself an animal lover. Every year, with loud trumpeting, she sends off a five-pound postal order to the RSPCA and another for three pounds to the Donkey Sanctuary. 'The poor dumb creatures,' she would say. 'I feel so sorry for the poor dumb creatures.'

'You haven't touched your food, dear.' Mrs Maundy bustles about me. 'Waste not, want not. That's my motto.'

I have no appetite but, to avoid a lecture, I apply myself with as much enthusiasm as I can summon.

There is a clatter of cups and saucers as Herbert bangs his fists on the table and levers himself upright. Though this is an habitual flourish of his, the signature with which he ends every meal, it has never ceased to jar. I sit, tensely expectant, waiting for it to happen. This morning it is particularly bad. My nerves ripple in a radiation of fine, needling pain. The goose pimples rise. My ear drums reverberate with the lingering echo. I shut my eyes, biting on my lower lip.

'So jumpy, dear. So jumpy.' Mrs Maundy pats me on the back. She seems to be amused. Bending down confidentially, she whispers, 'We will wait till they all clear out, dear. Then you can tell me what's on your mind.' However, it is a whisper calculated to carry. The tenants glance up furtively.

Herbert jumps up noisily from his chair, dabbing his lips with a spotted handkerchief. 'I'll be off now, mother. See you later.' He goes out from the dining-room. Mrs Maundy follows him with her eyes. Herbert's footsteps thud ponderously along the hallway carpet. The front door opens and slams. The walls shake and ornaments rattle. In a sense, I am glad there is at least one person in the world who frightens Mrs Maundy. I regard it as salutary. Still, that is cold comfort to me. Between the two of them, taunting mother and dead-eyed son, I feel trapped.

One by one the others finish their breakfast and Mrs Maundy removes the dirty plates and glasses, piling them on the draining-board. These successive departures and Mrs Maundy's journeys between dining-room and kitchen are like the swings of a pendulum ticking away the seconds to the doom which is about to devour me. I am seized by panic and try to eat more quickly. The intention is frustrated. Husks of dry toast lodge in my throat and almost succeed in choking me. I cough and splutter.

'I hope you're not dying, dear,' Mrs Maundy calls out from the kitchen amid a clinking of cutlery. 'Remember our little secret. You're only allowed to die *after* you've told me.' She stands in the kitchen doorway and laughs.

The last of the tenants has finished. He rises, bids Mrs Maundy goodbye and departs. I am alone. Alone with Mrs Maundy! She comes in from the kitchen to take away the remaining plates. I struggle to my feet as she does so, pushing my plate aside. The taste of oily egg circulates nauseatingly at the base of my throat.

'Are you *through*?' she asks, staring in disbelief at my plate.

'I'm not very hungry this morning,' I manage to say. 'My stomach is upset.' I hold on to the chair for support. My legs feel unsteady.

'Ungrateful old man,' she says. 'You don't appreciate what I do for you. You wouldn't get as much as what's left on your plate in most establishments. They will give you a continental breakfast. Have you any idea what a *continental breakfast* is?' She breathes indignantly at me. 'What I provide costs me a pretty penny, let me tell you.'

Murmuring apologies, I run out of the room. My legs make the decision rather than me. Mrs Maundy pursues me to the foot of the stairs. 'Wait!' she cries. 'You still haven't told me that little secret of yours.'

'I have no secrets,' I reply, pausing on the first landing. 'I have no secrets at all. . . .'

'It will all come out in the wash, I expect,' she says. 'Never mind.'

What relief courses through me when I finally reach the haven of my own room. I lock the door and collapse against it, fighting to steady my nerves and ward off the nausea. There is a burning tightness in my chest. I listen to see if Mrs Maundy has followed me. But I do not hear that slow, heavy tread. I relax somewhat. I cross to

the washbasin and examine my face in the shaving-mirror. How pale
and wild and hunted it looks. Not the face of a man in serene old age. I
open the window wide and thrust my head outside. The fresh air is
reviving and I inhale deeply. The morning is clear and crisp and the
blue sky is without a cloud.

It occurs to me I should go for a walk in this lovely weather. It
would probably do me good to get out of the house for a bit. To taste
once more my dwindling freedom. I dress hurriedly and sneak down
the stairs, hoping to avoid Mrs Maundy and her inevitable questions.
But, as luck would have it, I stumble on her in the hall.

'I thought you were ill,' she says, blocking my passage.

'I'm just going out for a short while,' I reply, hating myself for
behaving like a prisoner. 'To the park. It might clear my head a little.'
She looks at me in sceptical silence. Then, like a jailer, she makes way
reluctantly. She watches me as I open the door and go down the front
steps to the street.

'Take care you don't catch a chill,' she shouts after me. 'At your age
that could prove fatal.'

The sunshine has lured many people to the park. After the walk, I
am tired. I sit on a bench and try to read the newspaper I have brought
with me. A chill wind is blowing. Bloated pigeons peck at the crumbs
a woman is scattering on the snowy grass. She laughs ringingly as the
pigeons swarm greedily about her feet. Several people are exercising
their dogs. In the blue distance beyond the farthest line of trees a mist
is forming, shot though by the copper sun. Suddenly I have the
absurd notion I am invisible and seeing everything in slow motion.
The dogs, the people, the pigeons, the woman's ringing laughter seem
unrelented elements of a fantasy in which I have no part. At one
moment I am a giant watching the antics of a pygmy race. At another,
I am the pygmy and they are giants and I am terrified of being
crushed. I have to remind myself where I am and what I have come
there to do. 'Only the park,' I assure myself repeatedly. 'Only the
park.' I do my utmost to concentrate on the newspaper. The words
refuse to yield their sense. They perform a blurring dance on the
paper. I try to recall the sound of Mrs Maundy's voice. But that too
possesses an alien quality and is soaked up in the hallucinatory
sensation. It is as though life itself – not simply *my* life – is ebbing,
rushing away from me into a black limbo. But the strangest thing of all
is how calm I am. I seem to be standing at a certain remove from
myself and noting, with a kind of dispassion, even my own terror.

Yes, it is that dispassion which is the strangest thing. I pinch my arm but the skin is numb and I feel no pain. My heart is racing and my head is spinning. What shame, I think, to die in front of these people. Without a name. Without a past. Another body. 'Help me!' I want to shout. 'I am dying without dignity. You must help me!' The woman with the ringing laughter scuttles towards me. 'Can't you see you're scaring away the birds?' Her words are like an antidote. The chaos recedes. The world gradually comes into focus again. I rise from the bench, leave the park and walk slowly back to my room, buffeted by a raw wind.

Mrs Maundy is cleaning the hall. 'The return of the prodigal son,' she says.

I do not answer her but go straight up to my room. Opening the window, I look out. The snow is melting. On the street the brown slush is furrowed by the tracks of cars. Water drips from the black branches of the chestnut trees. The weather has changed. This swift transformation of the white morning alarms me. Storm clouds flurry across the sky as if propelled by a malevolent god. The grey light is probing and harsh. Then I hear my neighbour opposite.

'You yellow bastards! You yellow bastards!'

I shut my window quickly and turn my back on him. Lying down on the bed, I close my eyes, praying for sleep.

I wake with a start. Someone is in the room. A prowling, hostile presence. 'Who is it? Who is there?' I raise my head cautiously from the pillow. Herbert Maundy is standing over me. He fixes me with his dead, blue-grey eyes. 'What do you want with me? I have done nothing to you.' He does not reply. His head inclines towards me until I can see only his eyes. They are as menacing and ominous as the sky itself. 'I've done nothing to you. If it's the rent your mother sent you for tell her I can pay. I'll find it and pay her in full.' He does not answer. I cannot escape the dead eyes of my Angel of Death. 'Why can't you speak? Why don't you *ever* speak to me? Say something. Say anything. You shouldn't frighten an old man ... a dying old man.' The awful eyes dim. They grow distant. Herbert vanishes as soundlessly as he came. For a time I lie there, unable to move. The room is cold and dark. It is late. Soon I will be called to account. The wallet ... the wallet. ...

I dash to the wardrobe and frenziedly ransack the pockets of my coat, my three pairs of trousers, my two jackets. Nothing. I drag a chair over and, hauling myself on to it, sweep my hands across the top of the wardrobe. Nothing. I fall on my knees and thrust my hands into the gap between it and the wall. I insert my arm as far as it will go. Nothing. Nothing but cobwebs and dust. Still on my knees, I crawl over every inch of the floor. Nothing. I lie flat on my stomach and grope under the bed. Nothing. Nothing. Nothing. If only I had some evidence one way or the other. The wine bottle for instance. I start to cry.

'What *are* you doing down there?' Mrs Maundy has made one of her silent invasions.

Why can't you leave me in peace, I want to say. Why can't you and your son leave an old man in peace. This is my room. I have always managed to pay the rent for it. Surely I can do what I like in here. On my patch of earth.

'I was hunting for my shoes,' I say. 'I can't seem to find them anywhere.' I haul myself effortfully to my feet.

She has that queer look again.

'What is it?' I ask. 'What are you looking at me like that for?'

'If you want to find your shoes it might help if you switch on the light,' she replies. She flicks the switch.

The light. I had not realised. And it is cold too. I had forgotten how cold it was. Clasping my arms about me, I shiver.

'I came up to see you earlier,' she says.'But you were asleep.'

'Asleep . . . yes, yes, I was asleep.' I do not look at her.

'Since you haven't had any lunch,' she says, 'I thought I would ask you to have some tea with me. Yyou must be hungry.'

'Tea,' I repeat stupidly. 'You want me to have tea with you.'

'I've baked a lovely cake.' She smiles cheerfully. 'With nuts and raisins.'

I fight my surging anguish. 'I'll be down in a minute,' I mutter. 'Just let me find my shoes and I'll be down.'

She points to the floor near the foot of the bed. 'There they are,' she says, not troubling to conceal her amusement. 'Now don't be long.' She wags her finger at me and goes, not closing the door.

Tea indeed! A lovely cake with nuts and raisins! I am too well acquainted with Mrs Maundy's little tricks to be taken in by these blandishments. She is planning one of her perverse games with me. I don't believe for a minute she is concerned about my hunger. Anyway, I am not hungry. Her acts of 'kindness' do not fool me. Their purpose is clear enough. To fox me. To throw me off my guard. I remember the day, some months ago, when, out of the blue, she came up here and presented me with a book of crossword puzzles. 'To keep your mind occupied,' she said. 'It's bad for old people to get bored. The Devil always finds mischief for idle hands.' But then, like now, it wasn't genuine concern for my well-being that prompted her. Not at all. Her joy consisted in watching the confusion into which this act of apparent generosity threw me. Her invitation to tea isn't very different. She knows something is wrong and, most probably, she knows it is to do with the rent. Mrs Maundy can sniff these things out. She is an extremely clever and observant woman. However, she won't come right out and say so. That isn't her style. She must have her fun first. Play cat and mouse with me. And only when she has wearied of the amusement will the trap be sprung without further ceremony.

'Yoo hoo up there! What are you doing?' Mrs Maundy's strident tones drift up from the hallway. 'The tea will be undrinkable if you don't come down straight away.'

'Coming! Coming!' I shout back. I try to make myself as decent as I can as quickly as I can. My fingers are fumbling and awkward and my palms are moist. I feel feverish. The journey down the stairs is like the journey of a condemned man to the scaffold. Mrs Maundy is waiting for me in the hall.

'Ah! There you are at last, you old dawdler.' She hustles me into the sitting-room. Two arm-chairs are drawn up in front of the small, brown-tiled fireplace. The banked-up coals glow orange in the grate. A round table on spindly legs is placed between the chairs. I see the virgin cake, the teapot sheathed with its woollen cap, two cups and two saucers, a shining knife. They are arrayed like the instruments of my impending execution. The room is crowded with furniture. I sink down in one of the arm-chairs and gaze at the fire. My doom sounds faintly in my ears like the crash of distant but approaching thunder. Mrs Maundy, chattering gaily, pours the tea and cuts meagre slices of the cake.

'Isn't this nice and cosy? After a hard day's work to relax in front of a cheerful fire with a cup of tea.' With a self-satisfied grunt, Mrs Maundy settles herself into the chair beside me. The springs creak. She sighs. 'It's so good to be able to put your feet up at the end of a hard day.' She glances at me out of the corner of her eyes. 'But I don't suppose you know what bliss it is. I mean, having nothing to do all day you wouldn't appreciate it.'

I remain silent, staring at the fire.

'Just think how lucky you are,' she adds. 'All you have to worry about is paying the rent. That apart. . . .' She waves her hand.

On the mantelpiece, occupying pride of place, is a photograph in a gilt frame of a bland, smooth-featured man, probably in his thirties. I grasp at this straw. 'Mr Maundy?'

'No,' she replies shortly. 'That is a friend of mine. He died during the war. I married Mr Maundy just after the war.' 'After' is spoken pointedly. 'He was in the Merchant Navy. His ship got torpedoed.'

I do not say anything. She seems irritated and speaks with a mixture of harshness and indifference.

'I've never been beyond these shores and never wanted to,' she says. 'I was happy to stay at home. But he – he was a great traveller.' Her eyes rest briefly and lovelessly on the photograph. Is she praising him? Or is she cursing him? I cannot make it out. Her tone is impenetrable. 'They finally got him though.' She speaks almost with triumph. 'Whoosh! Through the water it went.' Her arm dives towards the fire. 'Whoosh! A direct hit. And that was that.' She blinks reproachfully at me. 'You're not eating your cake. Is your stomach still upset?' She grins slyly at me.

I nibble at the edges of the yellow slice she has rested on my saucer. She watches me intently. Any moment now, I think. It will happen at any moment. The front door opens and closes with a bang. The house shudders.

'That will be Herbert,' she says absently.

I listen to Herbert's ponderous footsteps thudding on the carpet and ascending the stairs to his room.

'I wonder what it feels like to drown,' she says. 'To know you're going under with no hope of rescue – like my friend must have done. To have the water closing about you. Unable to breathe. Sinking deeper and deeper.' She is all harshness now. Herbert moves noisily overhead. 'Which is the worst way to die? By water? By fire?'

How mercilessly she taunts me.

'Are you afraid of dying?' She bites into her slice of cake and chews methodically.

'I try not to think about it too much.' My palms are moist. The thunder rolls nearer.

'Don't you now?' She arranges herself more comfortably. 'But you should prepare yourself. My friend wasn't prepared. But Mr Maundy was. I saw to that. And I tell you the same things I told him. I keep telling you. . . .'

'I know you do.' I answer, turning towards her. 'You torture me
with it.'

'Torture you, do I?' She seems mildly astonished. She laughs.
'What an odd fellow you are. I try to help you and you call it
torture.'

'Yes. You brought me down here in order to torture me at your
ease. While putting your feet up. . . .' Again I have that strange feeling
of dispassion. I jump up from the chair. The thunder rolls and crashes
deafeningly about me, one with Herbert Maundy's resounding foot-
falls. 'You brought me down here to play cat and mouse with me. But
I won't allow it.'

'Cat and mouse!' She shakes with laughter.

'If you know I can't pay my rent, why don't you say so straight out?
Get it over with instead of. . . .'

'So,' she says, 'now we have it. From your own lips. I said it would
all come out in the wash, didn't I?' She wags her finger at me. 'You've
squandered all your money in the pub and now you can't pay my
rent. You're begging for my charity.'

'Never! Never would I beg for your charity. That would be a fate
worse than death by drowning and fire put together.'

'You ungrateful old man! After all I've done for you. . . .' She is
shouting at me.

'Don't you dare shout at me.' I am standing by her chair. A raging,
black cloud envelops me. 'You're quite right. I squandered my
money. Every last penny of it. And I'll even tell you what I squandered it on. *Who* I squandered it on. I spent it all on a woman. . . .'

'You liar!' Mrs Maundy is not smiling now. She rises from her
chair. 'What woman would so much as look at you? You – you with
one foot already in the grave. . . .'

'I spent every last penny I possessed on a woman I picked up in the
pub. On a woman of the streets. A common whore!'

She stares at me with speechless venom.

'I brought this common whore back to your house. Back to *your*
respectable house! And . . . and I. . . .'

'Your brain is rotting,' she says. 'You lost your money. Your wallet.
I found it out in the hall. Lying there. . . .'

She wants to make me believe it's a dream. She has invented
another of her perverse games. But I will not be cheated. I cannot be
cheated like this. 'Show me! But you can't show me. I won't be taken
in by your tricks any more.'

'You're mad,' she says. 'Mad! I'm going to let them come and cart you away.'

She retreats as I advance on her. But she cannot go very far. Not in this small room crowded with furniture. She cowers against a table. I bring my face close to her. 'A common whore entered your house, Mrs Maundy. Smelling of rotting roses!'

Mrs Maundy has such a comical expression. She is babbling away. What a commotion there is on the stairs. I have never been able to cope with hysterical women. Herbert is bearing down straight towards me with those awful eyes of his starting out of his head. Mrs Maundy lies limp in my arms. Not me, Herbert. Not me. I'm not the one in need of attention. You are making a big mistake. It's your mother you should be tending, Herbert. But what is the good? He never sees what is in front of him. Why is he pinioning me like this? What have I done? All I can see is my Angel of Death with the dead blue-grey eyes. They are the colour of the pitiless sky itself. If Mrs Maundy would let me sleep, if only she would let me sleep, my nightmares would, I am sure, vanish into thin air.

Discover more about our forthcoming books through Penguin's FREE newspaper...

Penguin Quarterly

It's packed with:

- exciting features
- author interviews
- previews & reviews
- books from your favourite films & TV series
- exclusive competitions & much, much more...

READ MORE IN PENGUIN

In every corner of the world, on every subject under the sun, Penguin represents quality and variety – the very best in publishing today.

For complete information about books available from Penguin – including Puffins, Penguin Classics and Arkana – and how to order them, write to us at the appropriate address below. Please note that for copyright reasons the selection of books varies from country to country.

In the United Kingdom: Please write to *Dept. JC, Penguin Books Ltd, FREEPOST, West Drayton, Middlesex UB7 OBR.*

If you have any difficulty in obtaining a title, please send your order with the correct money, plus ten per cent for postage and packaging, to *PO Box No. 11, West Drayton, Middlesex UB7 OBR*

In the United States: Please write to *Consumer Sales, Penguin USA, P.O. Box 999, Dept. 17109, Bergenfield, New Jersey 07621-0120.* VISA and MasterCard holders call 1-800-253-6476 to order all Penguin titles

In Canada: Please write to *Penguin Books Canada Ltd, 10 Alcorn Avenue, Suite 300, Toronto, Ontario M4V 3B2*

In Australia: Please write to *Penguin Books Australia Ltd, P.O. Box 257, Ringwood, Victoria 3134*

In New Zealand: Please write to *Penguin Books (NZ) Ltd, Private Bag 102902, North Shore Mail Centre, Auckland 10*

In India: Please write to *Penguin Books India Pvt Ltd, 706 Eros Apartments, 56 Nehru Place, New Delhi 110 019*

In the Netherlands: Please write to *Penguin Books Netherlands bv, Postbus 3507, NL-1001 AH Amsterdam*

In Germany: Please write to *Penguin Books Deutschland GmbH, Metzlerstrasse 26, 60594 Frankfurt am Main*

In Spain: Please write to *Penguin Books S. A., Bravo Murillo 19, 1° B, 28015 Madrid*

In Italy: Please write to *Penguin Italia s.r.l., Via Felice Casati 20, I–20124 Milano*

In France: Please write to *Penguin France S. A., 17 rue Lejeune, F–31000 Toulouse*

In Japan: Please write to *Penguin Books Japan, Ishikiribashi Building, 2–5–4, Suido, Bunkyo-ku, Tokyo 112*

In Greece: Please write to *Penguin Hellas Ltd, Dimocritou 3, GR–106 71 Athens*

In South Africa: Please write to *Longman Penguin Southern Africa (Pty) Ltd, Private Bag X08, Bertsham 2013*

READ MORE IN PENGUIN

Penguin Twentieth-Century Classics offer a selection of the finest works of literature published this century. Spanning the globe from Argentina to America, from France to India, the masters of prose and poetry are represented in by the Penguin.

If you would like a catalogue of the Twentieth-Century Classics library, please write to:

Penguin Marketing, 27 Wrights Lane, London W8 5TZ

(Available while stocks last)

READ MORE IN PENGUIN

A CHOICE OF TWENTIETH-CENTURY CLASSICS

Orlando Virginia Woolf

Sliding in and out of three centuries, and slipping between genders, Orlando is a sparkling incarnation of the personality of Vita Sackville-West as Virginia Woolf saw it.

Moravagine Blaise Cendrars

In *Moravagine* a young French doctor, specialist in nervous diseases, releases a murderer from a lunatic asylum and joins him in his travels through Europe. With Max Jacob and Apollinaire, Cendrars was at the forefront of the modern movement, a poet, film-maker, nomad and novelist whose finest novel is a fiercely iconoclastic and original masterpeice.

The Living and the Dead Patrick White

To hesitate on the edge of life or to plunge in and risk change – this is the dilemma explored in *The Living and the Dead*. 'Scene after scene is worked out with an exactness and subtlety which no second-string novelist can scent, far less nail to paper' – *Time*. 'He is, in the finest sense, a world novelist' – *Guardian*

Tell Me How Long the Train's Been Gone James Baldwin

Leo Proudhammer, a successful Broadway actor, is recovering from a near-fatal heart attack. Talent, luck and ambition have brought him a long way from the Harlem ghetto of his childhood. With Barbara, a white woman who has the courage to love the wrong man, and Christopher, a charismatic black revolutionary, Leo faces a turning-point in his life.

Memories of a Catholic Girlhood Mary McCarthy

Blending memories and family myths, Mary McCarthy takes us back to the twenties, when she was orphaned in a world of relations as colourful, potent and mysterious as the Catholic religion. 'Superb . . . so heartbreaking that in comparison Jane Eyre seems to have got off lightly' – Anita Brookner

READ MORE IN PENGUIN

A CHOICE OF TWENTIETH-CENTURY CLASSICS

The Sea of Fertility Yukio Mishima

'Mishima's thrilling storytelling is unique; there is nothing like it. His flashing style is perfect for his dark motives and there are times when his words are so splendid, and his concepts so tragic, that reading him becomes a profound experience' – *Sunday Times*

Nineteen Eighty-Four George Orwell

'It is a volley against the authoritarian in every personality, a polemic against every orthodoxy, an anarchistic blast against every unquestioning conformist ... *Nineteen Eighty-Four* is a great novel and a great tract because of the clarity of its call, and it will endure because its message is a permanent one: erroneous thought is the stuff of freedom' – Ben Pimlott

The Little Demon Fyodor Sologub

Peredonov, a schoolmaster, is exercised first by the idea of marrying to gain promotion, later by arson, torture and murder. His descent into paranoia and sexual perversion mirrors the obsessions of a petty provincial society, tyrannized by triviality and senseless bureaucracy.

A First Omnibus Ivy Compton-Burnett
A Family and a Fortune • Parents and Children • A God and His Gifts

'Ivy Compton-Burnett is one of the most original, artful and elegant writers of our century ... She invented her own way of writing a novel; form and content (unlike her characters) make the happiest of marriages' – Hilary Mantel

Selected Short Stories Rabindranath Tagore

Rabindranath Tagore (1861–1941) was the grand master of Bengali culture, and in the 1890s he concentrated on creating a new form, the short story. His work has been acclaimed for its vivid portrayal of Bengali life and landscapes, brilliantly polemical in its depiction of peasantry and gentry, the caste system, corrupt officialdom and dehumanizing poverty.

BY THE SAME AUTHOR

The Chip-Chip Gatherers

With skill and compassion, Shiva Naipaul brings to life an unforgettable cast of characters in a small village in Trinidad. There is Egbert Ramsaran, an egomaniacal tyrant who dominates the tightly knit Hindu settlement; his son, Wilbert, bullied into passivity and failure; Vishnu Bholai, the downtrodden grocer without grace or hope; Julian Bholai, hoping to escape his father's fate by becoming a doctor; the beautiful, unpredictable Sushila, who briefly wields her seductive powers over Ramsaran; and her daughter, Sita, intelligent enough to know that escape is impossible.

'A compelling, tragic, painfully comic masterpiece' – *The Times Literary Supplement*

Fireflies

'*Fireflies* tells the story of Trinidad's most venerated Hindu family, the Khojas. Rigidly orthodox, presiding over acres of ill-kept sugarcane and hoards of jewellery enthusiastically guarded by old Mrs Khoja, they seem to have triumphed more by default than by anything else. Only 'Baby' Khoja, who is parcelled off into an arranged marriage with a bus driver, proves an exception to this rule. She is the heroine, and her story the single gleaming thread in Shiva Naipaul's ferociously comic and profoundly sad first novel.

'A masterpiece … anyone who misses reading *Fireflies* will miss an entirely delightful experience' – Auberon Waugh in the *Spectator*

North of South
An African Journey

Travel narrative in the classic tradition of Graham Greene, *North of South* is brilliant, comic, controversial – a scathing and intimate documentary on Africa and its people today.

'One of the best travel books to have appeared for many a year … Mr Naipaul is a modern George Orwell.' – *Sunday Times*

BY THE SAME AUTHOR

A Hot Country

Cuyama, a small country in South America, its spirit robbed by centuries of conquerers and colonizers, is poised on the brink of crisis.

Shiva Naipaul's passionate and evocative novel focuses on two casualties of Cuyama's post-Independence malaise: Aubrey St Pierre, dedicated to redeeming the sins of his slave-owning ancestors, and his wife, Dina. While Aubrey sits in his highbrow bookshop composing protest letters to *The Times* in London and New York, Dina stands aloof and passive in the face of an impending tragedy, which seems to her more personal than political. The fate of their marriage comes obliquely to reflect the fate of a nation, portrayed by Naipaul with intense sympathy, vision and elegance.

'Naipaul uses language like a scrupulous epicure: with relish and precision. *A Hot Country* is a work of art that delights with its craft' – *The Times Literary Supplement*